**Barry Pullen**

# SNAPSHOT

Limited Special Edition. No. 22 of 25 Paperbacks

Barry Pullen was born in Darlington in 1950, but as his father was in the RAF, he was soon on the first of many moves around the UK and abroad.

Barry also served in the RAF, visiting many different countries during his time in service.

After he left the RAF, he worked in Oman for eleven years, followed by four years helping to build the new Airbus A380 in Germany.

Barry now lives in Rutland with his wife and daughters, and their dogs, Misty and Rex.

After reading other people's work for years, he decided to write stories of his own. *Snapshot* is the first of these.

I would like to dedicate this to my wife, Rose. If not for her encouragement, it may never have reached the end.

# Barry Pullen

## SNAPSHOT

AUSTIN MACAULEY PUBLISHERS™

LONDON • CAMBRIDGE • NEW YORK • SHARJAH

ISBN 9781528907842 (Paperback)
ISBN 9781528907866 (E-Book)

www.austinmacauley.com

First Published (2019)
Austin Macauley Publishers Ltd
25 Canada Square
Canary Wharf
London
E14 5LQ

"You are a very lucky young woman, not many people bother to stop and admire the wonderful English countryside anymore."

Joshua was excited as he sat down beside the girl, in a small hollow halfway down the slope of a grassy field. He'd seen this view, looking over the vale towards Melton Mowbray to the left and Oakham to the right, several times on his journeys to and from work and knew, hoped anyway, that she would enjoy it also.

She, of course, would have preferred to have been anywhere else. She should be at home totting up her night's takings, in the warm, instead of sitting here wearing nothing but a smelly mac. She'd been working her corner the previous evening, hoping to get some business from the cars as they were forced to slow for the junction with the main road. If she got a second look she would adjust her pose to let them know that she was exactly what they had been looking for, hoping that they would stop and beckon her over. Business had been slow last night, so when he'd pulled over she'd agreed to use the back of his van, not something she would normally have done. Too risky with all the nutters around but, as he had looked eager and slightly nervous, she'd taken the chance, reckoning on ten minutes tops. She could be back on her beat within the half hour. An easy thirty quid.

What a mistake *that* had been.

She'd seen to his needs, which had taken her a lot longer than expected. He wanted to try all the positions, but there was one she would not do. She knew that some of the other girls didn't mind taking it up their bum but not her, no way. He'd looked disappointed when she'd refused to let him do that, but then he'd smiled to himself and told her OK, maybe next time, eh? After he *had* eventually come and rolled off her she thanked God and was getting into her jeans, wondering whether or not to call it a night, when his arm suddenly came across her face and he covered her nose and mouth with some kind of soft pad. Next thing she knew she was sitting against this bloody tree in the middle of this bloody field, with nothing on but a bloody mac. She must have sat there for a couple of hours before she heard his voice, just after the sun had risen. Her bum had gone numb, but when she tried to wriggle herself into a more comfortable position she felt a pain seemingly from inside, so she reckoned he *had* done her there after all. That was bloody uncomfortable but worse still there was a scarf tied round her head, covering her mouth and stopping her from spitting out whatever he had put in there. She was hoping it was just her hankie. The gag made it impossible for her to answer him but, without it, she would have started yelling, and she didn't think he wanted that. Her hands had been tied behind her, around a small sapling from the feel of it against her back.

She'd been rendered quite helpless.

All she could do now was sit and listen to him prattle on about how nice the bloody view was. She was desperate for a wee, but that was probably the least of her problems. She looked at him and her eyes were pleading for him to remove the gag. He leant towards her and she thought he was actually going to take it off, but he just made sure that the scarf was secure, then leant back and looked her in the eyes.

"A necessary precaution, my dear, but it will be removed soon, now just sit still and enjoy this wonderful view."

"While you can," he added under his breath.

*Fuck the bloody view*, she thought, *just get this over with so I can go home*.

He smiled at her before turning back to the vista before them, glancing sideways at her face every so often.

"You know, this is all so beautiful I think I'll take a photograph or two."

He stood up, took out his small Olympus camera and moved behind the girl. No matter how hard she tried, she couldn't turn her head enough to see him. He snapped several photos from this position before returning the camera to his coat pocket.

Now was the moment.

Reaching into the underarm holster he'd made from an old school satchel, he brought out his .22 target pistol. He calmly aimed it so that the barrel was pointing at the middle of her head, pulled the trigger, reloaded and fired again, before returning the gun to its hiding place. He wasn't worried about anyone hearing the shots, he'd heard noisier bird scarers.

Leaning down, he gently removed the scarf he'd used as a gag before wrapping it over her head and tying it under her chin, finishing off the illusion by placing a pair of oversize sunglasses on her. Cutting the cable ties from her wrists he carefully put the pieces in his pocket, before laying her hands in her lap. To anyone passing by on the path, several yards up from where she was sitting, it would appear that she was enjoying a rest.

"Bye-bye, my lovely," said Joshua, before climbing back up to the lay-by where he got into his van and drove home.

# Chapter 1

*God, this job is bloody boring sometimes*, Ashley thought. He was sat in the traffic car, parked up with just its nose showing, at the side of the A47 near the village of Tugby. There were compensations though, as his partner was Constable Tina Taylor. Ashley looked across at her and wondered, not for the first time, what she would be like in bed. She was a natural beauty with a figure that other girls spent hours in the gym trying to achieve. Long brown hair that was tied up in a bun, how he would love to free that and see it tumble over her shoulders, and the deepest green eyes he had ever seen. She was quite something, still single, putting all her energy into her job.

"So, Tina, another working weekend. Whose toes have you been treading on then?"

Tina looked across the car at her partner for the next two days and thought that it could have been worse. Ashley Smith was not bad looking and had the gift of the gab when it came to the ladies. According to locker room gossip, that wasn't the only thing he was gifted with. The only fly in the ointment, as far as she was concerned anyway, was that he always wanted to drive. She had passed the police advanced driving course over three months ago now, and would love to show some of these men just how capable she could be at driving the 'proper quick' police car.

Before she could answer, the radio crackled into life.

"Tango four, tango four, unit required to attend on B6047 just out of Tilton, heading towards Queniborough. A couple has reported finding a body. Can you assist, over?"

Tina pressed her mike button.

"Control from Tango four, we are close by and will attend, over."

10

Ashley started up the BMW, and as he pulled out onto the main carriageway he floored the accelerator while Tina flipped on the lights and siren. Three minutes later they were at the Tilton turn off.

"It's only a couple of minutes up here," Ashley said as he turned off the A47 onto the B road and headed towards the hilltop village.

Just after the village was a lay-by, of sorts and, standing by their car, a young couple. They started walking towards the police car as Ashley came to a halt. Tina turned the siren off, but left the blue lights flashing. The young woman was holding on to the man and as Ashley and Tina got out of their car the man started babbling, "We're pretty sure there's a dead woman down there," he said, pointing down the hill. "We only noticed there was someone there because we were watching a Kite and it landed very near to where she's sitting. We thought it was strange as they are normally very shy birds and tend to keep clear of human contact so we went down to have a look. When we called, she didn't answer and it was only when we got close that we noticed there seemed to be blood on her coat. She wasn't moving so I walked round in front of her to see if she had just fallen asleep and then I saw her face."

The woman started crying then and the young man looked at the two police officers, indicating, with a nod of his head, a gap in the hedge that gave access to the field.

Tina and Ashley pushed through the gap and started down the slope towards the figure.

Ashley reached the figure first and when he saw the reason for the Kites' seeming indifference, he couldn't help exclaiming, "Oh my God, her face!"

He stumbled away from the body, there was no disputing that fact, and tried to keep himself from heaving up the Subway he'd had for lunch.

Tina approached the figure and was prepared for something bad, judging from Ashley's reaction. She was not disappointed. The face had suffered at the hands of nature's scavengers and some of the features had been eaten away. There were two bloody sockets where her eyes had been and her nose was missing, all that was left was a knobbly lump of bone. *It could have been a pretty face before this had happened to it,* she

11

thought. There was a scarf lying on the ground beside the body, covered in what Tina guessed was blood, and a large pair of sunglasses. She looked closer at the head and noticed what appeared to be two small holes just below the crown.

*I don't think they were made by any animal*, she thought, then called over to her partner as she heard the ambulance approaching,

"They won't be any use to this one, but I reckon those two up there will need treating for shock. They looked well shaken up."

Her partner just looked at her, and nodded.

"Ashley, when you've stopped being a wimp get back to the car and radio that we need some assistance. And stop the ambulance men from coming down here. This is a probable murder scene now and we have to keep it from getting more contaminated than it is already."

She looked back at the body and noticed that there were no shoes on the feet. No handbag either. She would ask the young couple about that. It wouldn't be the first time that personal belongings had been taken before calling the police.

She went back up to the lay-by and told Ashley of these missing items. Going to their car she got the 'Police – Do Not Cross' tape out of the kit in the boot, tying it across the gap in the hedge, before walking over to the ambulance to talk to the young couple.

"Did either of you notice anything else at the scene, like a handbag, or shoes?" she asked, watching their faces for any sign of reaction to her question. There was none and they both said no together.

"There may be further reasons to talk to you both, so if you can give me your contact details, I will pass them on to the team who will be investigating this, then you can go."

Once she had this information she watched them as they got into their car and drove off. It wasn't long before the teams started turning up. First to arrive were Detective Inspector Tom Longman and his colleague, Detective Sergeant Charles, from Leicester CID.

DI Longman had been with the Leicestershire police for the last six months after being transferred from the Met. An officer with the Major Crimes Unit down there, he'd been badly injured during a raid on a suspect's house. The man, according to information received, was one of a gang involved in an armed robbery on a jewellers shop in Hatton Gardens. The raid had left a sales assistant dead and the owner in hospital with a cracked skull. The police had surrounded the man's house and Longman had been the second one in through the back door. As he entered the kitchen the suspect fired both barrels of his shotgun, killing the armed officer in front of him, and Longman had caught some of the blast in his shoulder. He spent several weeks in hospital, and was lucky that his arm had been saved, although he still had twinges when the weather turned cold. The suspect had not survived. As armed officers had run through to the kitchen from the front of the house he'd turned, still holding the gun, and they didn't hesitate, shooting him dead.

After leaving hospital Longman decided that, that had been one close call too many and had asked for a transfer. He hadn't expected Leicester, having requested Derby as it was nearer to the Dales, and his cottage. He was enjoying the slower pace, although there had been the odd challenge, and his life, and career, was slowly getting back on track.

Thirty seven, a well-built six-two, with short, dark hair and a rugged 'Old Spice' face, he'd had his share of female admirers but had never married. He didn't think it was because he hadn't met the right one yet as he never had been a believer in the 'love at first sight' adage. No, it was probably more accurate to say that he was quite happy with his lot. He enjoyed his cottage in the Peak District he'd bought the previous year, with part of a sizeable inheritance, after the death of his mother. His army father had died when he was small, killed in the Yemeni troubles. He'd no brothers or sisters, hence no nephews or nieces to call him uncle. He led a solitary existence away from his office, although there had been attempts to get him into a serious relationship on a few occasions. He wasn't a monk, and enjoyed female company, but there was no attraction for him in taking things as far as the altar. He was fastidious in his personal life and shaved every morning, although he generally looked as though he needed another by mid-afternoon. He invariably wore suits at work, casual clothes were for leisure he'd always thought.

"Come on then, Sergeant, let's see what this is all about, shall we," he said, turning off the engine and opening his door.

His partner, DS Michael – never Mike – Charles got out of the passenger side and wandered over to where Tina and Ashley were waiting. He was not quite the opposite of his boss but it came close. He'd joined the force the day after his twenty first birthday, meeting the then height requirement with nothing to spare. That was now thirteen years ago. He lived alone, not through choice, but because he was a chauvinistic bigot, and any relationships that he'd attempted to cultivate soon fizzled out when his true character started to show. He was thin to the point of being scrawny, and generally wore slacks and an old leather jacket.

He'd risen to Detective Sergeant on his ability to catch criminals, not his personal attitude. The only thing he and his boss really had in common, apart from the force, was that they were both still single.

"So, Constable, what have we got then?" he asked Ashley, giving Tina a quick nod. He was of the opinion that female officers should be behind a desk, not out in the real world dealing with proper police work, and was not subtle in showing his views.

Ashley did not like DS Charles too much, not many did, and fielded the question to Tina.

"Tina, sorry, Constable Taylor, saw more of the scene than I did, and as soon as she realised it looked suspiciously like murder I moved back up to the lay-by here to avoid any further contamination of the area. Sergeant."

This now forced DS Charles to ask the same question of Tina. It was quite obvious he would have preferred not to but he'd been left no option.

Tina told him everything that had happened since they had arrived, not forgetting to mention that it seemed odd that there was no sign of either the dead woman's shoes or handbag.

"Constable Taylor, I thank you for securing what is left of the crime scene after two members of the public and two police officers have trampled all over it, but when it comes to deciding whether something looks odd just leave that side of things to the professionals, eh," he told her.

Tina had to bite her lip as she knew that he would not have talked to Ashley in the same manner.

Mr Brandon, the ME, was next to arrive and parked up behind the ambulance. He got changed out of his shoes, donning a pair of wellingtons before getting his bag out of the boot. He ambled over to the detectives and asked Longman about the whereabouts of the body. The DI pointed to Tina,

"Ask Constable Taylor, Henry, she seems to have got everything under control and is the only one who has actually looked at the body properly so far."

He knew without looking that his sergeant was inwardly wincing at a female officer getting any kind of praise. For all his personal failings, Charles was quite good at reading crime scenes and had often noticed small things that others had missed. This was the only reason that Longman kept him on as his partner, but obviously he would never let Charles know that.

Tina told the ME where the body was, and also informed him that the track was quite dry so his use of wellingtons was not really necessary.

"Ever since my first call out I have worn wellingtons, Constable, and I probably always will. Saves the worry of wondering whether I should have or not if I put them on at the start, but thank you for your concern."

Turning back to Longman, he asked, "Photos taken yet, Tom?"

"He'll be here in a couple of minutes," was the reply.

Within a minute the police photographer drove up, followed by a minibus, and another police car. The forensic team had arrived, a normal occurrence when a body gets discovered, and the two constables who got out of the police car had been asked for by Longman. He knew that the field would need securing from the public; and the press, who seemed to be almost psychic whenever a body was found. The photographer got his camera bag out of the boot and came over to them.

"Morning, sir, where is it?" he asked Longman.

"Through there and down to the small copse, you can't miss it. A body sat by a small tree," Longman answered, indicating the gap in the hedge.

The constables were ordered to keep members of the public from the field.

"It only takes a siren to stop, and they come out of the bloody woodwork, hoping to see the result of a road accident no doubt," commented one of them as they took their positions either side of the gap.

Longman thanked Tina and Ashley for their good work and told them that they could go back to their regular duties.

"Drop your reports in to my office later, OK."

"Not a problem, sir," said Tina.

As they walked back to their car Ashley said, "Shit, that'll be another late finish."

Then, as an idea hit him, he continued, "I don't suppose you fancy a bit of supper after, Tina."

"Yeah, why not," she answered, thinking to herself that it might be nice to find out if the gossip was true.

"Tell you what, why don't you drive for a bit, I still feel a bit peaky."

"Ta," Tina said as she took the keys and got behind the wheel, smiling broadly.

The photographer took his shots and walked back to the two detectives waiting by the hedge.

"Okay, sir, I'm done; unless you need any more close ups," he informed Longman.

"I think you've taken enough, thanks. Copies to the incident room as soon as possible, please."

"You get off," said D.S. Charles, "I have a camera if we *do* need any more."

"My turn now, I think," said the ME.

He went down to where his skills were needed and started his preliminary examination. This was really to confirm that the woman was dead and to make an educated guess as to how long she'd been that way. The cause of death looked likely to be gunshot wounds to the back of the head but this would be confirmed on the autopsy table later. He did get a shock, of sorts, when he opened the raincoat as the woman had nothing at all on underneath. He also noticed that the wrists showed signs of some form of restraint, but he would be able to determine more once the body was on his autopsy table.

"OK, Tom, she's all yours for the moment. Looks like she's been here for a couple of days, judging by the damage done by nature. That puts time of death at sometime between Thursday afternoon and Friday morning. I'll be able to give you a more precise window after the autopsy, I'll be doing that this afternoon. Damn, it's just getting interesting in the open too." Henry Brandon was known for his love of golf, and was a good player by all accounts, captaining his local club and playing off an eleven handicap.

He went back to his car and changed back into his shoes before driving off.

"Wouldn't surprise me if he has a telly on the wall in the morgue," muttered Charles.

"Come on, Sergeant, let's take a look, shall we?" said Longman, as he handed a set of paper overalls to Charles before starting to get into his own.

They followed the forensic team who were already starting their search for any evidence left by whoever had brought the woman into the field. They were given the go ahead to have a closer look at the body by the sergeant in charge. Longman went to the body for a closer look whilst Charles, letting his DI carry on, stood back and just looked around. Charles preferred, whenever possible, to get the feel of the scene before getting down to the physical inspection. This one felt strange, even the positioning of the body felt wrong to him, in the open as it were, with no real attempt to hide it. Never mind that it was also naked but for a thin raincoat.

Why go to all the trouble of bringing someone here before killing them. The risk of being seen should have been enough to dissuade anyone from doing that, he was thinking, while studying the ground hoping to find something that shouldn't have been there.

There was nothing.

It had been so dry lately that there were no footprints or signs of a body being dragged.

Nothing.

He now moved closer to the body and saw immediately that this was a nasty one. The woman's face had been attacked, probably by scavengers, and her eyes were gone. Looking closer, he noted that there were indeed what looked like two small calibre gunshot wounds to the back of her head. He grudgingly admitted to himself that that girl PC had given quite a good account of things.

He looked at the wrists then, noticing that they had been tied with something narrow, and they had been bound tightly. She hadn't struggled, as there were no scrape marks from the bonds and the skin wasn't broken. *Curious*, he thought. The raincoat was the only clothing on the body. Ears were pierced but no earrings, and no rings on the fingers even though there were the ridges on the thumb and fourth finger of the right hand which indicated that rings were normally worn.

"Someone wants this one to remain unidentified for as long as possible, sir," he remarked to his DI.

"Let's hope that we can prove him wrong on that, Sergeant. Her identity may well prove to be a key factor in this if we're lucky, so we need to find out her name, and soon. According to the ME she's been here for maybe two days already," said Longman.

"Yeah, I know, that's two days for the killer to be feeling good about getting away with it."

Charles took a set of prints from the left hand, hoping that they would match a set on the police database. Contrary to popular belief, their success rate in finding identities from prints was quite low. Most of the population was law abiding and had never been printed, making the process of identifying a body more difficult.

All good detectives knew that they needed to get somewhere with murder cases within the first twenty four hours, before the clues disappeared, and this one had already passed that deadline.

DS Charles told his boss his thoughts so far and suggested that the autopsy would probably show that some kind of drug was involved, causing the woman to be relatively docile in the time before she was killed.

"Agree entirely, Sergeant, so will you do the honours with Henry this afternoon. I have an appointment with the ACC, I'm afraid."

"Not a problem, sir," said his sergeant, "it wouldn't do to keep her waiting. I'll see you back at the office later, after Mr Brandon's done his stuff."

Leaving the team to carry on, Longman and Charles returned to their car, divested themselves of the paper overalls, and made their way back to headquarters.

# Chapter 2

Kate Laxton, the youngest Assistant Chief Constable in the force at just thirty three, was sat in her office on this Saturday afternoon with a bit of a problem. She'd heard that one of her Detective Inspectors had been to the scene of a murder near a little village in the eastern part of the county and had requested that the police photographer take some shots of the general area as well as the usual close ups of the body.

She had also asked for the SOCO, DI Tom Longman, to come and see her as soon as he'd been to the scene. She was waiting for him now, with a forgotten mug of coffee on the desk. She had the posh cups and saucers but only used them when diplomacy demanded something better than her Ikea mug. Her intercom beeped softly on the desk and she pressed the answer button.

"Yes, Emma?"

"DI Longman is here, ma'am," said her PA.

"Thanks, Emma, send him in, and can you do a couple of mugs of coffee, please?"

She knew he also hated drinking coffee from little cups.

"No problem, ma'am."

Emma had a list of how her boss's regular visitors liked their coffee so didn't have to ask how the DI took his, just one of many reasons Kate liked having her as her PA.

There was a tap on her door and DI Longman came in, followed by Emma who removed the cold cup of coffee from Kate's desk.

"Afternoon, Tom, how was it?" Kate asked, getting straight to the issue at hand. Whenever she was one on one with any of her senior officers she preferred to use their name rather than their rank. It had taken some of them by surprise, but she had found that the conversation flowed easier and she ended up finding out more than she would have otherwise.

"Bad, ma'am, very bad indeed," he answered. He was old school and would never use anything other than ma'am or sir when talking to officers senior to him. He gave her a brief summary of what they had found at the crime scene, stopping when Emma returned with the coffees.

"Before you start giving me anymore, Tom," Kate said as Emma left the room, "there is something I need you to see."

Kate took a photo off her desk and handed it to him, noticing the reaction as he realised what it showed.

"This photo was taken at the scene where the body was found!" he exclaimed.

"That's what I was afraid of," she said.

"How do you come to have it here, surely the photographer hasn't been that quick?"

"That arrived in the post, or I should say in the post-*box* this morning," Kate explained. "There was no stamp and it was addressed to me personally. Inside was that photograph, and this," she continued, passing her DI a note.

Longman took it, unfolded it and read,

**THIS IS THE FIRST. NICE VIEW, AIN'T IT.**

"I see, I don't suppose that anybody saw who posted it."

"Unfortunately, no. The desk sergeant keeps an eye on the entrance camera screen, as and when, but he was distracted by the cleaner knocking over her bucket. Next time the mail was checked that was in there."

"This puts a different perspective on things, if it's true. Of course, it could just be an empty threat," Longman said, but seeing the look on his boss's face he continued, "but we will treat it as genuine. This person is making it personal to you, seemingly, ma'am. Do you have any idea as to why?"

"No, and I've been wracking my brains trying to figure that out, Tom. It doesn't seem to make any sense to me at all. I want to be kept up to date with this one, regular daily reports, and don't mention this," she waved the note, "to anyone."

"Not a problem, ma'am. There'll be something, there always is, that will trip this killer up. It's the autopsy this afternoon, my sergeant is attending it, so let's hope for something from that to help us."

"That's DS Charles, isn't it."

Longman nodded.

"He has a good reputation. Not a lot gets by him from what I've heard. With the two of you on this I feel more confident of a result already," she added.

Longman took that as his cue and stood up to leave,

"Don't worry, ma'am, we'll get him, or her," he added, before leaving.

# Chapter 3

Henry Brandon looked down at the corpse on his autopsy table and said a little prayer, as he normally did before opening up what used to be a living, breathing human being.

*What did you do to deserve ending up here*, he thought, before starting his examination.

Aloud, he introduced himself, his assistant and also mentioned that Detective Sergeant Charles was observing, speaking into the microphone above the autopsy table. As he progressed he would be recording his observations for the autopsy report.

He cleaned under the nails and put the scrapings into a small container. He had many different sizes of container, all ready for accepting his samples. He took samples of hair next, both from the head and the pubic area. His inspection now became far more intrusive as it was always hoped that semen traces would be found, and he checked her vagina and rectum, taking swabs from both outside and inside.

"No apparent signs of forced vaginal intercourse, no excessive bruising except for the rectum, which does show evidence of forced anal intercourse."

He forced her mouth open and found that there was a wadded ball of material inside. He removed it and it turned out to be a pair of panties.

"A pair of panties, found wadded into a ball inside her mouth," he said, putting them into an evidence bag. They would be checked later for any DNA traces that, hopefully, would not match her own. He also took several swabs from inside her mouth.

The only other conclusion he came to before starting on the head wound was that there did not appear to be any signs of the deceased struggling with her bonds. There were marks, of course, left by whatever had been used to secure her hands. He'd seen similar marks before and guessed that they'd been made by large cable ties. He recorded his observations for the benefit of the recording and proceeded to turn the body over, with the help of his assistant who'd been observing the autopsy thus far.

Once they'd turned it over the ME reported the presence of purplish, bruise-like discolouration's on her buttocks.

"Based on the lividity marks evident on the deceased I would opine that she was killed while sitting down, probably at the location where she was found," he stated. He now started his examination of her head, having noted at the scene earlier the wounds present there.

"There are two, small calibre, gunshot wounds to the back of the head, one inch below the crown."

He got a thin plastic rod from the small table behind him and inserted it into one of the holes, confirming the calibre as .22.

"The angle of entry suggests that the killer was standing behind and above the deceased when the shots were fired, so the deceased was probably sitting. There is evidence of powder round the two holes. I have no doubt that she died as a result of being shot twice, at close range, in the head; and probably at the location where she was discovered."

He removed the rod and replaced it with a pair of long, thin forceps. After a bit of fiddling, he managed to remove both bullets and dropped them into separate containers. They would be sent for ballistics checks to be carried out. These would confirm the calibre of the bullets and also, if they were very fortunate, they would match ballistics data kept on file. It could be that the gun had been used before and the bullets ballistic signature could be matched; but if not they would then have the data on file in case the killer used the same gun again.

The body was turned onto its back once more and when he reached for the scalpel DS Charles decided to leave. He'd never got used to seeing a body get cut open, exposing the internal organs. All that would be done now was the cracking open of the ribcage followed by the removal and weighing of the heart, lungs, kidneys and liver. The stomach would be next, opened up to divulge its contents which would be analysed. This often helped to narrow down the time frame during which death occurred. After that there would be toxicology checks to see if drugs had been used to subdue the victim. Finally the cranium would be sliced open and the brain taken out and weighed. Charles had often wondered why all the organs had to be weighed, since he could see no profit from knowing.

The DS had just gone out of the door when his phone beeped.

"DS Charles," he said.

"Hello, this is Charlotte, I have the results from the fingerprint checks on your female found this afternoon. Shall I send them over to your office?"

"No, I'll collect them from you," he replied, "I'm just leaving the mortuary at Leicester Royal so, traffic permitting, I should be with you in about twenty minutes."

He was always glad of an excuse to go to Charlotte's office as she was an extremely pretty long haired blonde. He wasn't stupid and knew he'd never stand a chance with her, but a visit to her office always cheered him up.

Like a lot of specialists nowadays, she wasn't a serving officer but was always ready to cover the odd weekend call, especially when it was as urgent as this one. He knocked and entered her office, hardly waiting for her to invite him to enter.

"What have we got then, Charlotte?" he asked right away.

"Well, her name is Anna Horton. She is, sorry was, twenty six on her last birthday. Last month she was picked up by vice for soliciting, her second arrest, by the way, in as many months. She didn't have a regular boyfriend at that time."

By regular boyfriend the DS knew that the word pimp could have been used.

"So it looks as though she was a bit of a novice at the game," continued Charlotte, "getting caught so easily. Some of these girls are just doing it to get a bit extra for their drug habit but she was clean. Said she was saving up for a new telly," Charlotte added, reading from the computer screen where she'd called up the details from the arrest log.

"Address?" he asked.

"She was living at 46a, Somers Gardens. That's in the Beaumont Leys area, I believe." "Yes, I know the area, not the best place to house hunt, that's for sure. Any information on next-of-kin?"

"Her mother died when she was just six, and her father moved to Edinburgh two years ago. She moved into her current address when he sold up. Said she didn't fancy living up there. This is all according to the information she supplied. We have his name but no address, unfortunately," said Charlotte.

"Can you give me a print out of all this?"

"Yes, thought you would ask so I already have. Here you are," she said as she passed him the copy.

He thanked Charlotte for her quick work and headed for the CID office, finding his DI had beaten him there.

Longman quickly read through the report, then picked up the phone and rang the number of a local locksmith. After getting confirmation that the man would be at the address within the half hour Longman put the phone down and, turning to DS Charles, he said, "Come on, Sergeant, no time like the present. Let's see what kind of woman this Anna Horton was, shall we? We may even find an address for her father if we're lucky."

Her address turned out to be the top flat of a semi, the door was on the side of the house and the locksmith was waiting when they drove up. As they parked behind his van he got out and followed the two detectives to the door. He saw straight away that the only lock was a Yale and had the door open within a minute, using a bit of flexible steel strip.

"Do you want the lock changing, Inspector?" he asked.

"Just wait here for a couple of minutes, please," Longman said, "there may be spare keys in the flat so if we can save the expense…"

"Yeah, I know, police budgets and all that," said the locksmith, with a sigh.

After having a good look round, the DI could not find any spare keys and reluctantly gave the locksmith the go ahead to change the locks.

*Bet that will be a hefty bill*, he thought, *Saturday evening too.*

They started to search the flat while the lock was being changed. Everything seemed to be in its place. Just a normal single girl's flat. There was a basket of laundry waiting to be ironed by the look of it, and dishes on the drainer. No ashtrays or any signs of drug use. The fridge had a tub of margarine, half a container of semi skimmed milk and an unopened packet of thinly sliced ham. There was an empty vodka bottle on the table, and several foil takeaway containers in the kitchen bin. An old sideboard in the living room contained assorted bottles of spirits, most nearly empty, in one cupboard and, surprisingly, some good quality glasses in the other. The only item of any real worth was a large screen television sat on a corner unit, connected to a Freeview box. The drawers contained what looked like bills, most with the red bars top and bottom denoting overdue payments. *No personal correspondence anywhere which was rather sad*, thought Longman, and when he looked around there were no family photographs either.

The overall impression was of someone living from one day to the next. No wonder that she'd occasionally sold herself to make a bit of extra cash.

*This was a very lonely girl*, he thought.

In the bedroom they fared little better. Apart from the normal clothing any young woman would be expected to own, the wardrobe also revealed a selection of outfits that would have done justice to an Anne Summers window display. This got the DS to thinking about the possibility that she had used the flat for her 'business', and with a bit of luck this is where she may have entertained her killer. Longman agreed, this flat would need a good going over by the forensic team. If there was anything here that could assist them it would be found. They collected the new keys off the locksmith, locked up and headed back to the station. On the way Longman phoned in his request for forensics, but was told that they weren't available until Monday.

They stopped at the front desk and gave the desk sergeant the name of Anna Horton's father, asking him to please get on to Edinburgh police to see if he could be traced. Once they were in their own office and had got themselves a coffee, the DI ran through what they had so far, then sat back and invited his sergeant to add his observations.

"Well, sir, it's not often that I'm stuck for ideas, but this has got me baffled so far. If forensics can't discover something from the samples taken during the autopsy then I fear this could take a while to crack. There's always one detail that gets them in the end, though, so let's hope it turns up sooner rather than later."

The DI knew what his sergeant meant by that, and silently agreed.

"There's not much we can do tonight, Sergeant, so I'm off home and I suggest you do the same. I'll see you in the morning, we can work out a plan of action then."

"OK, sir, that sounds good. I'll just tidy things up here and I'll be off. See you tomorrow."

After his DI had left DS Charles sat at his desk for a few minutes before getting up and writing all the details they had so far onto the whiteboard that took up most of one wall of their office.

An hour later he had finished and before leaving he read all that he had written before turning out the light and going home. He'd found, on occasion, that this started his deduction processes going whilst he was sleeping and more than once he had woken up with a completely new angle to pursue.

Next morning DS Charles was at the office before seven but, even that early, he found his DI had beaten him in and was perusing the wallboard.

"Nice job, Sergeant, now if only this could tell us who did the deed. Have you had any further thoughts about, how we should proceed?"

Longman had always been one to give his subordinates every chance to show their mettle, and more than once he'd been surprised by the insight shown when crimes were being discussed.

"Well, sir, we know that her house needs a proper going over by the team, just in case she did entertain anyone at home last Thursday night. They may find something. A house to house too, someone may have noticed any comings and goings. Can you get people in on a Sunday, sir?" he asked.

"I'll try, sergeant, but that may have to wait. If we can't get forensics till Monday I wouldn't hold out a lot of hope for a house to house. You know what the budgets like just now."

"Any news from Edinburgh about the father yet, sir?"

"Not yet, but it looks like she wasn't in contact at all after he left. It will be nice to find out why."

"She may also show up on the area CCTV recording. Richard Mapley's on duty there this weekend so I'll pop down to his office with Anna's photo and hope he can turn up some footage. He's been a great help to us in the past," Charles said as he picked up the phone and dialled a number from memory.

"Hello, Richard, it's Michael. We need a favour, if you can spare a few minutes to do a search for us."

"Is that a real few minutes or are you after another needle in our haystack of footage?" came the reply.

"If I bring you a photo, along with the subjects starting address, do you think you could see if she shows up anywhere? She may have been soliciting near her address, but if we're very lucky she could have been picked up in the busier streets."

"OK, Michael, bring it over. But I'll warn you now that, with all the vandalism, there are a lot of our cameras out of action, God knows when they'll be fixed. Fortunately some are still working, so keep your fingers crossed."

As the DS put the phone down it rang straight away.

"CID office, DS Charles speaking," he said, holding it to his ear. "Oh, hello, Mr Brandon, what can we do for you?" he asked.

"I think you both need to come and see me, Sergeant. I have the results of the forensic checks on that young woman who was brought in yesterday, and some of them are quite interesting," he heard the ME say.

"Right, we're on our way."

He put the phone down and told his DI what the ME had said. They dropped the photo off at Mapley's office, he would call them as soon as he found anything, and quickly made their way to the mortuary.

The ME was in his office, waiting for them.

"Hello, Tom, Sergeant," he said as they entered, "come in and take a pew. I think you'll be quite pleased with what has been determined so far."

The two detectives sat opposite the ME and waited for him to continue.

"I've narrowed down the time of death to between midnight on Thursday and dawn on Friday. Can't get it closer than that, I'm afraid."

*That time frame had been expected as the killer would have been less likely to be seen during the hours of darkness*, thought Longman.

"As you know, there was a wadded up ball of material in her mouth. It turned out to be a pair of panties, which we are pretty sure were hers. Her DNA was present on them, and some of her pubic hair also which tends to confirm that suspicion. More interesting was the discovery of semen, both on the panties and the sample we swabbed from her mouth."

At this both detectives sat up a bit straighter, this was a major step forward in the case.

"I thought you'd like that piece of information," said Brandon. "There were no traces of semen on either the vaginal or anal swabs, by the way, although her anus did show signs of forced penetration," added the ME.

"And before you ask, we have already done the check on the DNA database and have a match. His name is Alan Massey."

"I know Alan Massey, sir," said DS Charles. "He's a bit of a lad. I arrested him last Christmas after a fight at a pub. He'd punched one of the barmen who'd refused to serve him and it so happened that I was there at the time. I couldn't stop the assault but I managed to subdue the little bastard and kept him that way until the uniforms arrived. I wouldn't think he would have the nerve to shoot anyone but we'd better find out. How do you want to play it, sir?"

"I think we had better assume that he could be armed, which means that we go in with an armed response team. I'll have a word with DCI Haddon and get things moving. Hopefully everything will go smoothly and we get the suspect in for questioning with no hassle but it doesn't hurt to be fully prepared," answered Longman.

"Before you leave, detectives, there is more," said the ME.

"The deceased had been drugged, probably to make her more manageable. I found traces of a benzodiazepine, Valium, in her blood, and a trace of chloroform as well. That would explain the lack of defensive marks, and would have also allowed the perpetrator to rape her, knowing he would meet with no resistance, before killing her. The cause of death was either one of the two gunshot wounds, certainly. My full report will be sent to you tomorrow."

"Once again, Henry, my thanks for your speediness with your procedures," said Longman, knowing that it could sometimes take a lot longer to get DNA matching. He didn't know it but the pathologist's brother in law had fast tracked the check.

"I just hope it's the end of it when we bring in Mr Massey."

# Chapter 4

Josh lowered his window and shouted at the car in front that had earlier pulled out from a lay-by, causing him to brake sharply. He'd caught up to it at the next set of lights.

"You fuckin' wanker, don't you know where your indicators are!"

It was a young guy in the car and, yes, it had to be an Audi didn't it. Josh was half hoping that the man would get out as he had 'just about had enough' for today. The number of drivers who would not use their indicators had been getting to him for quite a while now. They weren't as bad as tailgaters, oh no, but they still *annoyed him*.

Then he remembered that he had a passenger and decided he didn't need the aggravation, so was quite happy to see the lights change and the young man, in his penis extension, roar off down the road.

"Sorry about that, my darling, but sometimes these rubbish drivers really get me going."

His passenger looked at him but didn't speak. She couldn't, because he'd stuffed her mouth with her own panties before sticking some heavy tape over it. He could see her in the mirror on his visor, sitting in the back of his van, tied to the ladder struts, naked as the day she was born.

They'd met quite by accident on Friday, in Boots. He'd gone to work with a headache that had stayed with him all morning, so during his lunch hour he'd gone in search of some pain relief. While he was studying the choices of headache pills, she'd stood beside him. She wasn't much to look at really but she did have a great figure, and long black hair. When he started to dither about which tablets to get she gave him some advice.

"I always use these ones, they seem to work real quick," she'd said, giving him a smile.

"Well, I haven't tried them before," he'd said, "but how can I not? When such a beautiful girl has recommended them so nicely."

Her face immediately started to flush with embarrassment, so he apologised if he had offended her.

"No, you haven't," she'd said, "it's just that I don't get many compliments like that."

They had started chatting then and he found out that her name was Lucy, she was twenty nine, and had dropped her car in for a service that morning and was wasting the time until it was ready, by wandering the shops. Her car would take most of the day, though, as they'd rung her up to tell her that the rear brake pads needed replacing and they weren't due to be delivered until the early afternoon. After chatting for a while he told her about a nice country pub he knew of and suggested that they go and grab some lunch, his treat, and carry on their chat there.

She accepted, and once they were out in the country he'd stopped in a lay-by on a quiet road and asked her for a kiss. She readily agreed and he reckoned she'd not been with a man for a while, the way she hungrily kissed him. He tentatively put one of his hands on her breast and through the material of her t-shirt and the soft bra she had on he could feel her nipple hardening. She started moaning and her hand went to his crotch and she gently rubbed him through his jeans, getting him hard.

"Shall we get in the back," he suggested.

"Mmmm, yes please," she answered.

He'd made up his mind that she was to be his next victim while they had been chatting in Boots so it didn't really matter whether she agreed to have sex with him or not, as he was prepared for both eventualities. He was a little surprised, though a bit disappointed in her, when she had so readily agreed. She climbed over the seat into the back of the van and as she did he noticed that she had a perfect little bottom. This was going to be most enjoyable, for him at least. He followed her into the back where she sat on the single mattress he had laid down one side of the van and watched as she started taking off her things. He had been right about her body, it was perfect.

As her bra came off he found himself looking at two beautiful nipples standing erect on her firm breasts. Her jeans were next and then her panties, which she threw at him, telling him to get a move on. He took off his own things and when she saw his erection she gasped,

"God, will that fit? It's huge."

"Don't worry, Lucy, it'll fit, but I hope you don't mind if I wear some protection. I have a particular rubber that I like because it has an arse tickler on it, which I think you might enjoy."

He was watching her face as he said this and she gave an involuntary little shudder as he mentioned her arse getting tickled. He knew that he was going to have a great time with this one and wondered if she was a virgin in that respect.

Afterwards it was a simple matter to reach into the container at the end of the mattress, before pressing the prepared chloroform pad over her mouth and nose. She struggled but was no match for him and eventually she went limp and he laid her back down on the mattress. This had got him excited again and he turned her onto her stomach and admired her perfect bottom before roughly taking it once more. He decided that her long black hair needed shortening, and used a pair of old scissors from his tool kit to cut it so that it would hang only as far as her shoulders. She'd eventually woken up, still in his van, her mouth filled with a wad of something and taped shut. She was still naked and felt quite sore where he'd taken her from behind. She wondered why he'd cut her hair, she could see it lying on the van floor, and this got her thinking about what was going to happen to her now. She'd enjoyed the sex, well most of it anyway, and once he'd dropped her off that would have been the end of it. Goodbye, thanks for the scampi and the sex. No problem.

However, she didn't think that dropping her off was on the agenda, never mind lunch.

She was right.

After about ten minutes Josh pulled off the main road onto a country lane. Five more minutes saw him turning onto a single track lane that led into a small wood. There was a fire lookout tower in the heart of the trees that hardly ever got used anymore and he stopped his van and sat there for a few minutes looking around, making sure that they were alone.

"Okey-dokey, out we get," he said as he moved round to the back of the van. He climbed inside and cut the cable ties he'd used to secure her. He took a mac out of a bag and told her to put it on. She shook her head but changed her mind when he pulled a gun out of his jacket and pointed it at her.

"I said put the mac on, sweetheart. Don't make me use this thing, please."

She hurriedly put it on and got out of the van. He pointed at the ladder that gave access to the tower. She took the hint and climbed up. Standing at the bottom of the ladder, he watched her as she climbed up.

*What a waste*, he thought, looking at her perfect backside.

"Right over to the far corner, please, my dear, and face away from the trapdoor," he instructed as she climbed through the opening.

He climbed up onto the platform and sat in the opposite corner.

"You can take the mac off now. No, don't turn round yet," he quickly added as she started to turn towards him.

She shrugged out of the mac and it fell to the floor behind her. He reached over, picked it up then dropped it out of the trapdoor.

"Turn around now and face me," he instructed.

She turned round and he shot her in the heart. Her face only had the time to register surprise before he had reloaded. This time he aimed between her eyes and fired. She slumped into the corner, her blood slowly forming a little pool where she sat. After a moment she went still and he checked that she was dead. That was the only trouble with a .22, it sometimes took a few moments for the victim to die. He would have loved to have a .44 Magnum but they are not something you can buy readily in England, and they are far too noisy anyway.

"Pity, that was the sweetest piece I've had for a long time," he said, before taking out his camera and taking some shots of the view from the tower.

"I don't think you will be as quick to find this one, Kate…"

# Chapter 5

At that moment the subject of his thoughts was sitting at her desk ten miles away.

Kate Laxton was thirty three, very young for the post she'd held for only two months. She was quite slim but in a healthy way. She'd no use for diets and had always eaten whatever she fancied without having it turn to fat. Being raised a vegetarian had helped and she always had a well-stocked fruit bowl in her office. Her hair was jet black and cut just above her shoulders. She had the most piercing blue eyes and a ready smile, was a brown belt at judo and, unusually for a woman, a very good shot with the longbow. Married to husband Richard, an architect, there were no children yet. They'd talked about this before her promotion and had nearly decided that she would put her career on hold and try for a child. She knew of career women who could juggle both but that wasn't how she had been raised. If, and when, she had a child of her own she would gladly stop work to devote all of her time to it. This latest promotion was the best thing to happen so far in her career, but it had made any decision even more difficult. If the truth were told she would have to admit that, so far, her career had always made the decision for her. Being fast tracked up the promotion ladder had put any thoughts of stopping to raise a family on the back burner. Now, just when she had thought that she could start being a mother instead of a police officer this had happened.

She'd met Richard at the press launch of the plans for the new police station, to be built on the outskirts of Leicester. It would include a state of the art traffic monitoring centre and a large custody suite with twenty cells, reflecting the rising crime rate in the city. They'd clicked straight away and after a few months they announced that they intended to wed. There had been no honeymoon, Richard had been kept busy as the new police station had proved to be a perfect combination of good design and functionality, and he'd been asked to collaborate with architects on the continent. His design lent itself to interpretation, only slight alterations being necessary to accommodate their particular criteria. She'd managed to spend a week with him, before having to return to her job. During these frantic first years of their marriage, when most young couples would have been saving up for the pushchairs and cots, they'd been far too busy to think about having children.

Now, just as they 'were' starting to think about it, she'd found herself in this new job which had come like a bolt from the blue. The position of Assistant Chief Constable for the Leicestershire area had been hers for the taking really. The Chief Constable had been forced to take early retirement due to developing prostate cancer; *that* caused a lot of black humour in the ranks, as is usual in any uniformed service. This meant the move up to the top job for his ACC at the time, Chief Superintendent Harold Judson, which had, per se, created the requirement for a new assistant. He'd immediately thought of Kate and had asked her to attend an interview which had been a mere formality as she was the ideal candidate for the job. She was the youngest Chief Inspector in the force and had got there on merit. Her mind soaked up knowledge like a sponge, and this, combined with her near photographic memory, had proved invaluable during her career thus far. Not everyone was happy with this latest appointment, however, and with some she knew it was because she was a woman. There'd been quite a bit of friction at the start of her career but once it was realised how good she was, and how hard she worked, most of her colleagues ended up changing their attitude toward her. She hoped that she would end up getting the same level of support in this latest promotion. The press, of course, had made the most out of her appointment. The local papers carried her picture on the front with a full story detailing her career on a two page spread inside. Even the nationals took an interest as she had become the youngest ACC in the country, and was a woman to boot. This latter fact had caused some tongues to wag. Some of the older officers thought that she wasn't ready for the responsibility of her new office and she knew that she would have to tread carefully to avoid embarrassing herself. They would love to be able to say; 'Told you so'. The only weird thing about accepting the appointment was that she had been instructed to undergo a very strict medical, had even been put under the surgeon's knife while a biopsy was performed after a routine X-ray had shown a slight shadow. They told her that she'd had sarcoidosis, a self-limiting disease that affected nearly everyone at some time in their lives, but it came and went without treatment, so was very rarely noticed. It was a coincidence that she happened to have had it at the time she was checked.

Kate had known that she wanted to be in the police, ever since primary school. She was a lively, bright girl and had achieved good results in her exams. She applied to join the police and was accepted. During basic training she was consistently at the top of her entry in both the academic and physical aspects of the course, getting her noticed by the forces own 'talent scout'. This was a consultant who visited every course on the lookout for promising candidates, and he believed that he had definitely found someone out of the ordinary with Kate.

When she finished the course, getting the honour of not only being above her contemporaries in all aspects but also the distinction of achieving the highest overall score ever given, she was requested to present herself at New Scotland Yard for an interview. No matter how hard she tried she couldn't find out why she had been summoned, so on the appointed date she had shown up at the desk in the foyer of the iconic building that was the home of Britain's police force to so many.

Showing her very new warrant card, she introduced herself and handed her letter of referral to the desk sergeant. He checked her name against one of his many lists and, finding it, directed Kate to a door.

"Through there, Constable. Halfway up the corridor, on the right, you'll see a room with a Candidates Waiting Area sign on the door. Wait in there. Someone will come for you."

He pressed the release button for the door and Kate went through. Finding the small room, she took a seat and waited.

After ten minutes a head poked round the door,

"Constable Laxton?"

"That's me," replied Kate, getting up.

"My name is David Wright," he said, coming into the room and shaking her hand, "and I'll be interviewing you today along with some of your superiors in the police. I'm not a policeman, by the way, so you can call me David. Do you know why you are here?"

"Not really, no. I know I did well on the course so maybe it's to do with going on specialist courses, but that's just a guess."

"Not too bad a guess, as it happens, but it's not just any course you'll be offered, Kate. Follow me and all will be revealed."

Kate followed him along the corridor to the lifts, and they took one up to the fifth floor. Turning right, he led her to a door and, opening it, ushered her in and indicated for her to take the chair that faced a large conference table. Behind this sat three senior police officers; a Detective Chief Inspector Markham and two Chief Superintendents, Judson and Gillard, according to the name plates in front of each of them.

David Wright took a seat between the latter two and introduced his fellow interviewers before going into the reason for her attendance.

"Your performance on the basic training course was outstanding, Constable Laxton, do you mind if I call you Kate, by the way?"

"Not at all," Kate answered.

"Good. Well, every so often someone joins the police force who the instructors feel have the necessary personal qualities and commitment to go further up the promotion ladder than most. They call us and we then monitor this individual's progress to see if their opinion is justified. Most of the time it is, and that's when the people in this room come into the picture. You, Kate, have the qualities that will be needed in our next generation of senior officers. If you agree with what we'll be offering, you'll have the chance to develop these qualities and progress through the ranks a lot quicker than most."

This now had Kate's full attention and she wondered what was coming next. Obviously there was some kind of fast track promotion scheme on the table, just how it was going to work exactly, was still to be explained.

Chief Superintendent Gillard cleared his throat before addressing Kate.

"Constable Laxton, what we are proposing is seen as a sensitive issue in some quarters, so if you decide that it is not for you it must not, *under any circumstances*, be discussed outside this room. Is that understood?"

"Yes, sir."

"Good. Historically, there have been instances where a promising officer has left the force due to their frustration with how the system operates. Sometimes their talents are simply not allowed to develop because they are at the wrong end of the rank structure. We don't want this to happen with you. We believe that it would be best for the force if you stay, so in order for *your* talents to be fully realised we propose that you are given every opportunity to progress through the ranks at a rather faster pace than most. The first stage in this procedure is for you to complete a split university degree course in Law, and Psychology of Human Behaviour. We believe that these are the best subjects for you based on your performance in the course examinations that you took during basic training. This will be sponsored, of course. After all, we wouldn't want you to leave university with a huge debt, would we now?" he said with a smile.

While Kate was digesting this bombshell the DCI leant forward and fiddled with his name card. Kate looked at him, her attention caught, as was the intention.

"Please don't think that this is an easy ride you are being offered, Constable. You will need to work hard at university, the course is quite challenging I've heard. Afterwards you will face resentment from your peers as no matter how much we try to keep this low key, someone will discover the truth of your seeming 'fast track' rise through the ranks. Not everyone shares our views, I'm afraid, thinking that the only way one should be promoted is by the old criteria of 'doing your time' in the mundane jobs. We honestly believe that there are certain officers that deserve the opportunity to bypass some of these aspects of police work. You are one of them, Constable, so think hard about what is on the table here," he leant back again, but kept his eyes on her as she assimilated this information.

"My turn now, I think," said Chief Superintendent Judson, "although I doubt that I can really cause as much of a surprise as these two have done."

He looked at the sheet of paper in front of him on the table before continuing,

"We have put together a probable career projection for you, Constable, and it could go something like this: finish university, then on to the inspectors course and then into a supervisory office role here, at New Scotland Yard, for up to a year to learn the administration side of police investigations, etc. While you are doing this there will be opportunity for you to attend various seminars on police related topics to broaden your knowledge. Chief Inspector by the time you reach thirty and then, if you still show the aptitude and willingness, a transfer to an operational role, running a full station anywhere in the country, dealing with cases at first hand. We expect, with hard work and determination, you will be an asset to the force, and that dedication will be rewarded." He paused before continuing, "We do not expect you to give us an answer now. It's a lot to think about, and it will mean quite a change to your circumstances. Have you any questions for any of us, Constable?"

Kate had only one question really, so she asked it.

"Where do I sign?"

# Chapter 6

Detective Inspector Tom Longman looked at the faces of the officers gathered in the briefing room and thought, not for the first time, how young they all looked. Most of those present were at least ten years his junior, and sat waiting for the briefing with a kind of nervous excitement. It was not often that the armed response team got mobilised as things had quietened down recently. The last time they had been called on was when a gang of armed robbers had holed up in a barn out in the sticks. That stand off had ended peacefully with not a shot being fired, thankfully. The gang had realised that giving up was the better option, and when their weapons were checked they were found to be empty and no evidence of any ammunition was found. They'd used their weapons for effect only, but still got fifteen years each because in the eyes of the law they were considered to have been armed when they did the robbery.

"Right, settle down. I would first like to remind you all that even though you have the latest, and best, in protective wear, you still need to be careful. There is *always* the chance that the suspect could have other weapons, so be prepared for anything," he began, then having got their attention he continued, using a large diagram drawn on the whiteboard for reference.

"The suspect, Alan Massey, lives alone as far as we are aware. His house has two entrances, here and here," Longman pointed them out on the drawing, "apart from the windows, and is on two floors. The front door gives entry to the hallway with stairs leading up to the two bedrooms and bathroom, and two internal doors, one giving access to the front room, the other leading into the kitchen. There is an external door in the kitchen that gives onto the back yard. It is not a large house, so there are not too many places to hide. We will be going in at three am when, hopefully, he will be asleep. This will be a quiet approach, so until the doors get breached no talking once we have parked up our vehicles. DS Ryle of the ART will lead the team through the front door, and will proceed upstairs to, hopefully, apprehend the suspect quickly and safely. DS Charles will follow them in. DCI Haddon has asked to come with us and he and I will follow the team through the back door." He paused for a moment, and looked round at their faces, before delivering the last part of his briefing, 'There must be no doubt as to the correct procedure to be followed here. There is a real danger that the suspect is armed, so be prepared. Any questions?"

As expected, there were none – so the armed team left to check their kit and the rest of them settled down to wait the couple of hours before they were due to leave for the suspects house.

DCI Haddon steered Longman to one side and they stood against the wall drinking the obligatory coffee.

"You OK with going on this operation, Tom?" asked the DCI.

"Yes, sir, no problem. Let's hope that this goes well, it would be nice to wrap it up quietly, if you know what I mean."

"You think he did it then?"

"Seems that way, going by the evidence we have so far, sir."

"Well, if it does turn out to be this Alan Massey, he's been quite stupid. He must know that we have his DNA on file, and to leave the sort of traces that we found from him on the body…well, it seems too good to be true."

"Most criminals 'are' stupid, sir, and we'll hopefully be able to find out soon if Mr Massey is typical of the breed."

The police cars, and one large transit bus, had parked up in the empty car park of a pub on the next street to the one where the suspect lived. The armed response team were all kitted out in full protective rig, from their helmets right down to their specially reinforced boots. No chances were being taken with this operation. The personnel not in the immediate entry teams were to stay back until the suspect was in custody before they would enter the house and search for any more evidence that may help tie him to the murder.

At five to three the armed team set off and by the hour they were in position at both doors. On the stroke of three they forced both doors, and rushed into the house, shouting.

"Armed police, stay where you are and put your arms above your head."

The team that had gone through the front door stormed upstairs and split up to enter both bedrooms. In one of them they found a very puzzled looking Alan Massey starting to sit up in bed, alongside a girl who was reaching for her clothes off the floor at the side of the bed.

"Don't move, and put your hands on your heads, both of you," said DS Ryle.

"Sod that, I'm getting my t-shirt on at least, you lot 'ave seen enough," said the girl, pulling it on before sitting back against the headboard.

"Suspect is secure, sir," said the DS into his radio, "we'll get him into the front room. There is also a female here."

"Thanks, sergeant," said DCI Haddon into his radio mike, then turning to Tom he continued, "Time to meet Mr Massey, Tom."

They went up the path and entered through the broken front door. DS Ryle and his team were already in the front room with Alan Massey, and a girl who looked to be about sixteen or seventeen sat on the sofa. She had managed to pull her jeans on as well as her top, but he was dressed only in his underpants.

"Look, she told me she's over sixteen so why all the strong stuff, I've not done nothing wrong," Alan Massey said.

"Alan Massey, I'm arresting you in connection with the murder of Anna Horton. You do not have to say anything, but it may harm your defence if you do not mention when questioned something that you later rely on in court. Anything you do say may be given in evidence. Do you understand?" said Longman, looking hard at Massey's face as he delivered the caution.

Alan Massey just sat there, looking stunned.

"Right, get him out of here," Haddon said.

Once the suspect had been allowed to put on the paper suit they had brought he was led out to the police car now waiting in the road outside.

Longman then turned to the girl. "And what's your name, young lady?" he asked, pleasantly.

"None of your bloody business," she answered, not showing any signs of being overawed in the presence of so many police.

"You have been caught in the company of a suspected murderer so it is my bloody business!" he shouted. "Now, I'll ask you again, what is your name?"

She had shrunk back at his outburst and quietly muttered, "Linda Grant, and before you ask I *am* over sixteen."

"That's as maybe. What are you doing here with Alan Massey, Miss Grant?"

"Thought that was bloody obvious," she said, then noticed his face and continued quickly, "he was in the pub earlier and we both fancied each other so we ended up back here. He's not my boyfriend or anything like that. What was all that about anyway, the murder and all?"

"Nothing for you to get excited about, but you will be required to come down to the station to make a statement, so if you would like to get yourself fully dressed, we'll continue this chat later. We'll wait outside the door."

After she'd got properly dressed she was led out to a waiting patrol car.

Longman turned to DS Charles. "Right, let's get the team in to search this place. Forensics will need to take his clothes as well, they might tie him to the victim. Did you notice that he went very quiet when I mentioned Anna Horton? Let's find out why."

Back at the station they had Alan Massey taken to an interview room and DCI Haddon conceded the interview to Tom and his sergeant.

"You saw the victim, now it's time to find out if he's the one who killed her."

Longman and Charles went into the room and Alan Massey started speaking before they had sat down at the table.

"What did you mean about Anna being dead, I only saw her last Thursday and she was fine then. I know Anna, course I do. Everyone does round here. She's a good sport and doesn't charge too much either."

Before he could carry on Longman held up his hand and told him to shut up.

"Mr Massey, this interview will be recorded so if you could wait until we are ready before saying anything else, please, it will save us asking you to repeat yourself."

He pressed the button to start the recording, stated the date and time and named himself, DS Charles and the suspect then started his questioning,

"Now, Mr Massey. How well did you know Anna Horton?"

"Only as a customer. You do know she's a prossie, don't you?"

"Was, Alan – you don't mind me calling you Alan, do you? – was. She is dead, as I think you know."

"No, I didn't know. She was fine when I left her on Thursday night."

"And what time was that, Alan?" asked Charles.

"Just after we'd left the pub, about eleven I suppose. We'd gone round into the alleyway at the side of the pub car park 'cause she was going to give me a blow job. It was my birthday, see, and she said as a treat I didn't have to wear anything. She'd always insisted that I put a johnny on before. Anyway, afterwards I paid her the twenty quid and she went her way and I went to the takeaway."

"Which takeaway was that then?" asked Charles.

"Same one I always use, the Khyber on Melton Road. Got my chicken tikka and went home. Took a taxi, as it was my birthday. Didn't want to use my car that night 'cause I knew I was going to have a few drinks. I haven't seen her again since then, honest."

"Which way did she go, Alan?"

"I think she was going to try for some more punters so she would have probably gone to the bus stop to get a bus into town. That's the other way from the takeaway, just down a bit from the pub," Massey said.

"Did you see her get the bus?" asked Longman.

"No, I told you. I went the other way. She wasn't there when I went past in the taxi though."

"Do you remember how much later that was?"

"Not exactly, but the takeaway wasn't busy so it can only have been about fifteen minutes."

"Which taxi firm was it, Alan?" Charles asked.

"God knows, I just asked the takeaway bloke to order me one. It was outside waiting when I'd got me meal. I got in and it took me home. The driver was a Paki, sorry, Asian," he put in quickly as he saw Longman's face darken.

Longman reached over and turned off the recording equipment.

"Stay where you are, Mr Massey. We may need to continue this little chat later," he said, and got up from the table, closely followed by Charles.

Outside, in the corridor, Longman turned to his sergeant.

"His story will be easy enough to check. If he did get a taxi from the takeaway we may be looking at the wrong man for this one."

"I think I'm in agreement, sir, he doesn't give me the impression of being able to hurt anyone, much less kill them. His car will be checked over as a matter of course, but now we know where he claims to have seen Anna last we can narrow down the CCTV search. I'll get on to Richard Mapley and let him know where to look. There's good coverage of Melton Road, so if the cameras were working we should be able to pick her up and see if she met any more customers."

"Right, I think we had better keep Mr Massey here for the moment. The girl can stay too, they might be in this together. Certainly wouldn't be the first time. Tomorrow, sorry, 'today', will be a busy one and it's nearly dawn now, so I think forty winks are in order."

"If it's all right with you, sir, I'll get back to the CCTV people and see what they can come up with. I wouldn't be able to sleep anyway."

"I'll be in the office then, Sergeant, so if you do get anything you can reach me there."

DS Charles was humming to himself as he entered the supervisor's office, something from the charts but he wouldn't be able to name the tune if his life depended on it.

"You're in a good mood, you got your man yet?" said Mapley.

"Nah, but I've narrowed down the area and time scale for you to check. If your cameras were working we may find out where she went and, if we're very fortunate, who else she met that evening."

Charles filled him in as they went from his office to the terminals where they could call up footage from any of the hundreds of cameras in their area. Mapley turned the screen on and fed in the numbers for the cameras that covered the whole of Melton Road, starting with the cameras near to the pub that Massey said he had been in when he met Anna Horton. The screen was split into four and once Mapley typed in the times they were interested in they started watching, waiting to see either Massey or Anna appear.

"There he is, with Anna, coming out of the pub car park," said Charles, pointing at the bottom left screen.

Mapley pressed a button and it expanded to fill the screen. As they watched they saw the girl wiping her mouth before spitting on the pavement. Massey said something to her and they both laughed before he obviously said cheerio and walked away from her.

"That's the right direction for him to go to the Khyber," observed Charles.

Anna Horton stood still for a few moments before walking to the bus stop which was only just in the picture.

"The next camera down will have the whole of the stop in frame," said Mapley, pressing buttons.

The picture that came up was virtually unwatchable, the image was blurred and only the basic outline of the bus stop could be discerned. They leant forward and thought they could just make out a figure.

"That *could* be her," said Mapley. As they watched, a vehicle that looked to be the size of a small delivery van drove slowly into view, then stopped. It moved off again after half a minute but there was no way to tell even the make from the bad image, let alone the registration number.

They couldn't be sure that the bus stop was empty when it had gone but it seemed to be that way.

"What kind of van was that, Richard?"

"Could have been anything from a whole range of vans, Michael, but it looked to be the size of a Transit. I can't be more definite than that, I'm afraid. Let's check the footage from the next few cameras down the line and see if they show a better image, shall we?"

Mapley called up the next camera, fed in the time and they looked for a whole minute but the van didn't appear in the picture at all.

"It must have gone into the pub car park," said Mapley, "I'll check the cameras to see when he left."

They watched the recordings that covered the next hour, then the image went black.

"Bugger, the bloody camera failed. Sorry, Michael."

Without being able to determine when the van left the car park they knew it would be impossible to trace its movements. Unfortunately for them Leicester, in common with large cities everywhere, had white vans to spare.

"Never mind, Richard, at least we can let Massey go, and his date. Pity, it would have been nice and neat if he'd been the one. I don't suppose you know if the pub has its own cameras?"

"They didn't last week. We had a bit of a punch up reported in their area and it spilled over into their car park, that's how I know."

"Oh well, guess it's back to the drawing board. Thanks for your efforts, Richard. See you soon, no doubt."

"Anytime, Michael, we're always here."

DS Charles left him with his screens and headed back to his own office.

He wasn't humming this time.

Longman had been busy on the phone while Charles had been with Mapley. The taxi firm closest to the takeaway had confirmed that Massey had used one of their cars to go home, and that he was alone. He had been bragging to the driver about his special birthday treat, so he'd stayed in the driver's memory a bit longer because of it.

Charles filled his boss in with the CCTV evidence, or rather the lack of it. All they knew now was that it looked like Anna Horton had got into a white van of unknown make, before being taken to the field where she was found, and there shot twice in the back of her head.

"At least it looks like Massey is telling the truth, sir, probably a first for him," said Charles.

"Yes, Sergeant, and, although it doesn't help us a great deal yet, it seems that this white van may be involved. It could be just another customer so I think that we need to have a meeting with the press. An appeal for the driver of the van to come forward, I think, although if he indeed was a customer and is married I doubt that we'll get any response. Maybe someone saw something. Anything at all will be a help on this one."

# Chapter 7

Josh was watching the early evening local news while eating his chicken 'ding' and nearly choked when a pretty young girl reporter started talking about the discovery of a woman's naked body in a field. He quickly turned the sound up and heard the copper as he answered the reporter's question about the identity of the dead woman.

"At this time we are not releasing the identity of the deceased. However, we are keen to talk to anyone who was in the area of the Red Lion public house on Melton Road between the hours of ten pm and midnight last Thursday evening. We especially want to talk to the driver of a white van who may have parked in the car park of the public house at about eleven pm that evening. We are also asking if anyone saw a white van parked at the side of the B6047 just before Tilton on the Hill, on the Queniborough side of the village, later on that same night or early on the Friday morning. There is a dedicated phone number to call which is 0116 225 5222. All information will be treated with the strictest confidence."

Josh turned the television off and sat for a few moments thinking hard. He knew that the woman would be found eventually, but from what the copper had said it seemed as though they knew the identity of the girl which was more than he knew as names were not generally traded between customers and whores. All he had wanted was the sex and the satisfaction of killing the girl afterwards. She had looked a little like that bloody Kate Laxton and it had been her that had been in his mind when he'd pulled the trigger. *If only it had been*, he' thought, before remembering that his aim was to make her feel inadequate as a copper first.

There had not been any registration number read out, but he knew that if they had discovered that they would have been banging on his door by now, so that was not a worry. His van, along with thousands of similar vans, was not marked with any firm's name, which made it completely anonymous. This time it seemed as though he had been lucky, he would have to be a damn site more careful in future.

*First things first*, he thought, it was time to make a call.

He finished his meal quickly and left his house, walking down the road to a telephone box. He rang the number that had been scrolling along the bottom of the screen while the copper had been gabbling on and waited for it to connect.

"Leicester police, this is Constable Martin, please say your name and address and the reason for your call?"

"Just shut up and listen. You want information about that lass that got herself killed? I did it, and I fucked the bitch before I killed her. If you don't believe me I can tell you how she died. Two shots in her pretty little head. And you can tell that cow that's in charge of you all, that she's only the start. I've already done the next one but I'm not telling you where. You'll get the photo, *you* work it out."

Josh hung up and went back to his house.

He lived alone in the house, where he had grown up as the only child. He had never married, he could never hold any relationship together long enough to enable it to develop. His parents had died when he was seventeen, killed when their car was hit head on by a fuel delivery lorry. The driver had suffered a heart attack at the wheel and his lorry carried straight on instead of going round a bend. Josh's parents were just unlucky that day to be coming the other way. That had been twenty years ago now. As the only child he'd inherited the house and also received a sizeable settlement from the lorry driver's insurance company. His parents had both been lawyers, with their own offices and a very wealthy client base, and after the funeral a lawyer had been appointed to look after the firm's interests until a buyer could be found. Eventually a large law conglomerate had shown an interest and eventually bought the firm, along with all the clients, for a sizeable sum. At the age of seventeen Josh had found himself to be a very wealthy young man.

. He still missed his parents, of course, and fondly remembered his childhood. His parents had never really finished with the hippy scene. They'd been at the famous Woodstock Festival and, even though they had become lawyers and joined the 'other side', still believed in free love and peace to the world. He would always be able to sing the words to 'With a Little Help from my Friends', having heard it hundreds of times played at full volume on his parent's stereo.

Josh had grown up in a cloud of fantasy. He'd quite often walked in on his parents indulging in sex, often in a haze of funny smelling smoke. At first he'd been too young to realise what they were doing, of course, and had been told to leave quickly. By the time he reached his teens he knew though, and would watch them without being seen. He'd also found out that the funny smelling smoke was probably pot. He had tried a puff of one of the fat cigarettes once and it made him feel all funny, which had amused his parents.

"One day you'll get a different effect," they'd told him.

He hadn't mentioned it to them then but one of its effects had been to make his penis go hard. He'd gone to his room and looked at it, then stroked it until he went a bit light headed. He'd watched in wonder at the stuff coming out of the end. That had never happened before. He tried to make his penis go hard again but it wouldn't so he resolved to get another of the 'cigarettes' from his parent's room. He found that, while puffing on these, he could play with himself for a long time before his penis let loose with the white stuff, while he fantasised about doing to the girls at school what he'd seen his parents get up to in their bedroom.

Once he'd brought one of his classmates back to his house.' He was fourteen and she was just coming up to her fifteenth birthday. He'd told his parents that they were going to help each other with homework and took some sandwiches and pop up to his room. After they'd eaten, and drunk the cans of pop, he'd shown the girl one of the 'cigarettes' and asked her if she wanted to try it. She'd agreed and they'd both got a bit high and, as he'd hoped, his penis went hard. He'd asked her if she'd ever seen a hard willy and she'd said no, so he'd unzipped his trousers, got it out and showed it to her. She'd touched it and it twitched which made her giggle. She'd touched it again and made it twitch again. He'd told her to wrap her hand round it and move it up and down and when she did that the sensations he'd felt were unbelievable. He'd asked her if she felt funny anywhere and she'd told him that she felt a bit strange 'down there'. He'd put his hand on her knickers and started rubbing her while she was rubbing him. Very soon he'd ejaculated and stopped rubbing her as it happened. She'd grabbed his hand and put it back, telling him to keep doing it. Not long later she shuddered a bit and asked him to stop. He'd carried on and she kept jerking against his hand and tried to pull it away because she said the sensations were too much. He'd kept his hand there though, rubbing her through her panties and watching her face start to contort. In pain or pleasure, he didn't know and didn't really care because he found that his penis had started to get hard again, so he pushed her over onto his bed and pulled her panties down. He put one of his hands on her neck, holding her down, and tried to put his penis inside her but before he could he ejaculated again. He immediately felt embarrassed and said sorry, and the girl pulled her panties up and told him she had to go home now.

"Don't worry, I won't tell," she said. "It's not like you actually fucked me, anyway."

"Can we try again? I've never done it properly," he'd asked, "and seeing as you know the 'f' word I suppose that you've done it loads of times."

"Cheeky bugger," she'd said, but, remembering how surprised she had been at the size of his penis, she agreed.

"Tomorrow afternoon, then," he'd said.

The rest of that term had seen her, and some of the other girls too, regularly joining him for 'homework' sessions after school. She'd obviously told her friends about the size of his penis, and they couldn't wait to see it. He was happy to oblige, and although stroking it was all some of them wanted, he did get to have proper sex as well sometimes. That was when he realised that the rougher he got, the better it was for him.

Yes, his early teenage years were definitely worth the memory.

He left school as soon as he could and got a job in a video store. He chatted up the girls and occasionally got them back to his place for sex.

After the death of his parents he had left his job and travelled, always to the countries whose tourism depended to a large extent on the sex industry. He had become addicted to it, and now that he had the means, he was determined to try all the various ways of enjoying it that were available in the world. His favourite holiday during this year had been Thailand, where he'd found that his sexual tastes were easily satisfied.

He needed to dominate his partner during sex, and the girls of Bangkok were ready and willing to go along with his demands. Their only thoughts were for the money and they would accept that occasionally the missionary position was just not exciting enough for some men. Indeed, they are known throughout the world for their expertise in satisfying all manner of requests, from women as well as men. He could never go back there though. On his last night he had been walking back to his hotel for a change of clothes, when a street girl had approached him.

"I stay all night with you, ten thousand baht," she trilled, sliding her hand into his trouser pocket and giving him a squeeze.

He looked down at her and thought that she was the most perfect girl he'd seen since he had arrived in Bangkok ten days' earlier. Her hair was jet black and hung to her waist. She wasn't tall, but not many Thai girls were, and she had a firm looking body that invited thoughts of a carnal nature. Good shape, too, which made a change. A lot of them were so thin, with small bums and breasts, it was like shagging a skeleton.

"OK, but we'll have to be quiet going into my hotel. Nobody must see you," he told her.

"No problem mister, you go and I follow, five minutes, OK."

"Room 517, the Imperial," he told her and headed for his hotel.

He went into the lobby and got his key from the desk, then used the lift to the fifth floor. He got to his room and thought that there was no way she would actually come to him, although it would have been a nice end to the holiday. He laid some fresh clothes out and was about to start his shower when there was a soft tap on the door. He wrapped a towel round his waist, went to the door and looked through the peep hole. She was standing there, looking from side to side so he opened the door and pulled her inside the room.

"See, mister, I come."

*Not yet, but you will*, he thought, as he looked at her, his erection already starting to grow.

She looked down at the bulge pushing at the towel he'd wrapped round himself and smiled.

"You happy to fuck me," she squealed, and pulled the towel off before kneeling down and kissing his now erect member.

He let her carry on and was almost going to let himself come but he withdrew from her mouth and told her that he wanted to see her naked too.

"No problem, mister," and was out of her dress and panties in a flash, but as she knelt down again he told her no, he wanted to do other things.

"Anything you want, I do for you, no problem."

That was just what he wanted to hear and for the next few hours he was treated to the realisation of many of his fantasies.

Until he killed her.

He was taking his pleasure from behind and her hair had fallen down either side of her neck, *such a beautiful neck*, he thought, and before he realised what he was doing he had grasped her neck in one of his hands and started squeezing. She started bucking and reached for his hand to stop him but didn't have the strength in her small body to prevent him strangling her. His excitement increased as fast as her struggling grew fainter and as he finally came he released her and she fell onto the bed. She didn't move so he shook her but there was no response. He checked her breathing but there was nothing, she was dead. He'd strangled her. He wondered what to do now, this was something new. His instinct for survival cut in so he got dressed and sat down on the end of the bed. He had to get rid of the body, and quickly. He wasn't sure if Thailand had the death penalty but he certainly didn't want to find out. Even if they didn't, the thought of being incarcerated in one of their prisons for the rest of his life didn't exactly fill him with joy. Getting up from the bed, he went into the corridor outside his room and looked for a suitable hiding place. There were several store cupboards at the end near the lifts and he quickly discounted these as they would be in constant use by the housekeeping staff. He did find a small room, at the other end of the corridor, with cots stored against one wall. There was a cupboard behind the cots that looked big enough for the girl's body to fit. It didn't look as though the cots had been moved in some time as they were dusty as hell, so he went back to his room and waited for the hotel to go quiet. This being Bangkok he had to wait until nearly three am before the noises of giggling and shrieking street girls being brought back for some tourists pleasure had stopped. He dressed the girl and carried her body to the store room. Moving the cots to one side, he folded her into the cupboard. Replacing the cots he cracked open the door an inch, to check that the corridor was still empty, before returning to his room where he showered, then packed ready for leaving.

No, he definitely did not wish to return to Thailand.

That was twenty years ago now but he still got an excited thrill when he remembered how he had felt in that far off hotel room.

He'd tried his hand at different jobs, more to keep from getting bored than any need for the money. He was having a drink one night with one of his co-workers from the bottling plant where he'd been for a month when the guy told him that the police were looking for recruits.

"I think I'll go for it. I've always liked the idea of being in uniform, and the policewomen look sexy as hell in theirs," he'd told Josh.

Josh thought for a minute, the images of young female police recruits in their uniforms swirling round in his head.

"Think I'll join you," he'd said.

He thought he really wanted to do something with his life and this seemed as good a path as any to follow so the next day he went, with his colleague, to register his interest at the local police station.

He got through the selection process, his mate didn't.

Eventually he was called to attend the training course and arrived full of confidence. There were fifteen others on the course, including three females. One of them was a real looker too, with short black hair framing an oval face. He resolved that he would try to know her better, a lot better, before the course ended.

He was OK with the physical aspects of the training, he had always been relatively fit without having to try too hard. When it came to the theory, however, he started to flounder. He couldn't remember enough to pass the paper examinations and was continually having to take resits. What made it worse was that one of the girls on the course, and it 'had' to be the looker, always came top. Her name was Kate Laxton and she'd rebuffed 'all' advances, not just his, but he didn't see that. If he couldn't have her he resolved to beat her in an exam, just once. The instructor helped as much as she could but a fortnight before the half way point she took Josh to one side and explained that if he failed this exam he would be back coursed. No one ever wanted that. It got round the force and wherever the person ended up he would always find that the whole station knew that he, or she, had started police life as a failure. He had to pass this exam, no matter what. He'd got to know the clerk in the school office quite well as he had handed his resit paperwork in at her office often enough. She was nothing to look at, quite frumpy really, and always looked at his arse whenever he went in. He knew this because he had turned round quickly once and caught her. She made a joke of it but he could see her face had flushed. He wondered just how far she would go, as she had a wedding ring on the appropriate finger and really didn't look as though she would cheat on her husband. He decided to find out and went to see her, ostensibly to get some notes. He leant over her desk and spoke quietly so she would lean forward.

"You have a lovely cleavage, love, I would like to go to bed with you right now, and put my dick between those," he'd said, looking at her breasts.

*He would get one of two reactions*, he thought. Either she would shrink back and start yelling at him or she would ask him to repeat himself. He hadn't counted on what she did do, though.

Without a word she got up, went to the door, locked it and then dropped her panties to the floor before sitting on the edge of her desk with her skirt round her waist and telling him to get a move on. He was soon giving her his best and it was only a couple of minutes before she came with a moan and a shudder.

He couldn't help himself and came also, which hadn't been his intention at all.

"I've wanted you ever since I first saw your nice bum weeks ago. That was better than putting it between these, wasn't it?" She'd said, giving her breasts a shake.

He visited her each day for the next week and when he thought that she would do anything for him he told her that he needed to see the question paper for the big examination that was approaching.

"Uh, oh. No way can I do that. It would be more than my job's worth," she'd answered.

"Oh, come on, love, no one would know."

"I've said no, and I mean it. Now come on and sort me out, it's been two days."

"Not on your life. I've only been shagging you to get those questions so now I'll get you to let me see them without having to please your fat body. If you don't show them to me I'll tell everyone what we've been up to, starting with your husband."

"You bastard."

"Call me what you like, 'sweetheart', but you *will* show me those questions. Tell you what," he said, opening his fly and showing her what she'd asked for, "I'll let you have this one more time too. You can't say fairer than that."

He was right, she couldn't help herself and, opening her filing cabinet, she passed him a set of papers. He quickly photocopied them and then, true to his word, dropped his pants and let her have what she craved.

When the day of the exam arrived he couldn't help but feel a bit smug. He'd show that Laxton who was the best. He'd done the test in his room, with the help of the textbooks that wouldn't be allowed inside the examination room. Time after time he had read the answers until he had them locked in his head. As they all filed into the room he was humming to himself.

"Feeling confident, are we?" asked Kate.

"Yes, I think I may have finally cracked the secret of studying. Good luck," he replied, smiling. Inside he was thinking that this time he would beat them all, *especially you, Kate bloody Laxton.*

As soon as he opened the paper his smile evaporated and he could feel the familiar sensation of failure. The paper in front of him was totally different than the one whose answers he had memorised. He was stumped. He couldn't think of anything except what he would do to that bitch of a clerk. He fumbled through the exam, knowing that he had cocked up once again.

As soon as it was over he went to the clerk's office, finding her at her desk.

"What the hell are you playing at?" he shouted. She looked terrified and he carried on, spittle flying from his mouth in his rage. "You knew, didn't you, it was the wrong fucking paper. You'll be sorry now, you bitch, *everyone* is going to know about your liking for cock now. Starting with your husband!"

Before he could say more the door flew open and he was grabbed from behind and forced into a chair by one of the instructors, who held his head in an arm lock.

'You'll not say a word to anybody, sunshine, if you know what's good for you. If I were you I would resign from anything further to do with the police right now. You wouldn't make a good copper anyway, you can hardly remember your name. Do you understand, Josh?" the man said, giving Josh's neck a squeeze.

"Fine, I didn't like any of your stupid rules anyway. And *you*," he spat, looking at the clerk, "were a lousy screw." He yelped as his neck was crunched by the instructor, who then released his hold and told him to get out.

"Thanks, Len, I didn't know who to ask. I knew he'd be back to see me after the test and, alone, I wouldn't have been able to stop him," the clerk said.

"Not a problem, Mary. Not a problem."

"Do you fancy a cuppa, Len, I hate having elevenses on my own," she said, moving round the desk.

Josh had tried several jobs since then and for the last three years he'd been working for a small delivery firm. It suited him as he could never have worked in an office or shop environment. That would have sent him potty. It didn't pay very well but money wasn't a problem, he just needed to do something. The nature of the job meant a lot of travelling and spending nights away from home. His hotel rooms were paid for by the company but not his extras. Not surprising as these extras were the women he either bought or, if he was lucky, chatted up enough to get them into bed. His perfect choice would have to be the bored wife looking for some fun on the side, as if he got a bit too rough who were they going to complain to without revealing what they had been doing.

And he nearly always got rough.

He'd realised after the Thailand holiday that inflicting pain on the woman, or girl, during sex increased his excitement and although he hadn't killed again, till now, he knew it had been close sometimes.

Josh opened the door and entered his den. This had been his father's 'at home' office when he was alive and Josh still used the big old desk, but now it was 'his' computer that sat there, connected to a high quality printer. He switched both on and, when prompted, entered his password. He opened his documents folder and selected the album icon. A new box opened with his albums listed by date. There were only two.

He selected the latest date and the photographs that he had taken from the lookout tower opened as thumbnails. He started them up in a slideshow and went through them one by one until he found the one he wanted. It showed the spire of a church far in the distance, above the trees that filled most of the shot.

He printed this off and, going back to his desktop, selected Word and printed off his second message to ACC Kate Laxton.

**WHERE IS THIS? YOU MAY NOT KNOW, KATE, BUT NUMBER TWO DOES**

He trimmed the sheet of paper to the same size as the photo and sealed them both in an envelope, using a stencil to print her name. Picking up his car keys, he left the house and drove to the local police station. This, like many local stations, was only open at certain times so there was no one to see him post the envelope in the box outside the front door. He went back to his car and headed home, stopping off on the way to ring the police information number again.

"It's me again, the killer," he said before the operator could start talking. "Check all your local station post-boxes. I've left you a message, Kate."

He rang off before the operator could do or say anything. The operator reported this call to her supervisor who immediately called the duty inspector who in turn called DI Longman. Everybody had been told, after the first call, that if any more calls of a similar nature were received he had to be told immediately, and no one else.

Longman went down to the control room and found the duty inspector, Mark Statham, already making a list of all the local stations that were closed at this time.

"There're only eight, but they are spread around a bit. Do you want any help, sir?" he asked Longman.

"We were trying to keep this under wraps a bit, about the messages to the ACC. It seems that he wants everyone to know, though. Can I use your phone?"

He rang the ACC's office, and after a couple of rings it was picked up.

"Assistant Chief Constable Laxton."

"Hello, ma'am, it's DI Longman. We've had two calls from the suspected killer of Anna Horton." Longman read out the messages that the operator had received. "'There are eight stations to check so to save time do I have your agreement to use the area cars. I don't think that the personal side of this can be kept under wraps any longer."

"Of course, Tom, but it's only two days since we found Anna Horton. If this is another murder let us hope that he is not starting a killing spree. Please get it to me as soon as you can."

An hour later Longman was in the ACC's office.

"This doesn't look good, Tom."

"No, ma'am. We need to identify where this photograph was taken, and soon. There is always a chance that he's bluffing, of course. It is a bit soon after finding the other one for him to kill again. In my experience there is normally a longer gap between events while the murderer savours the kill. I don't suppose anything has come to mind as to why there is the personal touch, ma'am?"

"No, but it seems as though he is definitely taunting me. Challenging me, us, to find him. And we will, Tom, we must."

"I have sent DS Charles off with a copy of the photo, ma'am. He knows someone in the city council who is a bit of an expert reading maps and hopes that, having the spire of a church visible in the photo, it will be possible to identify the location. It's been taken from height, either up in a tree or some kind of tower or pylon, so we are confident that we will find it sooner rather than later."

'If he *is* operating in our area still."

"Yes, there is that. He knows that some of our stations are not manned round the clock, which probably means he has local knowledge. I doubt that he would stray too far out of our beat, ma'am. He wants us to find his victims, I'm sure, but at the moment it's all on his terms. We need to find this place and hope there are some clues."

While they had been talking DS Charles had arrived at the council buildings. He parked up and was on his way towards the entrance when a young man sped past him on his bicycle, nearly catching his sleeve.

"Hey, mind where you're going, you idiot,' Charles shouted after him.

"Bollocks!" the man shouted back, as he sped off round the corner of the building. Charles mentally noted the man's clothing and hoped he would see him again. He hated cyclists that didn't follow the rules, they spoilt things for the ones that did.

As he turned the corner his wish was answered. There was a girl, she looked to be in her late teens, sitting on the path rubbing her arm and crying. The idiot who had been on the bike was just getting to his feet and was looking at the damage done to his pride and joy. He'd quite obviously collided with the girl before slewing off the path and into a bench. His bike had taken the brunt of the impact, the very bent front wheel testified to that. Charles told him to stay where he was and helped the girl up, asking her if she was OK.

"Yes, I think so, but my arm hurts quite a bit."

Charles guided her to the bench and she sat down with a sigh. He had a quick look at her arm and couldn't find any broken skin but it was swelling up quite quickly. He took out his phone and called for an ambulance.

"Better to be safe than sorry, eh."

He turned his attention to the young man, asking him just what he thought he was playing at cycling so fast on a pathway.

"I always go fast, keeps me fit. I've never had an accident before."

"Well, I hope you have some sort of personal insurance, son, because if I was her I would sue you for starters. Now, what's your name?" Charles asked.

"I don't think that's any of your business, mate."

"Oh, I think I can make it my business, 'mate'," said Charles, producing his warrant card and showing it to the young man.

'Shit, just my bloody luck. OK, my name's John Smith, and before you ask for it, here's some identification. For some reason you lot always think I'm taking the piss when I give you my name." He handed Charles a council I.D. pass.

"OK, Mr Smith, first off I'm going to ask you to moderate your language. It's not big and it's not clever to swear, especially at a police officer. I need you to make a statement as to exactly what happened here. I shall be getting the girl's version also and, going by the way you sped past me and shot round the corner, I think I can guess what she will say. Have you been in trouble with the police before?" Charles asked, thinking about what the man had just said.

"Yes, but nothing serious."

"What do you call 'nothing serious'. Just remember, I can check."

"Riding my bike on the pavement, twice," said Smith, quietly.

"Not learned your lesson yet, have you? I shall be reporting you and, going by your own admission, you will probably receive at the least an official caution this time. I wouldn't be at all surprised if you were asked to complete, at your expense, a safe cycling course."

Charles started taking notes and as he did the ambulance arrived. The medics looked at the girl's arm and concluded that it was not broken, just badly bruised. They strapped it up and gave her some painkillers, telling her to see her own GP if it got worse. The young man had torn his jeans but had no injuries at all.

"You're lucky, Mr Smith. This young girl can still take you to court, so I would make my apologies to her now, if I were you."

"Yeah, you're right," the young man said, then turning towards the girl he continued, "Sorry about running into you and that, and I'm glad you're OK really and that, OK," he said.

"That's OK, no real harm done. But you could buy me a coffee."

The young man picked his bike up and walked off with the girl. Charles wondered what the world was coming to before carrying on into the council buildings and finding his way to Alan Holmes' office.

Once he was settled into a surprisingly comfortable modern chair with a mug of filter coffee – "I hate that instant crap," his host had stated – he produced the photograph and explained what he wanted.

"This could be just about anywhere," said Alan Holmes. "I would suggest that, going by the close proximity of the tree tops that it has not been taken from a pylon, so I think to myself, 'What structure could be built close to trees?' and one answer comes to mind straight away."

He paused before continuing and Charles wished he would get on with it. He'd known Alan since school, they'd been in the same year and had both been in the debating society in their final year. That was a rather posh title really for what was, in effect, an after-school activity that normally degenerated into a shouting match. Alan had always been the one who stretched his subject out and hated being interrupted, which maddened the rest of them. He also never shortened any of his phrases, as though he was scared of apostrophes. The fact that his opinions were usually proved to be the correct ones didn't help either. Charles knew exactly why Alan had paused so to humour him he asked the question,

"And what answer was that, Alan?"

"Obviously, Michael, this photograph was taken from the platform of a structure built within the group of trees. It is difficult to ascertain exactly how large the wood, or indeed forest, may be, but, if I can identify the church, it will be relatively easy to determine the direction of said church from the point of origin. Of course, knowing then which church this is will also provide us with the height of the spire so, by using a simple formula, it will only require a straightforward calculation to work out the distance of the church from said point of origin."

He paused again, as though inviting comment, but Charles just looked at him, knowing that he would continue anyway.

Holmes produced a small magnifier from his desk drawer and studied the church spire, before leaning back to look at the photograph again.

"Well," he started, "it looks familiar, believe it or not. I am sure I have seen a similar photograph to this. I just need to remember where and when. Leave this with me and I will call you when I have anything. I am positive that I know this church, and once I have remembered where it is located I will be able to ascertain, using ordnance survey maps, the exact location from where this photograph was taken. "But," he added after a short pause, "I need to have absolute quiet to release the memory."

Charles thought that this was laying it on a bit, but he knew that they needed all the help they could get so he said his goodbyes and Alan showed him out, with the promise that he would ring as soon as anything came to mind.

Once he was back at the office and cradling a cup of coffee he gave his DI a progress report. "I'm hoping that your Alan Holmes can help, Sergeant, but we need to be proactive about this. I'm asking for all of our patrol cars to be on the lookout for any sort of structure in or near any trees, and to check if they find any. I think you will agree that there will be another body at this location, and the sooner it's found the better, for the investigation anyway."

"Agree entirely, sir, and I'll ask for a list of missing persons that have been reported in the last week or so. If indeed there is another victim it will probably be female but, as there is no way of knowing if he's just targeting women, I'll get a full list. It could help us to identify the victim and hope that something links her, or him, to this case. What we don't want is for this killer to be randomly selecting them. If only we could figure out the ACC's involvement…"

"Well, I'm off to see her now. There must be a connection between her and the killer, and that connection needs to be identified. She must have known this person at some time, either during her time so far in the force or even as early as school. She would have had her fair share of admirers and maybe there is one who never got invited to be her friend. I'll see you later this afternoon. Let's hope for a break, eh," said Longman as he got up to leave.

# Chapter 8

'Stop fussing so, Barney, we'll be off soon,' said Rosemary Philbeam as she got her coat from the hall cupboard. She loved the early mornings at this time of year, especially when it was warm enough for just her lightweight jacket to be required. The summers seemed to be getting shorter as she got older, so days like this were to be enjoyed and treasured. Barney, of course, loved being out at any time of year. Smells were smells and, although spring and summer provided a rich variety of them for his sensitive nose to investigate, any season would do for him. He sat on the mat inside the door, eagerly anticipating his walk. Barney was a ten-year-old black Labrador who loved his long afternoon walks in the lanes and footpaths that littered this part of the county, near to Peatling Magna, a charming little village on the south side of Leicester.

Rosemary opened the door and Barney trotted out, his nose already sniffing the air for any new smells from yesterday.

"Where to today then, Barney?" she asked, as she locked the front door. "All the way down the lane, or the footpath?"

Barney held his head up and gently tugged his mistress towards the gate that led to the lane, but after only a few yards he turned left towards the stile which gave access to a public right of way across a large field that had been left fallow.

Rosemary knew that whenever she let Barney choose the route for their afternoon walk he would always go for the footpath across the fields. He loved the openness and knew that he would be let off the leash to investigate any unfamiliar, but interesting, new smells. At the other side of the field was a wood and Rosemary herself loved it there as, at the other side of it, the trees gave way to a wonderful view towards their sister village of Peatling Parva.

They eventually reached the wood and Barney was doing his usual, sniffing away, and as she passed him on the path he kept on sniffing at the foliage that grew below an old firewatcher's tower. Nowadays it was used more for bird watching. And by the local youth, she reckoned.

"Come on, Barney, it can't be that interesting," she said, carrying on. Her dog ignored her and kept sniffing at the ferns so she went over to see what he'd found. He looked up at her as she got near and she noticed straight away that his nose was stained red.

"What have you done to yourself, Barney? Come here and let me see."

She looked at his nose and checked for any cuts as she was always finding bottles or cans at the side of the footpaths. She'd petitioned the parish council several times to make more bins available, without success. 'Budget constraints' was the latest excuse. After wiping the blood away with a tissue she couldn't find any cuts. She went back to where he'd been sniffing and saw what looked like blood covering some of the foliage.

*Now how in the world did that get there*, she asked herself. She looked round but couldn't see any evidence of a dead animal. She looked up then and thought that maybe an owl or something had taken a kill on to the tower to feed. *There seemed to be rather a lot of blood for the sort of animal that could have been carried there by a bird of prey though*, she thought. Her natural inquisitiveness took hold and she tethered Barney to the base of the ladder and climbed up to see what, if anything, had happened on the platform above. As she reached the top of the ladder she could hear the flies buzzing.

*This might not be very pretty*, she thought, but as she was nearly at the hole where the ladder went through, giving access to the platform, she carried on. As she put her head through the hole she came face to face with a young, naked woman. Her eyes seemed to be staring right at Rosemary, who nearly lost her grip on the ladder. Before she climbed down the ladder, a lot quicker than she had gone up it, Rosemary had noticed that there was a trail of blood down the woman's face, coming from a hole between her wide open, but unseeing, eyes. Her chest was covered in blood too. And flies, she noticed, were everywhere.

"Oh, dear, Barney. What to do? I knew I should have put my phone on charge. Come on, boy," she said, untying the lead from the ladder, "we need to get home quickly."

They were back in the house within ten minutes and Rosemary dialled 999.

"You have reached the emergency services. Which service do you require?" asked a female voice.

"Police, and an ambulance probably, I don't know," she replied.

"Can you give me your name and address, please?"

Rosemary gave the operator her details and told her what she had found and roughly where.

"Can you stay there, please? We will send officers to you. Will you be able to show them where you found this woman?" she was asked.

"Yes, yes, of course. I'll wait here then, shall I?"

"Someone will be there very soon," said the disembodied voice, then all Rosemary heard was the dial tone as they hung up.

The operators had all been told to report any calls to Longmans office that mentioned finding, or claiming responsibility for, missing women or bodies.

She immediately rang DI Longmans office.

"CID, DS Charles here."

"Sergeant, Constable Allen here. We have just taken a call from a rather distressed woman who claims she has just found the body of a woman on a platform in a small wood. Have you got pen and paper and I'll give you her address."

"Go ahead, I'm ready."

At that moment his boss was sat in Kate Laxton's office. Kate had been busy during the last few hours since his last visit.

"So, ma'am, whose names have you got on your list?"

"Not too many, I'm afraid, Tom. I have done two lists. This one has the names of all the officers who were on my entry course. It's not too often that a woman, or *girl*, gets the highest marks overall and maybe someone has gone off the rails and wants to make me think that maybe he is better than me if he doesn't get caught. I admit that this theory is the most outlandish, but you did ask me to come up with anyone who might hold a grudge," she said, and then continued, "and this one is a list of the criminals I have helped put away."

She passed the two lists over and Longman looked at the second one first as he thought it more likely that this was an act of revenge by someone she had put inside.

"Out of those names there are seven who have finished their sentences, two have died in prison, and the rest are still serving their sentence. I have annotated the list accordingly."

"The two that died in prison?" he asked questioningly.

"One from natural causes, cancer. The other one was a paedophile and he was got at, in the shower when he should have been alone. His killer is still inside, and will be for another ten years. The family of the kid he had abducted, raped and killed petitioned for his killer to go free but didn't get anywhere."

"Understandable, when you think about it, but a futile hope," Longman said.

He was about to start going through the other names on the list but was interrupted by his phone ringtone.

"Excuse me, ma'am," he said, then into his phone, "DI Longman."

"Sir, another body has been discovered. The location could match the photo as it's on a platform in a small wooded area near Peatling Magna, that's south of Leicester," he heard DS Charles say.

"Can you get a team sorted out, Sergeant? I'll meet you at the car in five minutes. I'll call the ME," he said.

"Another body, Tom?" asked Kate.

"Afraid it looks like it, ma'am. On a platform in a wood near Peatling Magna."

"I want to come with you on this one, Tom. I live in the next village along. This is starting to feel very personal indeed. Of course, he might *not* know my home address, but I think you must agree it would be quite a coincidence otherwise."

"Hmm. Fair enough, ma'am, I'll just give Henry a call and we'll be off."

They met DS Charles at the car and if he was surprised to see the ACC accompanying his boss he didn't let it show.

"Shouldn't take long, sir, it's only five miles," he said as they got into the car. "A mobile patrol was in the area and has

71

been told to go to the callers address and stay with the lady until we get there. The forensic team are on their way. The lady's name is Mrs Rosemary Philbeam. She lives in Peatling Magna and has agreed to guide us to the platform where it was discovered," he continued as they set off.

They pulled up outside Rosemary's house fifteen minutes later and she was there at the door, waiting for them. She made her way down to the gate as they reached it and introductions were made.

"We'll have to wait a few minutes more, Mrs Philbeam," said Longman. "The forensic team will be meeting us here, so that we can all go to the wood together. I don't suppose that there is a track across to it?" he asked, hopefully.

"There is a track from the road leading into the wood, but while I've been waiting I called the farmer who owns the field, and he has given permission for you to drive across it if you would prefer not to disturb the surface of the track. The field's not due to be ploughed until next week, so it shouldn't be too bumpy," she told him.

"That's very good of you. A lot of people would not have thought to do that," he said.

"Yes, well, my husband was a policeman for many years and I suppose these things rub off on one," said Rosemary.

"That wouldn't be Commissioner Bob Philbeam, by any chance?"

"Why yes, did you know him, Inspector?"

"He was in charge of the first CID office that I joined in London, oh, about twelve years ago now," he answered, "How is he? I heard that he had retired but didn't realise he lived round this way."

"Robert died last year, Inspector. Heart attack. He missed the old life terribly and never really adapted to the slow pace of village life in the 'sticks' as he called it."

"I'm very sorry to hear that, Mrs Philbeam."

"Thank you, Inspector, it was a rough time for a while, but Barney here has been a wonderful companion and our walks are helping me to carry on. One must, or who knows what would happen."

As Rosemary was talking, the forensic team turned up in their van, quickly followed by Henry Brandon, the ME.

"Would you like to join me in the car, Mrs Philbeam?" Longman asked.

"That would be fine and, please, call me Rosemary."

She locked her front door after shooing Barney inside and telling him that she wouldn't be long, before joining Longman and DS Charles in their car.

They drove up the lane to the gate leading into the field, followed by the forensic team's van and the ME's car. As Charles was driving, Longman got out and opened the gate, closing it once all the vehicles were through. He climbed back in the car and they bumped gently across the field towards the small wood on the far side.

They parked up just before the wood and Rosemary led them through the trees and stopped at the edge of a small clearing. In the middle of the clearing stood a wooden platform that had been used as a fire lookout tower years ago when the wood was a lot larger. It had a rough wooden ladder giving access through a trapdoor. Rosemary pointed to it,

"She's up there, Inspector. It was her blood on the ferns here that got Barney's attention. I was worried that whatever might be up there was lying injured, so I climbed up to look. Sorry if I may have disturbed any evidence."

"It is all very dry, Mrs…Rosemary," he told her, "I doubt if there were any footprints to disturb, and if you hadn't gone up we would not have known about the woman."

They put on protective overshoes and the white paper suits before going over to the area directly below the platform that the dog had investigated earlier. While the forensic team were securing the area with crime scene tape DS Charles, with their permission and under instructions not to touch a thing, climbed up and put his head through the trapdoor to 'See what I can see' and try to get a feeling about this one. As his head went through he stopped for a brief moment, before continuing through the opening onto the platform floor.

The sightless eyes of the young woman seemed to look straight through him as he quickly took in the scene. There were flies crawling all over her where the blood had trailed, most of them around the two holes that the bullets had made. There had not been any scavengers at the body yet, thank God, which should make the process of identification easier. He noticed that, again, there was no jewellery at all on the body. The ears were pierced and, again, there were the tell-tale marks on the hands that showed rings were normally worn.

*This killer is nothing if not consistent*, thought Charles.

There was always the possibility that, once they had discovered the victim's identity, a family member could describe any jewellery that was normally worn and a watch notice could be put out to the pawn shops and second hand jewellery dealers in the area. He didn't hold out a lot of hope, though, as there were so many of them in Leicester and not all of them would be cooperative.

But first, the identity of this woman had to be found, and quickly.

A quick look round the platform didn't reveal anything out of place. It would have been nice to have found a spent bullet casing or anything that showed someone else had been up here with the victim but there was nothing. Charles had seen enough and went back down the ladder.

"The platform is rough wood planks, sir, so there are no footprints to be photographed, which is a pity. Nothing there but the body as far as I can gather without moving it, so if the photographer is here he can start doing his thing."

One of the forensic team who had been waiting patiently for Charles to finish his preliminary look got a camera out of one of the hard cases and made his way to the ladder. He took photographs of the blood spattered ferns and the ladder, before climbing up to get more of the platform and its grisly occupant. He came back down after a couple of minutes.

"My turn," said the ME.

"Give me your bag, Henry, I'll follow you up," said Longman.

"That's very kind," said the ME, handing his bag over and climbing up to the platform. Longman followed and stood in the corner opposite the body while the ME conducted his examination.

"Naked, as before, but no coat this time, Tom. It looks like she has been shot twice, once in the chest and once in the head. Anything else will have to wait until after the autopsy. I would say that death occurred here, she bled from both wounds before her heart stopped."

"Any idea as to time of death, Henry?"

"Can't be precise yet, but as rigor mortis has set in at least twenty four hours. The autopsy will allow a more accurate time frame, insect larva and all that nice stuff, so I'll let you know as soon as I can, Tom."

"Thanks, Henry," said Longman, and climbed back down to the ground. The ME followed and requested that the forensic team bring the body down as soon as they could. As one of them climbed up to the platform he called his office and arranged for the mortuary wagon to come and collect the body. The forensic team should be just about ready by the time it arrived, he reckoned.

The two forensic technicians left on the ground started to search for any evidence around the bottom of the ladder, taking photographs from every angle as they methodically noted their progress.

It was easy to follow the trail of bent or broken ferns from the tower to the track, but there were no signs of any vehicle having driven down it lately.

"It's been very dry though, sir," said one of them to Longman, "so it's possible that whoever did this 'could' have used the track. We'll check all the way down to the road, just in case. There has to be something, there nearly always is."

Longman wanted, no, correct that, needed them to discover something to help him find the killer, so he wished them luck in their search.

"Can I have a word, Inspector, in private?" Kate asked.

"Of course, ma'am," he replied, and they walked a little way back towards the cars.

"I've been thinking hard about this, Tom, and the more I do, the more I'm convinced that this killer is someone I've known in the past. There were a few raised eyebrows when I got this promotion, and we both know that if a copper goes off the rails their experience in dealing with crime means that they know how not to leave clues. I think we need to list the other officers who were in my training entry and see where they are now, and how far they have got in the promotion stakes. It's almost as though, by linking these deaths to me, whoever is doing this is trying to make *me* feel guilty."

75

"It's possible, ma'am. But I think that this person has always had a problem following our conception of normal behaviour. In my experience revenge can take many forms, and they are usually more direct than this and rarely involve third parties not related or connected to their victims. Your idea will be checked on, however, as we cannot rule anything out at this stage. I wonder, though, if we need to go further back. Any ex-boyfriends from school that may be envious of your success, perhaps? In fact, anyone who wanted to go out with you but either never asked or got turned down."

"Oh, come on, Tom. That really is clutching at straws. I didn't tend to run with the crowd at school and have only ever had one real boyfriend as such. You can check him out if you like, we still exchange cards every Christmas. He lives in Lincoln, on a canal boat I believe. Last I knew he was still single, if that is relevant," Kate said, "and I doubt that he would feel inferior to anyone any more. He's a lottery winner, won nearly a million a couple of years ago. That enabled him to buy his boat and pursue his hobby."

"Which is?"

"Photography," Kate continued quickly, "But not landscape, before you ask. He does architectural photography and is very good, by all accounts."

"You seem to know a lot about him from just exchanging Christmas cards," Longman stated, with a smile.

"Yes, Tom, I suppose I do," said Kate. She wasn't going to tell him that she still saw her ex-boyfriend occasionally, theirs had been an intense relationship while it lasted and they were still good friends. He, unlike her, had stayed single. When she asked why once he'd told her, with a wry smile, that all the good ones were already married. *There was no way he could be involved in this*, she thought. *No way at all*.

They wandered back to the group and Longman left Kate talking to the ME, who had finished his initial examination and was putting his shoes back on. He went over to join his sergeant, who was talking to one of the forensic team.

"We have some tyre tracks, sir, and they are recent, according to Phillips here."

"Good. Will it be possible to identify the type of vehicle, do you think?" Longman directed the question at Phillips.

"We can normally determine the size of the tyre if we have a full rotation of the wheel, sir, and from that we can tell you the type of vehicle, although not the specific make. The tread on this one is very well defined so we do know that the tyres are probably quite new. Tread patterns can be matched like· fingerprints, as there will always be an imperfection unique to that tyre. This is only relevant if the vehicle can be found, of course."

"Anything you can tell us will be most welcome," Longman said. "Have you found anything else at all, no shell cases from the gun for instance?"

"No, sir, although we have yet to go over the ground with the metal detector. There is always a small chance that either the killer or his victim dropped something. I wouldn't hold out too much hope though, it would be most unusual to be that lucky."

"Well, good luck."

Longman turned back to Charles. "Right, Sergeant, let's take the ACC back to headquarters. It's time we started to find out a bit more about any of the boys that were in her class at school, and we also need to talk to this chap she knows in Lincoln. There are also all of the officers who were on her police training intake. Did they all make it through? She did come top of her entry so maybe that caused some resentment among her male colleagues? I know," he continued as Charles began to interject, "that is probably going to be a waste of time, but I promised that every avenue would be investigated."

"Actually, sir, I was going to say that it was a good idea. It wouldn't be the first time that a copper has crossed the line. Committing murder, however, would not be usual, and committing murder just to cause another to feel guilty would definitely be a first in my book."

"That's not all, Sergeant. There will also be a list of ex-cons that have done time on the evidence provided by our ACC, plus those who are still serving their sentences. It looks like a busy time ahead. Let's hope that we get some time to make progress before this killer strikes again, which I'm afraid he will probably do unless we can stop him. We don't need any more bodies."

Longman noticed that Kate had finished talking to the ME so he indicated that they were going to leave. She came over and Longman held the car door open for her.

"Thank you, Inspector," she said as she got in and settled herself on the rear seat. Longman closed the door and went round to the other side before getting in and joining her. DS Charles started the car and they slowly made their way back across the field to the gate. Once they were back on the road and heading towards Leicester, and headquarters, Longman asked Kate what her feelings were now that she had visited one of the crime scenes.

"This makes it a little more real, if that makes any sense, Inspector. I know I asked to come along today, but my intention was simply to try and get the feel of a crime scene again. I won't interfere, you are in charge of this investigation. I can assist, though, by providing any help you require. So if anyone starts giving you any trouble about resources on this case direct them to my office, Inspector."

"Certainly, ma'am."

They were quiet for the rest of the journey back to headquarters, each wrapped up in their own deliberations. Kate thanked them again once they were back in the building and headed for her office.

# Chapter 9

"Did you notice the similarity of this last victim to the first, sir?" asked Charles once they were back in the incident room. He had connected his camera up to the desktop and was in the process of downloading the photos of the latest victim onto his computer.

"Well, they were both young and attractive. Not out and out beautiful in the accepted sense but pretty nonetheless. Until we find out the identity of the second victim, and her way of life, we don't know if there are any more similarities. What have you spotted, Sergeant?"

"Might be nothing, sir, but if I'm right it will be another factor to consider," said Charles as he opened the photo file.

He soon had a close up of the second victim displayed on the screen.

Going into the case files of the first victim, Anna Horton, he found a similar photo and got them both onto his screen, side by side.

Longman looked, and then noticed what should have been obvious from the start.

"Good God, why didn't that strike me before now?"

The common fact that he hadn't noticed, the one that he had seen as soon as both pictures were displayed together, was the glaring evidence that both of the victims had jet black hair, cut so that it hung just above their shoulders.

Longman looked closely at both pictures before pointing to the one of the latest victim.

"Her hair's been cut, Sergeant, and not by a hairdresser. It looks like it has just been sheared off without any finesse. Look at the first victim and you'll see that her hair is also short, but has been properly styled to that length."

"Both of them are in a similar style to that of our ACC, sir," stated Charles.

"Yes, Sergeant. That fact hadn't escaped my notice. I would imagine that it won't escape hers either when she sees these photos together. I think a call or two is required here, we need to have patrols passing by her house regularly to keep an eye on things. She won't want that, of course, but she must accept it. This killer obviously has some kind of fixation about her, but can't approach her directly for whatever reason so he's hurting her by proxy. I think that if she saw him she would know him, and it would probably not be a friendly recollection. We had better get to work to find out why? And why now?"

Charles got himself comfortable and reached for his phone. The first call he made was to the personnel department.

"Hello, DS Charles here. I need to see the personnel file on one of our officers which may assist us with enquiries we are conducting in respect of a double murder investigation. The officer concerned is our ACC, can you help?"

He was asked to hold the line while the person on the other end had a word with his supervisor.

"Hello, Sgt Charles?" asked a thin, reedy voice.

"Yes, I'm here."

"I'm Inspector Bradbury, and my assistant tells me you need to see the personnel file for ACC Kate Laxton as part of an investigation, is that correct?"

"Yes, sir. Myself, and Detective Inspector Longman of Leicester CID. We are investigating a double murder and have received messages, from a person purporting to be the killer, personally directed at the ACC. We would like to have access to her personnel file as it is possible that it could contain information that may help us," said Charles.

"I'm sorry, Sergeant, but that is not possible. There is a marker on the file and it can only be accessed with the authority of the Chief Constable," said the inspector.

"That's fair enough," said Charles, "only to be expected, really. I'll pass this on to my guv'nor and let him deal with it. Bye."

He made a face at the phone as he put it down, but the response from personnel was expected. In these days of data protection, personal information, especially when it concerned senior ranks, had become more and more difficult to access.

"Pass what on, Sergeant?" asked Longman, who had been studying the crime data on the whiteboard.

Charles told him and Longman immediately reached for his desk phone and called the Chief Constables PA.

"Good morning, DI Longman here," he said, "I need to see the Chief Constable as soon as possible, please."

He waited a few moments as the PA checked the appointments file.

"Half past three, that's fine. Thank you."

"Right, Sergeant, let's hope that the Chief agrees with our thinking. In the meantime, I'll see if the ACC will agree for us to check the records from her college days."

He decided that it would be better, and probably more productive, to go and see her in her office. He had a couple of hours before his appointment with the Chief Constable, and it was always possible that Kate had remembered some facet of her life that had caused a particular resentment from someone at the time. *This could be like looking for the proverbial needle*, he thought as he made his way down the corridor, *but it would be a needle that had to be found.*

He turned the corner that led to the ACC's office and nearly collided with Emma, the ACC's personal secretary.

"Sorry," they both said together. Longman stood aside as Emma gave a rueful grin and carried on.

Kate had seen the near collision from her office door and waited for Longman to enter her office before closing the door behind them.

"She's got a soft spot for you, you know."

"Don't be silly, I'm nearly old enough to be her father."

"That's as maybe, Tom, but you must admit she is attractive."

'That I cannot deny, but your secretary isn't the reason I've come here. I need to ask if you've had any more thoughts about the case, ma'am. I would also like the name of your friend in Lincoln," he held up his hands as Kate started to protest, "not that we think he has anything to do with this, ma'am, but he may have noticed things while you were dating. Guys who are taking out a pretty girl will notice if anyone else is taking an interest, believe me," Longman said.

'OK, Tom, his name is Richard Belton. He lives on a canal boat called, and this is true, believe me, 'Mine all Mine'. It's moored in Brayford Pool. I have his phone number, heaven only knows if it is still current but you can try."

Kate read the number off her mobile's menu for him.

"Thanks, ma'am. We'll go and see him soon and hope he can help. You'd better know, by the way, that I'm seeing the Chief this afternoon and I will be asking for permission to go through your file."

He noticed her lips purse as he said this and carried on quickly, "Of course, it will be only seen by myself and DS Charles. There is no chance of anyone else having access, trust me."

"Oh, I do, Tom. However, I would prefer just you having access to the complete file. If you find anything that may help, and I can't see how, then share that information with your DS, by all means."

"That's reasonable, and if you remember anything that could be relevant."

"I'll let you know straightaway," finished Kate.

"Yes, of course. Sorry, but sometimes it's difficult to switch off the 'I'm the copper and you're the civilian' side of things."

"That's OK, Tom," she said with a smile, "and, please, keep me updated."

Longman left her office and was walking back to his own when his phone rang.

"Longman."

"Sir," said his sergeant, "there's a woman at the front desk who says she might have seen the van earlier on the same night that Anna Horton was killed. I have asked the desk sergeant to show her to an interview room and get her a cup of tea. I presume you would like to see her."

"Most definitely, Sergeant, I'm on my way."

Soon they were both sat in the interview room facing a young woman who was probably only seventeen or eighteen but looked older as she had plastered her face with far too much make up. She was provocatively dressed in a very short skirt, in a leopard print design, and a boob tube top in a vivid red that ended a couple of inches before her skirt waistband, revealing a pierced navel that sported a small, chromed, safety pin. She had on a pair of knee length black patent boots and probably thought she looked sexy as hell. Both Longman and his sergeant thought that it was a sad reflection on the world when young girls paraded themselves looking like tarts.

"So, Miss…?" started Longman.

"Jones, and me first name's Vicky," the girl said.

"I believe you told the desk sergeant that you have some information for us."

"Yeah, I 'ave an' all. You can also tell the dirty bugger that I noticed him trying to look up me skirt while I was sat down, waiting to be shown in 'ere.'

"OK, Vicky. Now, what information?" asked Charles, hiding a smile.

"Well, I seen that appeal on the telly about if anyone 'ad seen that van and I did, see. I was on Melton Road on the night you mentioned, at about seven or eight. Waiting for me bus, like, when this van pulls up and the fella leans across to the side window and beckons me over. I thought 'e may be lost, like, and wants directions so I went over and 'e asked me how much for a quickie in the back of his van. I said I wasn't that sort of girl, and anyway, everyone knows you don't get in the back of a van with the punt…strangers," she quickly corrected herself, "so I started calling 'im a dirty bastard and 'e drove away, like. I did get 'is number, though," she said, "and the van was a Transit. I know that 'cause me brother's got one."

"Well done, Vicky," said Longman, knowing that it was what she wanted to hear, "and the number was…?"

"I can't remember all of it but the first bit stuck, like, 'cause it was a bit unusual. It spelt out blob. Can't remember the rest, though."

"That's a really big help," said Longman, writing down BL08 xxx.

"Did the van have any lettering on, like the name of a firm?" asked Charles.

"Nah, it was just white. 'Ad a sliding door on the passenger side though, if that 'elps."

"Anything you remember will help, believe me," Longman said, then asked, "could you describe the driver at all. We have a police artist that can help."

"Yeah, OK. 'E was a middle-aged fella, at least thirty-five. Lots of 'air, thick and wavy you know? 'Is teeth were quite bad, they looked as though there were too many for 'is mouth, if you know what I mean, and 'e had starry eyes. It was as though 'e was undressing me by just looking. Creepy," she told them. "If you 'ave your artist 'andy I can try to describe 'im better."

"You seem to have got quite a good look at him from such a short exchange," mentioned Charles.

"I've always been able to remember faces. Don't know why, or 'ow, it just 'appens."

Both Longman and Charles were thinking that at last they had a break. This could narrow the search down a lot. They waited with the girl until the police artist arrived and, after thanking her again, excused themselves. If they could get a good description this case may get resolved before anyone else got hurt.

As they walked back to their office, Charles was already on his phone to the DVLA giving them the details of the van and asking for a list of Transit vans, in the Leicester area first, matching the limited details they had so far.

"Well, sir, it looks like we've got a break," he said, as he returned his phone to his jacket pocket, "they will fax us a list as soon as they can of all Transits with BL08 as the start of their registration. Should be with us within the hour."

"Mm, we'll see, Sergeant. Tracking down this van from just a part registration won't be easy, but, together with a decent description of the driver, it shouldn't be impossible. When the artist has finished I want to show the result to the ACC. You never know, she may recognise this person. I suppose you noticed that Vicky Jones had short black hair?"

"Yes, sir, I did."

"She should consider herself a lucky girl, she could have been in that field instead of Anna Horton," said Longman.

# Chapter 10

Anna Horton's father sat in the same chair that Vicky Jones had sat in just an hour before. Longman was sat opposite and had quickly decided that he didn't particularly like Mr Horton.

He saw an untidy little man, in his late fifties probably but looking ten years older. His eyes were darting about the room as though he expected something to happen, and jumped slightly when Longman entered, DS Charles following him inside.

"Mr Horton?" asked Longman.

"Yers, that's me," he answered. "What's all this about then, getting me all the way down 'ere? The coppers told me that me daughter 'ad been 'urt, like. Where is she then?"

*Here we go again*, thought Longman. It was a nasty job, telling next of kin that their son or daughter had been killed. Road accident or murder, the reaction was never the same. Some people simply broke down and cried, others refused to believe it. The sight of their loved ones on the autopsy table, ready to be formally identified, brought it home though.

Seems as though the Edinburgh police had sidestepped this one.

"Mr Horton, I'm afraid that I have some bad news. Your daughter is dead. She was killed last Thursday evening."

Horton's reaction was to sit and stare at Longman for a few moments, before he quietly asked how his daughter had died.

"She was shot at close range, and before you ask, we don't know who shot her yet. It wasn't an accident."

Charles had been observing Horton during this exchange and came to the conclusion that Horton had nothing to do with his daughter's death. On hearing this last piece of information, he had slumped back on his chair.

"The stupid cow. I pleaded with her to come to Edinburgh with me. Start afresh, like. But no, she wanted to stay here with her mates, said she wouldn't feel safe in Edinburgh. We haven't spoke for a while, you know. I still send her a card for her birthday and one at Christmas, with a tenner. Oh God, what am I gonna do now? Can I see her?"

"Of course, Mr Horton. I will arrange it," said Charles, leaving the room.

Alone with Horton, Longman asked, "Who were her friends here, Mr Horton?"

"God knows. And me name's Cyril."

"What do you do in Edinburgh?" asked Longman, more to pass the time than through any genuine interest. He also was of the opinion that Horton knew nothing of importance regarding his daughter's life in Leicester, and probably didn't know that she was an occasional prostitute either. He made a mental note to get the sex outfits removed from Anna Horton's flat before her father went to empty it.

"I'm a groundsman at Hibernian football club," said Horton, with a hint of pride.

"Hmm. That must be very interesting," said Longman, distractedly.

"Yers, people don't realise just how much work goes into getting a football pitch ready week after week. You know..."

He was interrupted before he could get into full flow as Charles came back into the room and told Horton that he could see his daughter now.

"If you would follow me, please, Mr Horton, we will take you over to the hospital," said Longman.

Nothing was said on the way to the hospital morgue. Horton sat in the back of the car, with Longman beside him, and simply stared out of the window. They reached the hospital and Charles parked outside the morgue entrance, in the reserved space for just this occurrence.

"If you would care to follow me, please, sir," said Charles, as Horton got out of their car.

"I've told yer, me name's Cyril. Can't be doing with all this Mr Horton, sir, rubbish."

"Sorry, sir, force of habit."

The ME, Henry Brandon, walked up to them as they entered the morgue and introduced himself to Horton.

"I'm afraid that there is some damage to your daughters face, Mr Horton. Are you sure that you want to do this?" he asked. "Yes, I'm sure. If it is my Anna I need to, you know."

"I think I do," said the ME and led them to a double door that gave access to the viewing room. Anna Horton's body was under a thin sheet and as Horton stood at her side the ME's assistant pulled the sheet back enough for Horton to see his daughters face. It was not as bad as it had been when she was found in the field. *They had done a good job*, thought the ME, *of patching up most of the damage caused by nature's scavengers*. They had filled out her empty eye sockets and, with her eyelids closed, that part of the damage was hidden from her father, at least.

"Yes, that's my Anna. What happens now? I need to get back to work, my boss don't like us being absent, you know."

*What a cold-hearted sod*, thought Longman. *He's just identified his daughter's body and all he's worried about is losing some pay.*

"I'm sure he'll understand that you need to bury your daughter, Mr Horton. If you like we can contact him and explain that you are required here for another week. After all, there is the matter of your daughter's flat. The council will want her things removing as soon as possible so that it can be reallocated. Plus there are various organisations that need to be informed, like her bank and her employers."

"Oh, yers. I forgot that part of it. God knows how I'm gonna move her stuff. Can't the council buy it off of me, then?"

"That is something you will have to take up with them. I'm sure they'll be able to advise you of the best way to dispose of your daughter's possessions."

"If you would care to follow me, Mr Horton," said the ME, "I need some signatures from you and then I can give you the paperwork you will need to obtain a death certificate. You will need that to arrange the settlement of all those things that Detective Inspector Longman has just informed you about."

They dropped Horton off at a small, cheap hotel after getting his contact details. He hadn't really given them anything new to help with their investigation, so they were back to square one. It was time to start looking for any possible link from this end, and that meant going through the ACC's file, if the chief agreed.

"The chief constable is ready for you, Inspector, so you can go straight in," said his personal assistant, Dorothy Pagett, as Longman arrived at the small waiting area outside the chief constable's office. She was a middle aged spinster with steel grey hair and a matching personality. It was not a good idea to incur her wrath by arriving late, no matter who you were.

Longman went through into the inner sanctum and was immediately asked to have a seat.

"Hello, Tom," said Harold Judson, the chief constable. He was another senior officer who had embraced the concept of using first names when talking with his officers in a one to one situation. "What can I do for you?"

If Tom was surprised that Inspector Bradbury hadn't informed the chief of the reason for his appointment, he didn't show it.

"Hello, sir. I need to see the personnel file on your ACC. We, that is Sgt Charles and I, believe that there may be something in the file that could help us to determine why she is seemingly being targeted by our killer. He's taking pains to taunt her about the victim's location."

Longman proceeded to enlighten the chief about the various phone calls and notes, all directed personally at the ACC.

"We think that there could be a point in her career when she has caused someone to resent her for whatever reason. It could go back further, to her college or university days, we don't know. She has certainly reached her present rank very quickly, and that must surely rankle with those who have been waiting longer."

"I hope you are not implying that this murderer could be a serving officer.'

"No, sir, we don't think that," said Longman. Privately he added a 'yet'. "But it could be a former officer, maybe one who left because he was passed over for promotion in favour of a woman. There is still a lot of chauvinism out there."

"Oh, come on Tom. That really is clutching at straws. However, if you think it will help I will get you authorised to view Kate's file. How many people will need to see it?"

"Just myself, sir. If it throws up anything that needs checking out further I will let you know. I have already informed the ACC of the reason for coming to see you and that is what she asked?"

"Very well, I will contact Inspector Bradbury and get you cleared. Anything else while you have my ear, Tom?"

"Actually, sir, there is one other matter. I have asked our mobile patrols to run by her house during their shifts, but ideally I would like to get a team together to run a proper watch. There is nothing to suggest she is in danger, yet, but I think it would be wise to give her some measure of protection."

"Hmm. That one could be tricky. We are on a moratorium, as you know, in respect of overtime. I think that the mobile checks will have to suffice unless she is threatened directly. I would love to give you unlimited resources, as I hope you know, but my hands are tied. There is one other thing that I would like you to know, Tom, and this is not to be discussed with anyone outside this room. I was a member of the board that interviewed our ACC when she was a brand new constable. She had shown considerable promise during training and was plucked from the fold, selected for preferred promotion. She has not disappointed us in our selection. It wasn't expected that she would achieve her present position so quickly, but when my predecessor became ill and I was moved up I could think of no one better suited to be my deputy. She has progressed on merit, I hasten to add. I, personally, feel proud that our choice was vindicated. I've followed her career closely and believe me, when I say that I find it difficult to think of any reason why someone who knew her would do this. She's always had an enviable knack of getting even the most chauvinistic of officers on her side, Tom. I think when you discover the identity of this murderer, you will find that he will not be connected to the police force, serving or otherwise."

The 'news' about Kate's fast track promotion didn't come as a surprise to Longman. He knew of a few other officers who had had similar career paths. Some made very good senior officers, but, if pushed, he could name a couple who had abused their privileged status.

He thanked the chief again for agreeing to let him see Kate's file and left, heading back to the incident room.

He arrived back to find his sergeant studying a print out. Charles looked up as Longman walked in and waited for his DI to get a coffee from the machine before giving him an update.

"DVLA were quick this time, sir. We have a list of all Transits that were registered with the BL08 prefix. There are one hundred and forty six. I think we can discount forty of those straight away, though."

"Why is that, Sergeant? Surely we need to check them all out."

"Well, sir, these ones 'are' a bit distinctive. They have lots of reflective tape all over them and pretty blue lights on top," Charles said, grinning.

"OK, Sergeant, you got me that time," said Longman, joining in on the joke, "That still leaves us with over a hundred, although most of those will probably have some kind of lettering or logo. I suppose we'd better get busy. Let's hope he isn't using false plates – that would be a real bugger."

They studied the list of addresses used when the vans had been first registered and decided to start with the ones that were privately owned, before moving on to the businesses.

It would prove to have been the wrong choice.

There were fifteen vans registered to individuals, the rest were company owned. Two of those private owners were women so they decided to get those checked first. Longman picked up his phone and called the inspector on duty in the traffic office.

"Hi, Phil, Tom Longman here," he said, "I'm in the middle of a murder investigation that could involve a white transit van. I know, there are millions of the sods, but we have narrowed it down to one hundred and six. If I send you a list of the registration numbers, would you distribute it to all traffic control centres? I have a tentative description for you of the driver." He repeated the description given by Vicky Jones. "The police artist is working with a witness to get an image, as soon as we have it we'll fax you a copy. You will, great. A word of warning, though, Phil. The person driving the van may well be armed. So far the van can be linked to at least one murder where the victim has been shot with a .22 weapon, we think a pistol rather than a rifle. There's no reason to take any chances as I've an armed response team available if circumstances warrant their use. I'll fax you all the info now. Thanks again. Bye."

Longman turned to his sergeant as he put down the phone, "Right, Sergeant, time to go and see a few people."

"Ok, sir. I have the list of private owners. The first one will be a Mrs Planchett, she lives in Coalville."

It didn't take too long to reach the address and they found Mrs Planchett in her front garden, dead heading some rather large flowers.

"Mrs Planchett?" enquired Charles.

"That's me, but please, call me Dolly," said the rather brightly dressed Mrs Planchett. She was a tall, strong looking woman and had striking blue eyes, Charles noted.

Both Longman and Charles introduced themselves and proffered their warrant cards. Longman said, "Nothing to worry about, Dolly, but we would like to see your van, if we may? And we also need to know who is authorised to drive it."

"My van? Why do you need to see that? It hasn't been used in weeks," said Mrs Planchett, "and the only driver is myself. It's used for doing boot sales during the summer. The last one was over a week ago, and the next is this coming Sunday morning."

"I'm sure everything is fine, Dolly, but we do need to see it, please," said Longman.

She showed them round to the door in the side of the garage and unlocked it before standing to one side, allowing them access.

Longman and Charles checked the registration first, ticking it off against their list, before looking over the rest of the van. The windscreen was quite dusty, as though from non-use, which backed up Mrs Planchett's claim that it hadn't been used recently. It was unlocked, so they opened the rear doors to be confronted with stacks of cardboard boxes. They were all numbered, *obviously something to do with the nuances of boot selling*, thought Longman.

"Not our van, I think, sir," said Charles, "this stuff looks like it has been here for quite a while, and there's no room to swing a cat, never mind room for what Vicky Jones said he wanted."

"I agree, Sergeant, I think we can tick this one off the list."

They went back outside and found Mrs Planchett back in the garden, carrying on with her dead heading.

"Thank you for allowing us to inspect your vehicle, Mrs Pl…Dolly," said Longman. "We won't need to bother you anymore. It would be advisable for you to keep your van locked in future, even if it is inside a locked garage. There are a lot of opportunist thieves about."

"OK, Inspector, I'll try to remember. Goodbye," she said, without looking round.

They climbed back into their car and were on their way to the second address when the radio squawked into life. As Charles was driving Longman picked up the hand mike and answered.

It was Phil Cox, the inspector from traffic.

"Hello, Tom, thought you might like to know that one of our cars tried to pull over one of those transits on your list, but when they pulled up behind it and while one of the officers was walking up to the driver's door it accelerated away. At the moment it has two cars behind it and I've called for the helicopter."

"Thanks for that, Phil, where is it now?"

"Heading towards the M1, junction 23. I'll keep you posted. We follow at a distance now when suspect vehicles are on the motorway. Too dangerous trying to stop them unless we can get at least four cars to hem them in. Plus there's always the chance that, if it is the one we're looking for, he may have picked up a new victim."

"Yes, there is always that in the back of your mind. Do you want me to contact the ART?"

"Not yet, Tom. We don't know where he is headed yet but from the reports I have had so far he will probably crash before we can stop him. He is going far too fast to be able to keep control if sudden avoiding action is needed," answered Cox.

"OK. Keep me posted, please. Bye," said Longman, replacing the mike into its cradle on the dash. As this was a positive development in their investigation they decided to return to the office where they could keep up to date with the pursuit of what they hoped would be their suspect.

It would be a bitter pill indeed if this van just happened to be someone with another reason for avoiding being questioned, quite apart from being a bit too coincidental.

As they entered their office the desk phone started to ring. Charles picked up the handset, "DS Charles," he said.

He listened for a few seconds, before saying thanks and replacing the phone.

"That was the artist, sir. She has the picture ready for us and Vicky reckons it's a very good likeness," he told Longman.

"That was bloody quick, I suppose we had better get back down there. I'll just let the ACC know, she has to be shown the picture first. You never know, she might recognise him straight away," said Longman.

He phoned Kate on the way and wasn't surprised to be told that she would meet them at the interview room.

They arrived to find Kate already there, examining the picture.

"I'm not sure about this, Inspector, but there is a similarity to someone I once knew. If it 'is' who I think it is, this could be embarrassing for the force."

"I take it that the person you are thinking of is a serving officer, ma'am," said Longman.

"You would be wrong, Inspector. This man *was* an officer, albeit under training, when I knew him. There was a suspicion of cheating in an examination and after an investigation it transpired that he had befriended a clerk that worked in the examination setting office. She was married, but fell for his charms and they had an affair. He threatened to tell her husband about the affair unless she fed him the questions to an important examination. Believe it or not, all he wanted to do was get a higher score than anyone else, just once. He was suspended from training and, after a disciplinary hearing, was dishonourably dismissed from the force."

"But why should that make you the reason for him to start killing these women?" asked Longman.

"Inspector, you will be aware of this once you have read my file, but during training I was consistently top of my entry. I am able to soak up facts and have total recall. I'm not boasting about it, it's just something I have always been able to do. This did cause some resentment at the start from the others on the course, but most of them accepted that it was the way it went. This guy, though," she said, jabbing her finger at the picture, "if it's him, never did accept the fact that a woman could be better."

"I think we had better find him, and quickly. What was his name, ma'am?"

"You're going to like this, inspector. It's Joshua Jeremiah Smith." Kate saw his eyebrows rise just a bit at this and carried on, "we found it hard to fathom too. Turned out his parents were a bit religious, according to him, and he was always called JJ at school which he liked, so of course during training we all called him Joshua, which he didn't. Childish I know, but he *was* a bit of an arrogant sod."

Longman turned to Charles and was about to ask a question but his sergeant had already got the answer ready.

"Not on our list of van owners, I'm afraid, sir. That doesn't mean he doesn't drive one belonging to someone else. We could ring the firms on the list, he could be an employee."

"Well, let's get him in, Sergeant. There should still be a record of his last known address. With a bit of luck he won't have moved. Things may well be falling into place on this one already. Let's get back to the office and get a copy of this sent to traffic."

Longman was picking up the desk phone as he spoke and dialled the extension for Phil Cox at traffic.

"Hi, Phil, Tom here. We have an image of our suspect for you, it's just getting faxed now. How's the pursuit going?" he said.

"We've managed to get him to stop by forcing him into one of the service areas on the M1. He had thrown some bags out of the window on the slip road, hoping we wouldn't spot them. Don't these idiots know that we get it all on film from the in-car cameras? He doesn't fit the description you gave me though, I'm afraid. He's twenty three with a shaved head and glasses. The bags were recovered and it looks like cocaine, and quite a lot of it. It's no wonder he didn't want to be stopped," said Cox, "the van was empty, no tools, rope or anything that could be used to subdue anyone.'

"Ah, well, never mind. It was a slim hope anyway that we would get that lucky so quickly," said Longman, then continued, "we also have a name, well a possible name I should say, of our suspect. Joshua Jeremiah Smith. He was on the same training course as our ACC when she joined the force and was kicked off and out after being caught cheating. It's a long story but the description fits so we are now going to try and locate him and bring him in for questioning. In the meantime I would be obliged if you could circulate copies of the image to your officers and keep the van search going."

"That's not a problem, Tom, I'll be happy to do that. You never know, we might end up with more guilty parties that we might otherwise have missed," said Cox.

During this exchange DS Charles had been on the other phone to records, getting the last known address of Smith, J.J.

# Chapter 11

Emma Ponting had always enjoyed the fresh air and this morning the weather could not have been better, as far as she was concerned. She had started her run just before dawn as she wanted to get up on the peaks to see the sun come up. It never failed to amaze her just how beautiful it could be looking across the wilds of the Peak District around Bakewell. She was always glad to get the first few miles under her belt as they were on the path that ran alongside the busy main road between Bakewell and Baslow, which meant she had to endure the peeps from the lorry and van drivers. She wasn't vain, and knew she had a nice figure, but sometimes she just wished they wouldn't keep peeping their horns. She took in the view once more before turning onto the B road that would eventually bring her back to Bakewell, the last half of her run being across fields on a public footpath.

As she was passing Farmer Griffin's big field, as it was known, she was startled by a pheasant running out of the hedgerow, causing her to lose her rhythm and her foot twisted over. She felt the pain immediately and collapsed onto the verge. She knew that she needed to keep her trainer on and hoped that it would soon ease off enough to allow her to hobble home, where she could strap it up.

*Just what I didn't need, today of all days*, she thought.

She was expecting a visit from her future mother-in-law before lunch and was hoping to get back and have plenty of time for a tidy up first. She knew she wasn't the neatest of people and, living alone, there was no need to have her little semi tidy all the time. She had a clean-up once a week to get rid of all the magazines and clutter, which would always seem to magically reappear within a couple of days.

She had been going out with Alan for two years now and they'd set a date for their wedding last week. It was to be a winter wedding, followed by a honeymoon in the Seychelles.

She was jolted out of her reverie by a van coming round the bend rather fast. She scooted back a bit to make sure there was plenty of room for it to get by as the road was quite narrow.

Josh was late.

He had been asked to go to Manchester to deliver a piece of urgently needed medical equipment and had got caught up in a really bad traffic jam. Some idiot had run into the back of a coach and two lanes of the motorway had been closed. He'd decided to return to Leicester using the back roads as he knew that the A57 through Stalybridge would be absolutely chock full. Why the satnav always wanted him to use that route was a mystery. As he rounded the latest tight corner on this god forsaken back road, he caught sight of a young woman moving back on the verge, and noticed that as she did so her face was screwed up in pain.

He stopped his van and backed up to her. Switching off his engine he got out and went over to where she was sitting, warily watching him as he approached.

"You okay, miss?"

"Twisted my sodding ankle dodging a pheasant, but it will ease off soon, I hope."

"I've a first aid kit if you'd like it binding up," he offered. He was thinking to himself that it may prove to have been fortuitous, taking this back road. She was absolutely stunning, with the largest blue eyes he had ever seen, although her long blonde hair was wrong. That would need to be changed, they needed to have dark, if not black, hair.

She looked at him and saw what he wanted her to see, a middle aged man offering some help to a damsel in distress.

"OK," she said, "that's very kind of you. Thank you."

He went back to his van and opened up one of the back doors.

"You'll probably find it easier if you sit on the step here. Hang on, I'll give you a hand," he said as she started to struggle to her feet.

She took his arm and hopped to the van, sitting herself down on the floor at the back. Josh reached in, ostensibly for his first aid kit she thought, but before she knew it he was pressing a pad over her mouth and nose. She had been taken by surprise but started to fight him as soon as she realised what was happening. She raked her fingers across his hands but he was stronger than her and soon she was falling into a chloroform induced sleep.

"You bitch!" He said, licking the blood off his hand. "You'll pay for that, oh yes."

He quickly pushed her backwards into the van and closed the door before getting into the driving seat and moving off. He found a track that looked as though it gave access to the fields after a few hundred yards and turned onto it, following it until his van was well off the road and would not be seen. Switching off the ignition, he climbed into the back and looked at his victim.

*Time to see what that tracksuit is hiding, I reckon*, he thought, before soaking another pad in the clear anaesthetic and having it ready in a plastic container. If this one started to stir, he wanted to be ready.

He cut her things off and put the ruined clothing into a polythene bag. She wouldn't be wearing them again.

When he had done he looked at her. She was beautiful. Long legs, and an absolutely gorgeous figure. He felt the familiar excitement and decided that, blonde or not, unconscious or not, he was going to have her now. He undid his fly and released himself, before kneeling down and laying her on her back on the thin mattress he kept in the van. When he was done he immediately felt deep regret and disgust, but knew that this would soon pass and he would want her again. Not yet, though, he had to secure her first and get her somewhere safe.

Gagging her with her own panties, he tied her hands behind her back and ran another tie from them to one of the load hooks on the floor before tidying himself up and getting back behind the wheel.

He would have to go home, he'd left his pistol there as this trip was supposed to have been just a quick delivery. He'd hoped to go hunting for another victim soon; but as this one had fallen into his lap, so to speak, he didn't have to do that. It was a risk, but one worth taking, going back to his place. After he'd changed her hair colour to black and shortened it a bit she would be absolutely perfect.

Then he could kill her.

He decided to time his drive home so that he would arrive after dark. He would put a coat over her and carry her into his house, his drive went down the side and he could take her in through the kitchen door. He carried on down the track until he found a place to turn his van round, and was soon back on the road, heading slowly across the hills towards Leicester and home.

# Chapter 12

"25, Meadow Road, that's in the Dane Hills area, off Glenfield Road," said DS Charles. "A nice area."

"Come on then, Sergeant, no time like the present. Let's see if Mr Smith is at home, shall we?"

They were soon in their car and on their way, mentally keeping their fingers crossed that

Smith would be there.

Traffic was light and they made good time to Smith's address. The driveway was empty, not a good sign. Charles parked on the opposite side of the street and they walked over to the house. Longman pushed the button at the side of the door and heard the electronic 'ding dong' clearly. There was no response from inside so he tried again with the same result. Charles, meanwhile, was peering in at the window.

"Doesn't appear to be any movement inside, sir, and there are no lights on that I can see. I'll have a quick look round the back."

The door at the side of the house was half glazed and, looking in, Charles' couldn't see any obvious signs of it being occupied at the moment. He tried the door at the side of the garage that gave access to the garden and the rear of the house, but it was locked.

This reinforced their opinion that the house was empty, and they went back to their car.

"I think we shall have to come back later to see Mr Smith, Sergeant. Let's get a search warrant arranged, I don't think we'll have any difficulty obtaining authorisation. I'll ask the duty inspector to detail someone to keep an eye on this place. As soon as we get word that Smith has returned home we'll come back and see what he has to say for himself. In the meanwhile I'm off home for a shower and a sandwich, if you could drop me off."

"OK, sir, must admit I could do with something myself. Stomach thinks me throats been cut!"

Before they left, Longman got onto the duty inspector for the station that included Meadow road in its beat.

"Hello, DI Longman here. Can you spare an officer to keep an eye on a house in Meadow Lane, number twenty-five? No car, this needs to be covert surveillance."

He was obviously getting the story of manpower shortage from the inspector because he interrupted the inspector, "I'm sorry if you are shorthanded, but I wouldn't ask if it wasn't important. The occupier of that house could be instrumental in helping us solve a nasty murder case, I'm sure you know the one I'm talking about. You 'will', thanks. We'll wait for the officer and brief him here. He will not be in any danger, as soon as anyone shows up at the house we 'will' be there as soon as possible. No one is to approach the house under any circumstances as there may be weapons involved. Call us and we'll get there quickly with the ART. You will, thanks a lot, bye." Longman stopped the call and turned to his sergeant, "There'll be someone along in about five minutes, so I suppose we could wait until he arrives. I'd hate to miss our Mr Smith."

While they were waiting Longman rang headquarters and got things moving with the warrant.

They saw the police constable arrive on his bicycle a few minutes later and Charles got out to brief him. Once he was satisfied that the constable wouldn't play the hero he came back to the car and got behind the wheel. "He has our numbers so he'll call us directly anyone shows up, in a van or not," he told Longman.

"Right, home then please, Sergeant; and don't spare the horses."

Ten minutes later Longman was letting himself into his house. He liked the place, it was an old Victorian semi, built when rooms were made to accommodate proper sized furniture. There were bay windows to the front, both upstairs and down. He'd had a large conservatory built onto the rear, not because he needed the extra room but because he enjoyed the light and airy feel of it when he needed to relax with a good book or listen to his music. He was a big fan of the seventies and was also a country and folk music buff, with Johnny Cash beating Alan Jackson to the top of his collection.

He closed his front door and picked up his mail. Circulars seemed to make up most of the post he received and today was no exception.

There was only one letter with a hand written address so he opened it and found an invitation to a wedding inside. The daughter of his previous partner in the Met was going to be married next month, hence the invite. He remembered meeting the family when he had been persuaded to go to one of the barbecues his old partner was fond of throwing at least once a month during the good weather. He looked at the invitation again. Ah yes, he could picture Katy now. She was the middle daughter and definitely the most precocious, if his memory served him right. He put the invitation on the hall table and dropped the rest into the bin. He went into the kitchen and was about to fill the kettle when his doorbell rang.

*Who the hell could that be*, he thought uncharitably as he went to the front door.

The front door had leaded windows, as befitted the style of the house, and he could see a figure standing there. It looked like it could be a woman. If that's one of those bloody poll takers… he was thinking as he opened the door. He stopped short when he saw fully the face of his visitor.

'Helen…' he managed to say before the woman flung herself into him, bursting into tears as she did so.

"Tom, I didn't know where to go. I've left Alan," she sobbed, clinging onto him for dear life. He backed into his hallway, reaching over her to close the door. He gently prised her arms from around his neck and led her into his living room. She collapsed into a chair, still sobbing, and he felt a bit helpless, not knowing what to do to help her.

Helen Morrison had been a secretary at his last post, down in London. She must be in her thirties but had always looked younger. She was what the fashion trade called a 'clothes hanger'. She could, and did, wear anything and make it look good. Her hair was medium length, blonde – though Tom knew it wasn't natural – and she had lovely pale blue eyes.

The first time they had met had been at one of the numerous office parties, held to 'celebrate' a good result on a case, someone leaving, or just to unwind at the end of a long week. She had shown up one time and he'd thought that she looked stunning. He'd had a few beers by then, granted, but she'd been wearing a white trouser suit which showed off her summer tan to perfection. The blouse she was wearing under the jacket was cut low and showed plenty of cleavage, one of her best assets, she'd thought. Fair enough, she did have a nice figure but it had been the paleness of her eyes that had captivated Tom. They started chatting and before long they were sat in one of the booths that went along the length of one wall. He'd noticed the ring on her finger, and thought that she was just there to enjoy the company after a long week.

She, however, had a different agenda that evening. Her marriage had not been the wonderful life of wine and roses that had been promised during the courtship. Her husband, a probation officer, had been forced to work some funny hours and, unknown to her at the time, was sleeping with some of the girls in his charge.

It had come to a head when she'd gone to her doctor with a rash, and was informed that she had contracted a sexually transmitted disease, or, as she told herself, the clap.

She'd confronted her husband and he'd eventually blown his top at her.

"You're not exciting anymore," he'd shouted at her, "so I get it where I can. If you don't like it, tough!"

She hadn't slept with him since, and the rash soon cleared up with the appropriate antibiotics. That wasn't the point though, she could never trust him again. She missed the physical side of marriage, after all she was young and had a healthy sex drive, so the end of week drinks at the 'local' had become a regular date for her. She'd had the occasional one night stand but had set her sights on Tom Longman the first time she saw him. She'd worn her white trouser suit on purpose, she knew it looked good and it had worked.

They talked about anything that came to mind and didn't notice that most of the others in their group had left until Helen looked round and remarked that they seemed to be alone.

103

"Would you like me to see you home?" he'd asked, to which she'd replied, "Yours or mine, Tom?"

That was the start of an affair that lasted until he was transferred from the Met. He'd kept in touch although he never expected their affair to be rekindled. It was something they'd both needed at the time but it was over, he'd thought.

Until now.

Helen sat in his armchair and had never looked more beautiful.

"I'm sorry, Tom, but I didn't know where else to go. You don't mind, do you, if I stay for a few days until things settle down. Alan doesn't know where I am and I don't want him to know until I'm ready. It's definitely over this time. I could put up with him shagging around with any young tart that would have him, but finding him doing one of them in 'our' bed in the middle of the day was the last straw."

"Of course you can stay, Helen. I'm quite busy at the moment so you'll have to fend for yourself, I'm afraid, but there's plenty of food in the freezer and wine in the fridge. Now if you'll excuse me I really must get cleaned up a bit, I've been on the go since the early hours."

"Of course, Tom, and thanks. You don't know what it means to have someone like you to count on," she said, looking up at him with those pale blue eyes.

Five minutes later he was standing under the shower, letting the water wash the day off him, and thinking about Helen. She really was quite a woman, adventurous in bed and out of it too, he remembered with a half-smile. Why her husband had gone after young girls with a wife like her at home, Tom couldn't fathom.

He was deep in thought, the water rinsing the soap away, when a pair of hands reached round him and he felt her press against his back.

"Room for one more?" she said, dropping her hands onto his already stirring manhood.

He turned round and saw her looking up at him with a longing in her eyes.

"Please, Tom, please."

He grasped her round the waist and lifted her up, before slowly lowering her onto what she wanted. As he entered her she gasped, before wrapping her legs round him and giving in to the sensations that were slowly building in her body.

They let the water cascade over them as they moved against each other. It wasn't long until they were both ready and they came together, crying out with the sheer pleasure.

They soaped each other afterwards, before drying off and just as Tom was thinking of continuing in the bedroom his phone beeped.

"Longman."

"It's the duty desk here, sir. You asked to be notified if there was any movement at 25, Meadow Lane. The occupier has returned to the house, and is inside as we speak. I presume you will be going there yourself, but do you require any more officers?"

'Thank you, but no. I'll give the ART a call, the suspect in that house could be armed. Can your man at the scene stay until we get there?" Longman asked.

"Of course, can I tell him how soon you will get there, sir?"

"No more than fifteen minutes. Thanks for this."

"Not a problem, sir."

Helen had been watching him during this brief exchange and knew that she would have to wait for round two.

Tom looked at her, fresh from the shower and dressed in one of his large white dressing gowns. She looked sexy as hell but he had to get dressed and pay Mr Smith a visit.

"Make yourself comfortable, I've no idea how long this will take. If it's who we think it is I may be gone for quite a while."

"You go, Tom. I know how police work is, remember? I'll be fine. No one knows where I am," she said, standing on tiptoes to give him a kiss.

Longman rang his DS next. All he had to say was, "He's home."

"I'll be with you in ten minutes, sir, I'll swing by HQ and pick up the warrant first." Longman rang the rarely used number for the ART next.

"Hi, it's DI Longman here. Our suspect has returned to his house and my sergeant and I will be on our way in ten minutes. Should be there in fifteen, can you meet us there?"

Longman obviously received an affirmative answer, nodding his head as he cut the connection and put his phone down. He started to get dressed, watched by Helen. He really was quite a handsome man, she was thinking, and being a good lover also was icing on her cake.

Charles arrived outside just as Longman was giving Helen a hug and a kiss. Longman broke away as the doorbell went and gave her a rueful grin.

"Be back as soon as I can, we can catch up a bit more later."

"Just be careful," she said, remembering the reason why he had left the Met.

He went out and found that his sergeant had already returned to the car and as soon as his DI was in he switched on the lights and headed for Smith's address.

They arrived seven minutes later, traffic had been light, and found the ART already there, parked up in their minibus. Charles couldn't help himself and, laughing, pointed out that it was one of the ones off the list.

The beat policeman was standing by his bicycle, looking a bit overawed with the show of strength before him.

Longman went up to him, introduced himself and his sergeant, and asked how long the suspect had been home.

"Actually, sir, he isn't there. He did arrive home," the young policeman continued quickly, seeing Longmans face darken, "about half an hour ago. He backed his van in and carried something inside through the side door. Ten minutes later he came back out and drove away, heading back towards the main road."

"Could you see what it was that he carried in?" asked Charles.

"No, Sergeant, it had just got dark and it was all in shadow, but it looked quite large. He was cradling it, like, like you would a large dog."

"You're positive that he left not carrying anything?"

"Oh, yes. He came round the front of his van, got straight in and drove off, Sergeant."

"Thanks, you've done well. Not your fault that he's gone out, let's hope he returns home soon. You can get off now, you must be gagging for a cuppa."

"Thanks, Sergeant. The van registration is BL08 MWM. Bye, sir," the young policeman said to Longman, getting onto his bicycle and pedalling away.

"Well, sir, it looks like he has taken something, or someone, inside. As we don't know when he's coming back I think we should investigate. There could be someone in there, in heaven knows what state."

"Agree entirely, Sergeant," replied Longman and, turning to the ART leader, he continued, "can you stay here in case he returns. If it is who we think he may be armed. If we're lucky, his weapon may be inside, but best not to take any chances."

"Certainly, sir. We'll wait in our bus round the corner," was the reply.

"Come on, Sergeant. Time to do some breaking and entering," said Longman, striding out towards the kitchen door. He tried the handle first, finding the door locked. He used his elbow to break one of the frosted glass panels before reaching in and releasing the Yale lock. They entered a large kitchen/diner that was absolutely clean. No dirty pots in the sink and only a kettle and microwave on the worktop. They went through the door into another large room, this one was comfortably furnished with not one but three sofas, arranged round a coffee table. There was a large TV mounted on the wall opposite, with a cupboard containing what looked like a DVD and a Sky box. Not a lot of ornaments and no houseplants. Not surprising really, as Smith lived alone.

"Nothing down here, sir, maybe upstairs?"

"Up you go then, Sergeant," said Longman, following Charles up the stairs that were set against one of the living room walls.

They came to the landing and went into the first bedroom. That's where they found Emma Ponting, spread-eagled and tied to the four corners of the bed, face up. She was unconscious, gagged and naked. Charles went into the en-suite and found a large bath towel. Covering her up, he removed the gag before checking her pulse, finding it strong.

Longman was already on his phone, calling for an ambulance. He gave the operator the details, also adding that the patient was unconscious, probably from being subdued with some kind of drug. After being assured that an ambulance was on its way, he turned back towards the young woman. She was very pretty but there was something that didn't quite gel. Then he realised.

"Her hair colour is wrong, Sergeant. It should be black, not blonde."

"Of course, sir, I was trying to figure out why she hadn't been disposed of and left for us to find. Maybe Smith can't get it up unless the hair is dark. If so, why has he got her here?"

"Hopefully, we'll find out when she wakes up. It could just be a chance encounter that developed into an abduction. He may have been going to change her hair colour before leaving her somewhere, probably with another message for us."

"If that's the case she'll be blessing her hair colour for the rest of her life."

Longman was interrupted from saying anything more as there was the sound of a vehicle revving its engine hard outside, as it roared away.

They looked at each other, both thinking the same thing, *Smith!* and went to the window. They saw the tail end of a white van as it rounded the corner further down the street.

Longman was on his phone in a flash, getting onto traffic.

"DI Longman here, our suspect has just turned on to Glenfield Rd, heading west. The registration number is BL08 MWM. Proceed with caution, he may be armed. I have the ART with me and they will be assisting. I repeat, he may be armed."

He turned back to his sergeant, who was untying the bonds from the young woman's wrists and ankles. As the last one came off she began to stir, then cried out as she realised she was naked but for a towel.

"Don't worry, miss. We're police officers. You're safe now. There's an ambulance on the way to take you to hospital. You need to be properly examined by a doctor as it's probable you were drugged," said Charles. *And raped*, he thought, but he kept that to himself. "What's your name, miss?"

"Emma, Emma Ponting. Where am I? I feel terrible and I've got the mother of all headaches."

"Don't worry, Emma," said Longman. "You were abducted by someone who can't hurt you anymore. Can you remember where you were before you were made unconscious?"

"I remember twisting my ankle, up on the peaks, and a kind man stopped his van to help me. I can't remember anything else, sorry. I suppose that man wasn't so kind after all, was he?" she said.

"No, miss, he wasn't."

The ambulance arrived and they stepped aside to let the paramedics do their job. Soon Emma was on her way to the hospital; *thankfully not to the morgue*, both detectives thought.

Josh was annoyed.

He'd left the girl tied up and unconscious, there was no way she could have raised the alarm.

When he turned into his street he'd seen the police minibus parked just round the corner from his house. There was a car he didn't recognise parked opposite his drive so he reckoned that he had better leave the area and quickly, just in case it was all for him. He had to ditch the van, that was a definite. If the police knew where he lived they probably also knew the registration number.

Time for a change of plan.

He drove only as far as the next turn off, parking his van in a side street. He locked it before throwing the key over a hedge into someone's front garden. He walked slowly back out into the main road and headed for the bus stop a bit further up the street. As he walked a police car went tearing past, lights flashing and siren wailing. He smiled to himself, thinking that if he'd stayed with the van there would have been a good chance of being stopped, and he hadn't finished with high and mighty Kate Laxton yet.

Oh, dear me, no.

The jogger he had 'collected' would, unfortunately, be in the hands of the police and was, no doubt, on her way to hospital by now. Someone would pay for that, he'd been anticipating a couple of days with that one before he killed her.

Yes, someone would definitely pay.

He caught the next bus that came along and went all the way into the city centre, where he boarded a different bus that would take him to Groby, a rather nice suburb of Leicester. He'd rented a house, detached of course, in another name, paying cash to cover the first six months, there shouldn't be any need of it after that. Letting himself in he got a beer from the fridge before settling down to think about where to go from here.

He would have to change his appearance, that was certain. He'd prepared for this eventuality when he'd first started on his vendetta, hoping that he would complete the destruction of Kate Laxton before his identity was discovered. Never mind, it would still happen, though he would have to be a lot more careful in future.

He finished the beer and went upstairs to the master bedroom. Here he stripped off his clothes, making a mental note to burn them all, and went into the en-suite. He used a hair trimmer to cut his hair into a short crew cut before getting into the shower.

He'd bought a full wardrobe once he'd got the keys to the house and after drying off he got dressed in some smart chinos, a loose fitting shirt and deck shoes. On the top shelf of the wardrobe was the final part of his transformation, a dark wig. It was styled fashionably long and, looking at himself in the full length mirror, he was pleased with the result. A far cry from the baggy jeans, t-shirts and trainers that he'd been used to wearing.

*Try and catch me now*, he mused, before getting undressed and settling himself into bed.

Tomorrow was another day.

# Chapter 13

Longman and Charles knew that they'd come very close to getting their hands on Joshua Smith the previous evening. His van had been found in one of the side streets not far away and forensics had started on it early this morning. If there was any evidence tying it to Anna Horton or the second victim, as yet unidentified, it would be found.

*And then, Mr Smith, we'll find you*, they both thought. They had returned to the house to conduct a thorough search, accompanied by two constables. Charles took one of them with him to start upstairs, while the other one stayed with Longman.

"Right, if you start in here," Longman said, indicating the living room, "I'll do the kitchen."

While Longman was looking under the sink unit, Charles entered the kitchen and placed a large black bin bag onto the kitchen table. Hearing the thump as it landed Longman backed out from the cupboard and as he straightened up Charles said, "Found it in the spare bedroom, under some blankets on top of the wardrobe. There are items of women's clothing and two handbags in there, sir."

"Let's have a look, Sergeant,"

Longman took the bags out and handed one to Charles. He opened his and found a purse which had some cards in it, plus a couple of ten pound notes and three condoms.

"This one belongs, sorry belonged, to Anna Horton. No question really," Longman held up a driving licence. It was a new one and had a picture of a smiling Anna Horton in one corner.

"There's only one credit card in this one, sir," said Charles. "Miss Lucy Middleton. No photos, so we shall have to corroborate this with care. We don't want to upset any families.

I'll check with missing persons first to see if she's been reported to them."

"Yes, good call."

Longman found the keys to the garage hanging on a hook beside the kitchen door. Taking them, he went outside and opened up the garage. It was a tip and obviously had not been used as a garage for some time. There were sagging cardboard boxes stacked against the end wall. *They would need to be looked through eventually*, thought Longman, *and would probably fall apart in the process*. A chest freezer was plugged into one of the wall sockets and was humming merrily, its power light providing a steady green glow in the corner. He opened the lid and looked in, finding it half full of ready meals and pizzas. *No wonder the kitchen was spotless*, he thought, *if this was his diet*.

There were a couple of suitcases, piled one on top of the other, and he looked at these next. In the bottom one of the two he found the gun, wrapped in a towel and laying next to it was a box of ammunition. He read the wrapper on the box, 0.22 calibre competition standard rounds.

"Bingo," he shouted, "got you, you bastard."

The gun would have to be checked by ballistics but it looked to him that this would be a mere formality. There was too much evidence stacking up against Joshua Smith. All they had to do now was find him.

Placing the gun and ammunition into separate evidence bags, he carried them back into the house and placed them on the kitchen table, next to the bin bag.

"I'll go and see the ACC, update her on what we've uncovered here. Now that Mr Smith is without his van, it will be harder to spot him but, on the other hand, he won't be able to abduct any more young women. I think a TV appeal needs to be set up for tomorrow morning. If we can get his image out there, with a suitable warning, we may get help from the public. He may get rattled enough to make a mistake, and that could be what will help us catch him. We must get him in for questioning as soon as possible. In the meantime, Sergeant, let's get these evidence bags back to HQ, once forensics are finished with the van they'll want to go through this place. I wonder if there's anything more to be found. I really hope not, in a way."

"I know what you mean, sir," said Charles.

Longman was told to go straight in by Emma and as he walked through the door Kate Laxton was on her feet and started asking questions almost before he could close the door.

'What were the ART thinking of, parking their bus where it could be seen? I'll be having words with their Inspector," Kate started, then, hardly pausing for breath, she continued, "catching Mr Smith is our absolute priority, Tom. I've circulated his picture to all our stations. What did you find at his house? Anything that will help us to determine where he might be now?"

Longman cut in, "Take it easy, ma'am, please. I've a few more details for you. Nothing that will help us locate him immediately, I'm afraid. We got there before he could kill his latest victim. She has gone to the hospital to be fully examined. She was found tied to the bed, and naked, but can't remember anything since he offered to help her after she had fallen over. There is the possibility that he raped her whilst she was unconscious, the doctor will let us know on that score. We did find a weapon hidden inside a suitcase that was in the garage. It's on its way to ballistics. We're quite confident that it will match what we have from the first victim. We found nothing to indicate where he might be now. He abandoned his van quickly and has disappeared. I think we need to be pro-active now, ma'am..."

"Please, Tom, there are only the two of us in here. Call me Kate. I've always hated being called ma'am," she interjected.

"O.K, Kate," he said, feeling a bit uncomfortable as he spoke her name, "I would like to do a TV appeal for anyone who might have seen Joshua Smith recently. We have the drawing that the police artist produced from Vicky Jones' description, and the computer whizzes have aged the file photograph we had from when he first started on his training. I would like to show both pictures and hope we get a reaction from the public. Do I have your permission to go ahead, ma...Kate?"

"Of course, Tom," she said, inwardly thrilled that she had broken through and finally got him to use her name.

Longman thought to himself that if she wasn't married, he would have tried to get to know her better. He'd never used her name before for just that reason, and using it now had reminded him that she was a very good looking woman.

*Be honest*, he told himself, *she was as sexy as hell.*

"Penny for 'em, Tom," she said, with a half-smile, as though she knew what was going through his mind.

"Oh, sorry, I was miles away for a minute. Do you want to be there when we put the appeal on air, Kate?"

"Yes, please. I'll stay in the background though."

"Fine, I'll let you know when and where," he said, getting up.

Back in his own office, Longman contacted the liaison officer and asked for a press meeting to be set up for the afternoon. He wanted to get the TV appeal on the early evening local news report, knowing that it would be repeated during the following day.

After having been given a time to be ready for the cameras, he rang the ACC's office and Emma answered.

"The ACC is out of her office at the moment, Inspector, can I take a message?"

"Yes, please, Emma, could you let her know that the appeal will be getting recorded at four pm in the press room."

"Not a problem, Inspector. Four pm in the press room," she repeated, "bye."

Longman said goodbye and hung up. As he did Charles walked in and, before Longman could ask, he confirmed that the second victim was Lucy Middleton.

"She was reported missing by her parents after failing to return home the night before last. They even took a photograph of their daughter to the police station. I have it here, sir," said Charles, handing it to Longman, who looked at it and realised straight away that the young woman lying in the morgue was indeed Lucy Middleton.

Charles continued, "She'd taken her car for an MOT and when I checked with the garage they told me they still have the car. It had failed the first MOT and they'd had to change a brake part so they'd rung her up to explain that there would be a delay. She'd replied that she would do some window shopping and wait for their call. That was the last contact they had with her. When they called to say the car was ready there was no answer, sir."

"We'd better go and see her parents, Sergeant. This is one of the aspects of our job that I have never got used to, but as it's our case I prefer not to pass it on to uniform to break the news. Come on."

It was as uncomfortable as he had feared, both of Lucy Middleton's parents broke down and wept when Longman told them that their daughter was dead. What made it worse was that just one year ago her sister had been killed in a motorway pile up, so both their children were gone now. Longman managed to find out the family doctor's name from the father and got Charles to phone him. They waited until the doctor had arrived before leaving, both of them even more determined, if that was possible, to catch this monster in human form.

At ten to four Longman was in the press room, deliberating on how to deliver his appeal. Kate Laxton was sat in one of the three chairs behind a large table, facing the press and trying to appear relaxed. She was anything but as she knew that the two young women who had died had been killed by proxy. It was her that Joshua Smith wanted and she knew he would eventually try to get her too. In the meantime, how many more women would he rape and kill before they caught him? That was the question that she couldn't stop from going round in her head.

Behind her were two blow ups, one of Smith drawn from the description given by Vicky Jones. The second showed a computer aged photo of Smith, using the original photo from their files. They were very similar, a testimony to Vicky's observational skill.

"Good afternoon, ladies and gentlemen. I am Detective Inspector Longman, and this, as I'm sure you know, is Assistant Chief Constable Laxton. You'll have noticed the two photographs behind me," Longman turned and pointed to one of them. "This is a computer aged photograph of Joshua Smith and this one," he pointed to the second image, "is a drawing made from an eyewitness description. I think you will agree that they show the same person and we would very much like to speak to Mr Smith. We believe he may have information that would assist us with our enquiries into the suspicious deaths of two young women, and the abduction of a third who is now ·safe and recovering from her ordeal. If anyone has any information about the whereabouts of this man they can contact us on 01162255222. All information received will be treated with the strictest confidence. If you are watching this, Mr Smith," Longman leaned forward slightly, "I would very much like to speak with you, so please call the same number and ask for me. To remind you, my name is Longman, Detective Inspector Longman."

He leant back and waited for the questions he knew would be forthcoming.

"Katy Lee, Leicester Mercury. Can you tell us how the two women you mentioned earlier died, inspector?"

"They were shot."

As he had expected, this news shook the rest of them into life but, before they started shouting out questions, he held his hands up. As they fell silent again he carried on, "There is no need to build panic with your reports as we *have* recovered the weapon that was used in these killings." He'd heard from ballistics just before starting the appeal that the gun found in Smith's house was definitely the one used in the murders of Anna Horton and Lucy Middleton.

He answered some more questions before calling a halt, promising further updates as and when they became available.

Longman and Kate left the press room and went back to her office. Once they were both settled with a cup of coffee, efficiently provided by Emma, they talked about where to go from here.

"Hotels, guest houses and the like are being checked, ma'am. Sorry, Kate," he quickly amended as he saw her wince, "copies of the photos have been distributed to all stations in the area, so if Smith 'has' holed up in one of these establishments we should know before too long. If he's gone further afield we must hope that enough people watch the appeal on television, and that someone recognises his face."

There was one person watching the news later who knew exactly where 'Mr Smith' was at that moment.

Josh was sat in his armchair eating a supermarket pizza and occasionally sipping from a bottle of imported beer when the appeal got screened as part of the local news. He stopped chewing when Longman and *that bitch Laxton's* faces filled the screen. He listened as Longman asked for the public's help with locating him.

"So, it was you, Detective Inspector Longman," he spat the name out, "who prevented my little bit of pleasure. You'll pay for that, dearly. You'd like to speak to me? Oh, you will, but under *my* terms, inspector."

He started imagining how he could exact a fitting retribution on the policeman, finishing his meal while he ruminated. He would need to know where Longman lived, that was definitely the first thing he would find out in the morning. Now that he had a kind of agenda, he enjoyed another few beers before calling it a day and going to bed.

Josh had prepared thoroughly for the situation in which he now found himself. Not only was he able to change his style of dress and wear a wig, he also had another vehicle. Not a van this time, unfortunately, but at least it was an estate. He would miss the versatility he'd enjoyed using the firm's Transit, but that was over now, as was the job. He rose early the next morning and before long he was parked at the side of the road, with a good view of the cars arriving at the police headquarters. He had a newspaper and, if anyone asked, he was waiting for a colleague. He didn't have to wait very long before seeing Longman drive into the grounds. He made a note of the make and registration before starting his car and driving home.

That part had been easy. He'd found that there were people who could find addresses from registration numbers, for a price, so getting Longman's address wasn't going to pose a problem.

Smith put his car away in the garage and, after making himself a coffee, he turned on the computer. Finding the e-mail address he needed in his address book, he typed a message and pressed send. Now he would just have to be patient and wait for a reply. He had used this 'service' once before to find the address of a young man who'd cut him up on a roundabout and, to add insult to injury, had given him two fingers as he sped off. Josh had gone to the house late one night and poured a whole tin of paint stripper on the roof of the offending car. Definitely worth the hefty fee.

Longman had gone straight to the incident room when he left the ACC's office and found his sergeant already there, talking on the phone. He pointed to the mug on the table and mimed drinking. Getting the thumbs up from Charles he picked up the mug and, getting his own off his desk, went to the coffee machine in the corner and filled them both.

While he was doing this Charles had finished with his call and took the mug gratefully.

"Nothing yet from the trawl of hotels and guest houses. It's always possible that he's moved in with a friend. We know that he doesn't have any brothers or sisters, but what about uncles and the like, sir?"

"None that we know about. On his initial paperwork that he filled in when applying to join the force he left the next of kin box empty. When asked about it, he said he had no living relatives. It's all there in the paperwork we had sent across from records. No, Sergeant, if he's in our area he's living alone. I think we'll need to check on rental properties, although we'll have to accept that he may not even be in this area anymore. We need to have a word with his employer, that van was owned by a small delivery firm. I doubt that we will get anything that will help us to find him, but you never know. That's for tomorrow, though, I think I'll call it a day for now."

"I'll be here for a while yet, sir. Paperwork to do, and if we get any helpful calls from the public…?"

"Call me, if you think that they warrant urgent investigation. But try to give me a chance of a shower and something to eat, eh, Sergeant."

"Fair enough, sir. I think I'll go and get a takeaway myself. Can't be bothered sorting out something to cook, and I hate washing up."

Longman went home with a sense of anticipation, tinged with a small measure of apprehension. He'd enjoyed what had happened earlier with Helen, very much if truth be told. It had been a while for him, and he'd sensed that she had not had a very fulfilling time of it lately either. He wasn't exactly sure what his feelings were, or should be, regarding Helen. She was a very attractive woman, how her husband couldn't see that was beyond him. He was remembering just how attractive she had looked during their shared shower earlier and by the time he pulled into his drive he was feeling slightly aroused.

*Pull yourself together, man*, he told himself, *you're acting like a love struck teenager*.

He found Helen in the kitchen, busying herself at the cooker.

"Something smells good."

"Right thing to say," she said, not looking round as she stirred at whatever she was cooking in the pan. "I hope you like spaghetti bolognaise."

"Love it, especially if it tastes as good as it smells."

"There's a bottle of wine needs opening, a nice Chilean Merlot I found in your rack. It needs to breathe for a while, so you have time for a shower after you've done your thing with the corkscrew." She was looking at him and smiling as she spoke.

Longman felt a little shiver go down his spine. God, how could she make opening a bottle of wine sound sexy?

He went upstairs, got undressed and started the shower. While he was wondering if he would be interrupted during this one he heard the house phone ring. Cursing under his breath, he wrapped a towel around his waist and went into the bedroom to answer it.

"Longman," he said, sitting on the edge of his bed.

"Hello, inspector. Having a bit of time off. Tut, tut. When there's a killer on the loose, too. Before you ask, this is Joshua Smith. Yes, *inspector*, it's me. You spoilt things yesterday. I was hoping to have some fun with that one before I killed her. Never mind, there are more, there're always more. They'll have to wait, though, because I have other fish to fry first. You'll be hearing from me. And you can tell that big headed slut who's your boss – how do you like being bossed around by a woman, by the way? – I've not finished with her yet. She must pay for what she did, she *will* pay.'

Before Longman could start to speak the phone went dead as Smith disconnected the call. He immediately checked to get the number but saw 'number withheld' displayed. He hadn't really expected anything else. He wondered briefly how Smith had got his home number, it was unlisted, but knew that there were ways if you knew where to look, which probably meant that the man knew his address too.

It seemed like Smith was still in the area, or at least the area covered by the local news. Longman felt happier about that, as he really wanted to be the one who got him. Now he'd got Smith rattled, the chances of him making a mistake that would get him caught had just increased.

He was shaken out of his reveries by Helen coming through the door, wearing nothing but one of his shirts. She saw the look on his face and came and sat on the bed beside him.

"What is it, Tom? You look like you've seen a ghost."

"Helen, I think I'd better tell you a little about the case I'm on at the moment," he said, before giving her a quick resume. When he was done she looked worried, so he told her that there was no need to feel threatened.

"We have Smith on the back foot now. He's been forced away from his house, he's lost his van so will not be as mobile, and now he's just told me, unwittingly, that he's still in the area. Nearly every officer on the beat has a photo of him. If he shows his face we'll know about it. You'd better have a copy too, just in case he shows up here. No answering the door dressed like that, please."

"In that case, mister super-efficient policeman, can you help me out of this shirt? There's something I need to do before dinner. You."

The spaghetti was slightly dried up by the time they got back downstairs so Tom grabbed the wine and two glasses and nodded Helen back towards the stairs.

"What kind of woman do you think I am," she said, batting her eyelashes at him.

"My kind," he said, "back to bed, you hussy."

# Chapter 14

"It's as if he's disappeared off the planet, sir," Charles told Longman next morning.

They'd received nothing but negative results from the police stations whose officers had been checking hotels, guest houses and the like. If Smith was staying anywhere, it wasn't in Leicester. Reluctantly, they were forced to concede that he'd gone to ground. The only hope they had of catching him was if he showed himself, and Longman didn't think that Smith would be that forthcoming. The Chief Constable had agreed, when Kate had bent his ear, that the appeal for information should go national. The recording of Longman's appeal from yesterday was to be aired during the early evening news on both the BBC and ITV. It was to be repeated on the late news programme and also put onto the BBC's news website. Every effort was going to be put in motion to catch Joshua Smith.

"I think, personally, that he's still somewhere in Leicester," Longman told Kate Laxton later during their morning update in her office. "He said he hadn't finished with you yet, Kate. If he has gone further away from you it would make things more difficult than they need to be for him to have any chance of getting close. Needless to say, you're now being watched round the clock until we've caught him."

"No need for that, Tom. I know what he looks like and I can take care of myself. Resources would be better employed elsewhere, there are enough officers working on this already."

"Very well," Longman reluctantly agreed, "but if he makes any kind of direct threat that will change. We can't afford to lose you."

Kate felt warmed by Longman's concern, at the same time realising that she could well be in the firing line, literally, if Smith had procured himself another gun.

Josh had no need to find another gun. When he'd bought the target pistol he'd also bought a rifle. It, like the gun, had been made for target shooting, but because of its size he'd kept it at home. He never had figured out why he'd bought it, but it had felt like the right thing to do at the time. It had proved to be fortuitous as trying to get another pistol would be very difficult now. All the gun shops would have been put on alert and anyone wanting to buy any kind of weapon would be scrutinised most carefully. If the weapon concerned was a .22 alarm bells would most certainly ring. No, the rifle would have to do. It meant, of course, he would have to use this house as his base. Fortunately, the garage was built onto the side and had a door straight into the kitchen, so when he brought his victims home no one would see them. They certainly wouldn't hear them as they would be unconscious. He retrieved the rifle from its hiding place in the attic and checked it over. It was a good make, an Anshutz and, like the pistol, fired single shots. Putting the weapon into its bag, he placed it inside the wardrobe in the master bedroom, along with a box of ammunition. He intended that a certain policewoman would be seeing the business end of it soon. Josh wondered if she would beg him for her life. It wouldn't make any difference, he'd made his mind up she was going to die.

Nothing could change his mind.

He went back downstairs, deciding it was time for a coffee before going out for some fresh air. He turned the TV on while the kettle was boiling and caught the end of the weather forecast – much needed rain was due to fall during the evening – followed by the news. There was the usual doom and gloom about the economy, another multinational had posted bigger than expected losses and China was playing up again. He was about to turn it off when he saw Detective Inspector Longman's face appear on the screen. It was a repeat of the previous days broadcast and got Josh wound up just as much this time as it had then. He snarled obscenities at the image before grabbing his remote and punching the off button.

"I think you need to know that I'm still in business, Inspector!"

He went into the kitchen and made his coffee, bringing it back into the front room where he sat and planned the next phase of Kate Laxton's eventual demise. He needed another victim and decided to wait until it was dark before venturing out to find one. He knew where to look, any of the dark streets near to the railway station always had eager prostitutes ready to please. Finding someone was the easy part. Getting her to join him in the back of his car would be the challenge. He knew that most of the girls preferred to use hourly paid rooms, they thought they were safer doing their business that way. There would always, however, be one or two that would do their thing in the client's cars, and he only needed one. Preferably with black hair, but any colour would do as he still had the hair dye he'd bought for the blonde jogger. He had his chloroform pad ready in its plastic container, and had bought some tablets from an internet site that advertised them as the female Viagra.

''She'll do everything you've ever dreamed of, and like it,'' was how they'd been advertised.

It would be fun to see if they worked. He'd got himself quite upbeat about the evening to come, he would show them it didn't pay to mess around with Josh Smith.

Longman and Charles arrived at the offices of Smith's employer just as the staff started arriving for work. They parked in the visitor's slot and waited for a couple of minutes before entering the foyer where a middle aged woman was in the process of turning on her computer terminal. She asked them politely to bear with her as she got her desk ready for the business of the day.

"Actually, madam, we're police officers and we have some questions regarding one of your employees, so if you could be as quick as you can we would appreciate it," said Charles.

"Oh my goodness, what's happened? Has someone had an accident? Should I get the boss in here?" she said, getting quite flustered.

"Calm down, madam. Call your boss in please, it perhaps would be better if we saw him about this matter," said Longman.

She pressed one of the extensions on her phone.

"Mr Day, there are two policemen here to see you. No, I don't know what it's about. Can you come down and speak to them? OK, see you in a minute."

James Day came into the reception area within the minute and introduced himself to Longman and Charles. They showed him their warrant cards and asked if they could speak to him in private.

"No problem, Inspector, but my office is very small. Perhaps your sergeant could stay here, I'm sure Carol will be able to rustle up some coffee and a biscuit."

"That's fine by me, sir, I'm ready for a coffee, that's for sure," said Charles, thinking to himself that he would probably get some useful information off the receptionist while his boss was with the manager.

"That's settled then. If you'd like to follow me, Inspector."

Longman soon found himself in a cramped office upstairs from reception, thinking that the receptionist definitely had the best work space in this firm. When asked if he would like a coffee, Longman politely refused. Day poured himself a cup and sat down behind his desk.

"Sorry about the mess. Now, what can I do for you, Inspector?

"I believe your firm owns a white Transit van, registration number BL08 MWM?" he enquired.

"Yes, that's one of our delivery vans. Has it been in an accident? I wouldn't be surprised, he's a strange one is that Joshua Smith."

*Well, that confirms the answer to one of the questions he was going to ask*, thought Longman.

"What do you mean, sir, strange?"

"It's difficult to put a finger on it, but I always felt a bit uncomfortable round him. He worked well, although, thinking about it, he did seem to clock up more miles than he should have. He always explained the extra distance as being due to road works, diversions, or traffic jams and the like, that he tried to get round by going across country. I know that Carol downstairs didn't like being alone with him, she said she would catch him looking at her with a strange smile. Anyway, Inspector, what's happened?"

"We have the van, sir. It was abandoned by Mr Smith, who we would dearly love to talk to. Have you any idea where he could be? He's not at his house. Do you know him well enough to tell me where he would go?" Longman asked, not expecting any kind of positive answer.

"Afraid not, Inspector. Ricky might, he sometimes went down the pub with Josh on Fridays. He should be back sometime this afternoon, he had an overnight to Aberdeen. Shall I get him to call you when he gets in?" Day offered.

"Yes, please, sir." Said Longman, digging a card out of his wallet. "This will get me directly, any time at all. Do your employees have lockers here, Mr Day?"

"Of course, Inspector, but they are locked and I really don't think Josh would be happy if you opened his locker without his presence."

"Do you have keys, sir? I will stress that if there is anything to help us find him it could save him from getting into more trouble. We really do need to find Mr Smith, sir."

"OK, Inspector, but I'm not happy about it."

Day went to a cabinet and opened a drawer. He fished around and lifted out a set of keys.

"One of these will fit. If you'd like to come with me, Inspector, I'll show you where the lockers are."

There was a small sitting area at the back of the unit and there were five lockers against the back wall. Day opened the second one in from the left and stood to one side.

Longman looked into Smiths locker and saw that it was completely empty. Nothing at all to show that it had ever been used.

"Is that normal, sir?"

"Most definitely not. There should be a spare set of safety clothing in there for a start, never mind the old paperwork and bits and pieces that I would expect to find. This is a first for me."

"Oh, well, let us hope Ricky has some information that will help us locate the whereabouts of your driver."

"If he abandoned our van I would say that he is now an ex-driver, Inspector, and I can't say I'm sorry."

While Longman had been with her boss, Charles and Carol had been having an interesting conversation. To clarify, Charles had sat and listened while Carol told him about Smith. She quite obviously didn't like the man and made no bones about it.

"He used to look at me sometimes as though he was undressing me. It made me feel dirty just being in the same room. A nasty man, and untidy too. He'd been told time and time again to smarten himself up if he wanted to keep his job, but never did. It was as though he didn't care whether he worked or not. Mr Day wouldn't get rid of him though, drivers for this sort of work don't grow on trees, he would say. More like drivers who would work for peanuts don't, *I'd* say."

"Do you have a record of his trips, say for the last few months?" Charles asked her.

"Of course, Sergeant. I can print you a copy if you like," she offered.

"That would be fine, Carol, thank you."

While Carol was finding the details on her computer Longman returned with Day.

"Ready, Sergeant?"

"Just getting a list of Smith's trips, sir."

"Here you are, Sergeant. The last three months are listed, with recipients, dates and whether any of the trips involved staying overnight."

"Thanks very much, Carol. You've been a gem."

They thanked Day for his assistance and left. As they were walking to the car Longman told Charles what had transpired in Day's office, and Charles reciprocated, telling Longman about the receptionist's intense dislike of Smith.

"Let's hope this Ricky chap knows something that can help us," said Charles.

Josh left the house at eight and drove into the city. He knew where he was going to eat. He had a favourite Thai restaurant he always went to, their food was superb and reminded him of his long ago holiday in Bangkok. He parked up and walked the few hundred yards to the restaurant, finding it relatively quiet at this hour. Later on it, like most oriental establishments, would be heaving with people getting their food intake before hitting the clubs.

He was offered the menu by a beautiful young Thai girl with the blackest hair he'd ever seen. It was lustrous, thick and straight, and hung to her tiny waist. She gave him a beaming smile and greeted him with the traditional Thai greeting, 'Sa Wat dee, krap'. He responded and was shown to a table that gave him a view of the street. For the next hour and a half he enjoyed the food and the bottle of Singha beer that was served icy cold. By the time he had settled the bill and walked back to his car the time had crept on and it was starting to get dark. He sat in the car and waited for darkness to fully take over before starting his engine and heading for the seedy area that would supply him with what he needed. He found the street where he knew prostitutes would congregate and drove down it slowly before stopping against the kerb. He sat and waited, engine idling, and before long there was a tap at the window. He pressed the switch to lower it and a pretty young girl asked him what he wanted.

"That depends on what you can offer," he replied.

"Anyfing you like, within reason, but you 'ave to wear summing. I'm clean, see, an' I wanna stay that way. Normal is twenty quid, blowie is ten and the other I don't do."

"OK, how much to do it in my car. We would have to go somewhere quiet first," he asked, thinking that if he had anything to do with it she *would* do the 'other'.

"No cars, mister. I've got a room round the corner, we 'ave to use that."

"Sorry, it's in my car or not at all," he said and as she stood away he raised the window again and drove to his second choice, only a couple of streets away. He would cruise around for as long as it took, but he knew that if business was slow, one of them would take the chance on doing their trade in his car. It was just a matter of finding her.

It was his third try of the evening when he wound his window down and a beautiful, dark haired Asian girl poked her head in and said, "Forty quid, straight sex only."

He unlocked the passenger door and told her to get in. She slipped into the seat and as she did so her skirt rose up and showed her long legs off. She had a crop top on, no bra, and her nipples showed prominent against the tight fabric. She reached over and rubbed his crotch, but he told her to wait. He wanted to find somewhere to park up before they got down to business.

"Can't we do it here, mate?" She said, thinking that it wouldn't take long to make this old fart come.

"No," was all he said as he pulled out into the traffic.

"OK, mister, I can wait another few minutes. Better get prepared though," and as she spoke she raised herself up and pulled her panties off. She sat back down with her skirt round her waist and her long legs parted, turned slightly towards him. She knew he would not be able to resist having a look. He did, and saw she was completely hairless and pressed his foot a little harder on the accelerator. They were soon parked up in a dark side street, behind a big van that shielded his car from any light coming from the main road. The girl squirmed into the back seat and he got out and let himself in beside her. She pulled his zip down and took his erection in hand before giving a little gasp at the size of it.

"Don't worry, love, it always manages to fit somewhere," he told her, thinking that she was either a good actress or she was new to the game. She removed her top and sat on his lap, facing him. As she started rubbing herself against him, he stopped her.

"That might work with the young lads, love, but not with me. I don't mind wearing something, but this is going inside you. You decide where."

She thought for a second before reaching into her small bag for a condom. She handed it to him and asked him to put it on. He did so and she started to slide onto his lap again.

"No, love, I like to do it from behind. OK."

"OK," she said, and turned round, giving him a nice view of her ass.

*Very nice*, he thought, *I'll have that later*.

She lowered herself onto him, giving a sharp intake of breath as he entered her but was soon bouncing herself up and down on him, trying her hardest to make him come. She gave it her all and he actually thought she might even come herself, but knew he had to act before that happened. He felt for the plastic box in his jacket and quietly opened it, taking out the soaked pad. He quickly reached round her and pressed it over her nose and mouth, pulling her head back as she tried to fight him. Her struggling got less as the chloroform started to work and she was soon asleep. He gagged her, balling her own panties up and stuffing them into her mouth before tying her top round her head to hold them in place. He reached into the boot area and dragged a blanket over to cover her up. Satisfied that she was invisible to anyone looking in, he made himself decent before getting back into the driving seat and heading home.

As he reached his rented house he picked up the remote and used it to open the garage door, allowing him to drive in without getting out of the car. Once inside, he waited for the door to close before getting out and unlocking the door to the kitchen. Going back to his car, he opened the back door and found the girl still asleep. Reaching in, he lifted her out and carried her into the house, taking her straight upstairs and into the second bedroom that he'd prepared just for this. The bedroom contained a double bed and a chair. The chair was facing the bed and was bolted to the floor. He laid her on the bed and used cable ties to secure her wrists and ankles to the four corners. My God, she was gorgeous. He left the gag in place, he didn't want her screaming blue murder when she woke up. Knowing she would be thirsty he prepared a large glass of water, dissolving one of his tablets in it. It was time to see if they really worked.

He went downstairs and got a couple of beers before returning to watch her as he drank. He was stroking himself while he finished the second beer.

She started to wake up, struggling as soon as she realised she was tied to a bed, but soon gave up as the ties started to bite into her flesh. Josh leant over her and told her that if she promised to be quiet he would let her drink some water. She hadn't realised until he spoke just how thirsty she was so she nodded her head frantically. Josh took the gag off but left the panties inside her mouth. He showed her the hammer he'd brought up from the kitchen with the beers and told her that if she made any noise at all he would use it on her kneecaps. Her eyes went very wide at this, she knew she was in deep trouble now.

He removed the panties and held the glass of water as she drank greedily. She finished it all and he replaced the gag, before sitting in the chair and watching her to see if the drug worked. She started to breathe faster after a few minutes so he removed his clothes and stood in her sightline while he stroked himself to a full erection. She was looking at him and making little noises in her throat. He went closer and put himself in one of her hands. She started to rub her hand up and down, moaning.

*My God, they* do *work*, he thought to himself. The next couple of hours were passed in a frenzy of the most physical sex he'd had for a long time. He had to cut the ties as she was insatiable and tried anything and everything he suggested. She couldn't help herself, the drugs overriding any sense of revulsion she should have been feeling towards him. Eventually even he had had enough and he made sure she was secure again before going into his own bedroom where he showered and went to bed.

She couldn't sleep, the drugs were still coursing through her. She wanted more, and didn't care who gave it to her. Eventually, though, their effects started to diminish and, as they did, she started to feel a profound shame and disgust at herself for what she'd done. She couldn't stop herself from crying and lay there, sobbing. She must have finally slept as she was rudely awakened when the bedroom light was switched on, and *he* sat on the edge of the bed. He looked at her and decided that, beautiful as she was, she was not the one he wanted, needed. She'd been an interesting diversion and had confirmed that the drug worked, but he had no further need for her. She would have to die, of course. He would have to think about where he could leave this one. He wanted her found quickly as he would leave his next message to that bitch Laxton pinned to her body. He couldn't risk posting it at another station post-box, they were probably being monitored more closely now.

She was looking at him, pleading with her eyes for an explanation. He got up, reaching for a glass of water and she shook her head. She was thirsty as hell but there was no way she was drinking that stuff again, not now that she knew what it would make her become.

"Now, now, that's no way to repay my kindness, is it?" he said, removing the gag and the panties from her mouth. He showed her the hammer as she started to yell and it died in her throat.

"Please don't hurt me," she said, "I'll do what you want, but don't hurt me."

"That's better. Now, drink this all down, you must be thirsty," he said, tipping the glass towards her mouth.

She drank it all, thinking to herself that if it was drugged at least she wouldn't be responsible for her physical responses. Her body would undoubtedly respond, as it had last night, but she preferred the shame of that, to broken legs. It would be her body responding, but not her mind, she convinced herself. After a few minutes she hadn't felt anything at all and she realised that it had been just a glass of water after all. She started to say thank you but before she could get the words out he'd replaced the panties in her mouth and tied the scarf round her head again.

"Don't you try thanking me, love, I haven't finished with you yet. Don't get me wrong, I enjoyed last night as much as you did," as he said this he saw her face screw up in disgust, "but that was an experiment. I had to find out if the drugs worked. This morning, though, I'm going to have you as you are, feeling everything, but powerless to stop me. You're going to regret picking me as your forfeit."

He'd gone through her bag while waiting for her to wake up and had found that she wasn't a prostitute, as he'd suspected the previous evening. There'd been a piece of paper in her bag, instructions that as her forfeit she had to pick up a kerb crawler and shag him for forty quid. *Must have been quite a party if that was the type of forfeit given out*, he thought.

He quickly undressed and started on her, this time, unwilling body. His excitement grew as she writhed under him, trying to stop him entering her. It was futile and she finally gave up and lay there, unmoving, while he panted away on top of her. Afterwards she lay there crying, wishing she was dead. He hadn't used any protection at all and she wasn't on the pill. She'd heard of girls who'd ended up pregnant after being raped, resulting in them having to have an abortion. If that happened the shame would always be there, in her memory, forever reminding her of him.

He'd gone out of the room when he'd finished but she heard him come back in just before he pressed a pad onto her face. She was soon under again and he removed the ties, turning her over before securing her again.

She awoke a while later and realised straight away that she was lying on her stomach. She feared the worst now.

"Oh, you've woken up at last. I'm pleased about that as I was starting to get impatient," he said.

He had been admiring her backside while she slept and was more than ready, so he completed her shame while she tried desperately to shake him off. Finally he climbed off her, leaving her sobbing and broken on the bed. He collected his rifle from the other bedroom and came back in, standing at the end of the bed. Lifting the rifle to his shoulder he sighted on the back of her head, just above the neck, and pulled the trigger. The bullet struck home and she went still. Reloading, he fired again, aiming for the same place.

He checked her, but found no pulse. *It was a pity*, he thought, *she would have made someone a fine lover*. The drugs had released the inner her, a side she probably never knew she had, and never would again.

He couldn't move her until the night, and spent the rest of the day watching TV and checking his e-mails. The message he was waiting for arrived just after four pm. He wrote the address down and smiled to himself. It was time to make that inspector pay for his meddling. He would dump the girl's body tonight, somewhere where it would be discovered quickly. He needed the inspector to be at work when he visited his house, as his plan required a couple of hours inside the house.

At last it was time to move, and Josh went upstairs for the girl. He cut the ties before wrapping the body in a blanket and carrying it downstairs, through the kitchen and into the garage. He put the girl's body in the back of the car, covering it with another blanket, before going back in for the message he'd printed off earlier. Reading it again, he was satisfied that it would convey his intentions to the police bitch. He intended to leave the body sat in a bus shelter in one of the sleepy villages south of the city. It took him an hour of driving round until he found the perfect spot to leave the dead girl. The bus stops, he admitted, had not been a viable idea. He hadn't realised just how much traffic there could be during the night. Eventually he stopped in a layby that had some picnic tables in the area leading up to the trees. He was alone, the road was not too busy and as the parking area ran behind some trees he was not likely to be spotted by any passing traffic. He hoped that no one

would want to park while he was moving the body. That would
be very unfortunate.

He was lucky, and soon had the girl's body laying on one
of the tables, face up. He parted her legs and stapled the
message to the table between them. There was no need to take a
photo, the body should be discovered soon enough.

# Chapter 15

"The body of a young woman was found this morning by a lorry driver when he stopped for a break. Her identity cannot be revealed, but next of kin have been informed," the voice of the newscaster was sombre as she read the rest of the details, "The lorry driver had stopped for a break at a lay-by on the busy main road between Leicester and Newark. He noticed the body of the young woman laid on one of the picnic tables. Police are treating the death as suspicious. Anyone who used the road between ten pm and five am this morning are asked to contact Leicester police on the following number," the newscaster then went on to give the contact details for Longmans office.

Longman had been at home when the call had come in. The officers attending the call out to the lay-by where the body had been discovered had, once it was determined that she was indeed dead, called in the details to headquarters. The ME had been called and, on discovering the bullet holes in the back of the young woman's head, had reported back with the request that Longman should be informed as a matter of urgency.

Longman called his sergeant and asked him to meet him at the scene. Putting the phone down, he turned to Helen and ruefully told her that he had to go. She got out of bed, putting his dressing gown on and headed downstairs.

"I'll get you a coffee made while you wash and dress, you can take it with you."

She'd noticed that he had a couple of those travel mugs when she'd been looking for pots and pans the day before. She had the mug ready when he appeared at the bottom of the stairs a few minutes later.

"You're a sweetheart, Helen. I'm not sure when I'll be home, but I'll let you know as soon as I can, ok. Take care."

"Don't you worry about me, Tom, I'll be fine," she said, standing on tip toes as he bent down to kiss her.

He got into his car and set off for the lay-by. It was the other side of Leicester but at this time in the morning it was fairly quiet on the roads. It was only twenty minutes later that he pulled up in the lay-by, getting waved through the police tape that was preventing members of the public from gaining access. He found Henry Brandon, the ME, sitting in his car writing his preliminary report.

"What have we got here, Henry?" he asked, squatting down at the side of the ME's car.

"Another shooting victim, I'm afraid, Tom. Young girl, about eighteen or nineteen I'd guess, shot twice in the back of the head. From my first look the shots look as though they were fired with her lying down, on her stomach. As she was found lying on her back and there isn't any evidence of blood loss here I would say that she was killed somewhere else and then brought here to be discovered. There are traces of dried blood in the pubic area too. She was probably raped but I'll know more after the autopsy. Do you want to have a look before the body is removed?"

"Not really, Henry, but I better had. Has my sergeant turned up yet?"

"Yes, he's over at the scene now. Been here about five minutes," replied the ME.

Longman made his way over to the table area and saw his sergeant talking to a well-built man who was wearing overalls with his firm's name printed on the back, presumably the lorry driver.

"What did you do while you were waiting for the police, sir?" he heard Charles ask the man as he joined them.

"I went back to my lorry and got one of my blankets out of the back to cover the poor lass up. I know," he held his hands up, "I should have left everything as it was, but it didn't seem right, her lying there with nothing to cover her."

"That's all right, sir," said Longman, cutting in on the conversation, "anyone would have done the same. We can discount any hairs that your blanket may have shed, can we not, Sergeant."

"Of course, sir," said Charles, before turning back to the driver and continuing. "Did you see any vehicle leaving the lay-by, sir?" he asked him.

"No, the place was completely deserted, well except for…you know."

"Fine. Well, I think that's all for now. Can you come down to police headquarters later on and give us a full statement, sir?"

"Of course. Can I do my delivery now? I've got two on the lorry today. Half the load is for Newark and then it's over to Lincoln to deliver the rest. Should be done by three, if that's OK?"

"That'll be fine, sir, and thanks for your help. Do you want your blanket back, I see the paramedics have got her covered with one of theirs now?"

"No thanks, I don't think I could ever use it again. Can you dispose of it for me please?" the man said.

"I understand perfectly," said Charles, "Of course we can, sir."

Once the driver had left them, Charles turned to Longman.

"There was this, sir," he said, handing Longman the note found stapled to the table.

Longman quickly read the printed note, noticing straight away that the style of printing matched the previous ones.

**YOU WON'T FRIGHTEN ME OFF, INSPECTOR
LET THIS BE A LESSON
STOP INTERFERING, YOU CAN'T PREVENT ME FROM
COMPLETING MY PUNISHMENT**

This virtually confirmed his supposition that Smith was responsible for the death of this young woman. It also explained why his sergeant hadn't been treating the lorry driver as a suspect.

"Well, Sergeant, it looks like our Mr Smith hasn't finished his killing spree yet. I'd better come and see the scene, although I doubt it will throw up anything we don't already suspect."

As soon as Longman saw the dead girl he knew that this was going to raise the stakes as far as the media would be concerned. A maniac killing young women was bad enough, but now he'd killed an Asian girl the gutter press would have a field day. How had he managed to get her alone? Where did she come from? Who was she?

He knew that answers would have to be found, and quickly. There was no identification to be found here, naked bodies didn't come with name tags.

As Henry had finished his examination, Longman told the ambulance crew that they could remove the body from the scene now. They quickly got it into a body bag and placed it onto the gurney, wheeling it away and loading it into their vehicle. The ME followed the ambulance out of the lay-by, the body was going straight to the morgue where he would carry out the autopsy proper.

"Well, Sergeant," Longman said as they watched them go, "any ideas?"

"I've been thinking about that, sir. If he killed the girl somewhere else it could mean that he's in a house on his own. Renting a room, or using guest houses or hotels, wouldn't give him enough privacy. There's the noise issue too, even a small calibre weapon makes some noise and he wouldn't be able to use anything to muffle the sound because that would seriously slow the round. It may work in the movies with Dirty Harry type guns but not with a .22. I get the feeling that he has rented somewhere, probably detached, and because he just disappeared after we nearly got him I also think he rented it beforehand. Maybe he always had it in reserve, so to speak."

"Or maybe he had it ready to use on someone special, and didn't want to take the chance on using his own house," said Longman, thinking of Smith's fixation with his boss, Kate Laxton. "Whichever way you look at it, Sergeant, it seems a likely scenario. That means even more checking to do, there are quite a few letting agencies around."

"I have to agree, sir, but how many deal with detached houses, probably with garage attached. That would be the higher end of the market, I would suggest. In today's climate I wouldn't think there've been too many of those types of houses rented out."

"Let's get back to the office, Sergeant, and get cracking. There's also the identity of this young woman to determine. Please let someone be looking for her."

There were people looking for her alright, and they were scared. The girl had left them to do her 'forfeit' and they'd seen her get into a car, but instead of doing it there with the guy which is what they'd expected, the car had driven off and they only had enough time to make out that it was an estate, and dark coloured.

They'd flagged down a taxi but couldn't tell the driver where to drive to as they hadn't a clue where their friend had been taken, so went back to the club where they'd been celebrating the missing girl's success in being named runner up in the Miss Leicester contest. They all knew she should have won, and they'd been drinking heavily to drown their sorrows. The game of forfeits had always been a part of their evening and they'd got more daring with each successive party. This time, though, they knew they'd gone too far and tried to dissuade her from doing the forfeit, but she was adamant and would not back down. She never had before and, anyway, what harm could it do. She would probably be able to get whoever she chose to agree to have a feel while she gave him a hand job.

They sat on the wall outside the club, hoping that she would return and regale them with all the juicy details. After an hour they were really worried and decided that they should tell someone. As luck would have it, just as they were getting to their feet to go and find a policeman a patrol car turned into the street further up and headed their way. One of them waved and got the driver's attention and the car slowed to a halt beside them.

"Yes, sir, what appears to be the trouble?" the policeman asked as he rolled his window down.

He listened, and as he was told the sorry story he thought that youngsters today hadn't the sense they were born with. He took down the description of the girl and also her name and address.

"So, he said, "the girl's name is Aisha Pahman, she's nineteen and lives with her parents at this address." He pointed to the address he'd written down, getting a nod from them. "And she got into a car with a perfect stranger to have sex with him for a forfeit, and was going to charge him forty pounds for the privilege, yes?"

"Yes, officer," said the young man.

"And she's been gone for over an hour, yes?" he continued. Again they all nodded.

"Just how much has she had to drink tonight," he asked, thinking that the girl was most probably getting herself into more than she had bargained for by now.

"We've all had quite a lot to drink, it was a kind of celebration as Aisha had come runner up in the Miss Leicester pageant. She's a very pretty girl, officer, she shouldn't be in a car with a stranger."

*You've got that right*, the policeman thought.

"We'll keep a look out for her, sir, but she'll probably go straight home and get in the shower after he's done with her. Do any of you have a photo of Aisha?"

"Only the ones we took tonight on our phones, can we text them to your phone?" said the young man who seemed to be speaking for the rest of them.

"That'll do fine, sir, I'll give you the number and once you've sent it I will need to make sure that my number is deleted."

The picture that appeared on the police phone showed a girl with a beautiful oval face framed by dark, wavy hair. The policeman told them that the best place for them to go was home.

"She may already have done the same by now, and is tucked up in her bed fast asleep," he said.

"No, officer, she won't be. We always meet up after the last forfeit has been done, to share the stories. If she goes anywhere it will be back here. We'll wait, won't we?" he looked at the rest of them as he said that, getting nods of agreement.

"Fair enough, sir, but if she hasn't come back by morning I would suggest you contact her parents, just in case she did go home. If she's still missing then, let us know."

"OK, officer."

As he drove off, he thought that the lads would have a right laugh about this one in the morning when he went back to the station at the end of his shift. A beauty queen runner-up getting it on with a kerb crawler for a forfeit, dare or whatever you want to call it.

Stupid, he called it.

He passed by the club a few hours later and the group had gone, so he assumed that the girl had returned to them. Hopefully she would not have been upset or harmed by her experience, he'd seen what could happen to girls after being picked up by these scum who cruised round looking for cheap sex.

At seven he parked up in the police car park and strolled into the station. As he went through the door he could tell something was up, and it was an important something too.

"What's going on, Bob?" he asked at the desk.

"A girls body has been found in a lay-by on the Newark road, Stan," said the desk sergeant, "and as there was no ID at the scene we're trying to find out who she is.

There's a bit of pressure on this one, too, 'cause the girl's an Asian."

Stan's blood ran cold at that, and he quickly asked if there was a photo of the body yet.

"Not yet, but one's on the way. All the stations are getting it faxed through from headquarters. They reckon she was shot in the head, and are linking it to the others that have been found recently. What's up, Stan? You look like you've seen a ghost."

"I may have, Bob. There was a young Asian girl went off with a Kerber for a date last night and her friends were worried about her. I hope she's not the one. She's only nineteen and a bit of a beauty queen by all accounts. The only picture her friends had of her was taken on one of their phones last night, I transferred it onto mine just in case it was needed. Here, you'd better have it," he said, handing the phone over.

The fax machine seemed to take that as a cue and started chattering away. The desk sergeant peeled off the photograph and showed it to Stan, whose face told him what he was going to ask.

"That's her, all right," said Stan.

They checked the print out against the picture on his phone and agreed that they were of the same girl.

Picking up the desk phone, the sergeant pressed the numbers for headquarters and was soon talking to Inspector

Longman. After informing Longman that they had an ID on the dead girl he listened for a minute before saying, "Yes, sir," and replacing the phone.

"You'd better get yourself over to headquarters, Stan. The inspector in charge of these murder cases wants to see you. If I were you I'd dredge up anything that you might have seen that looked a bit suspicious, like, from last night."

Longman couldn't believe his luck, getting an ID on the girl so quickly was a real bonus for the investigation. Knowing where she had been picked up, and when, was the icing on the cake. The area concerned was covered by a myriad of cameras, some belonging to the council and others owned by the clubs and pubs in the area. The police knew that kerb crawling went on in the streets near the railway station and regularly used evidence from these cameras to convict drivers for the offence. He had sent Charles to see his friend in the CCTV department, hopefully they would turn up some footage of the car that Aisha Pahman had got into to do her forfeit.

*Quite a forfeit*, he thought, *it cost her her life.*

They had double checked her identity, going onto the local news website where they found photos of all the Miss Leicester contestants. There she was, smiling at the camera and looking like a million dollars.

"Who'd have thought that someone like that would end up going off with a stranger for a dare?" said Charles.

"She probably wouldn't have if she'd been sober, Sergeant, but from all accounts she certainly wasn't that," Longman informed him.

While Charles was investigating the video angle with Mapley, Longman rang Emma and asked if the ACC was available.

"Of course, Inspector, she's been waiting for you to come and see her. Do you want a coffee prepared?"

"That would be very nice, thank you, Emma."

He made his way to Kate's office and was ushered in by Emma, who placed a mug of coffee on the desk in front of Longman.

"Thank you, Emma," said Kate, as her secretary gave Longman a big smile before going back to her office.

"I tell you, Tom, she's got the hots for you, Emma has," said Kate, smiling.

"Yes, well, er, God knows why. I'm far too old for her, she needs to find a nice young man," said Longman, feeling slightly flustered.

'Right, down to business. What's the latest on the dead girl?"

"We've just got her identified, ma…Kate," he said, "she was a beauty queen contestant, came second in the Miss Leicester pageant. She'd gone with a kerb crawler for a dare, would you believe. The group she belonged to had a forfeit system and hers was to be picked up by a Kerber and get forty pounds for sex. I know, it's crazy what the young people get up to now but when she hadn't returned to the group after an hour they flagged down one of our patrol cars and reported her missing. They were able to give our driver a photo of the girl, but he didn't attach a great deal of importance to the affair. As far as he was concerned, she was probably back home and in bed. When he heard about a young Asian girl being found this morning he contacted us and the photo matched our body. Her name is, was, Aisha Pahman, nineteen years old and living with her parents. There are two Asian officers breaking the news to them as we speak, Kate. All in all, a sorry business. This was found stapled to the table where she was discovered." Longman passed Kate the note, which she quickly read.

"Still no idea where Smith could be, Tom?" she asked.

"Afraid not. Sergeant Charles is over at the CCTV offices trying to get any imagery of the area from last night. It may be that Smith's car will have been caught on one of them as Aisha was getting into it."

"I'm not banking on that, but it's about time we got a break on this case that will help. Smith seems to have been one step ahead so far, it would be nice to redress the balance in our favour," Kate said.

"I still think you should have twenty-four hour protection, Kate, Smith has made it very clear that he wants to punish you, and the latest note seems to point to him trying sooner rather than later."

Kate shook her head as Longman spoke, "No, Tom. If he sees a police presence all around me he might keep on abducting and killing more women. If he wants to try for me he'll have a surprise coming. Because I know he'll come I can be prepared. No, don't worry about me, Tom."

Longman told Kate about Charles' thoughts on what kind of place Smith may be using now that his own was out of commission. She agreed with them and authorised Tom to assign someone to check the letting agencies, with the priority on detached houses rented in the last two months. It was doubtful that Smith would have used his real name, but they could hope.

"The officer who was stopped by her friends is coming here; I doubt that he will be able to add too much to what we already know. Smith has done it again, vanished into a hideaway somewhere until he feels the need to surface," Longman told Kate.

"I'm sure we'll soon have the man in custody, Tom, he can't stay out of our sight forever."

Charles was sat in Mapley's office, looking intently at the screen in front of them both.

"OK, Michael, here we go. I have the recording from two cameras, both within spitting distance of the club where the pickup took place. Not brilliant quality but good enough to identify cars and their registration plates. From what you've told me the girl should be easy to recognise, not too many beauty queens are seen in this area."

Mapley started the playback of the recording and they watched the screen as the events outside the club for the previous evening unfolded as a slightly grainy, but clearer than Charles had expected, picture.

After about five minutes they saw the group emerge from the club and stand talking animatedly on the pavement. One of the girls, it looked like Aisha Pahman, was arguing with the rest and waving a scrap of paper.

"That must be her, with her forfeit," said Charles, getting a nod from Mapley.

"Here comes a car," Mapley said, leaning towards the screen.

Aisha went over to the car, a dark saloon, but as she reached it the car accelerated away, leaving her standing there giving it the finger.

Another car appeared and slowed to a halt beside her. She leant towards the passenger window and it must have been open because her head was half into the car.

"Pause, please," said Charles.

He looked at the still image and managed to determine the make of car, but not the registration number.

"That's a Mondeo estate, but the plate is unreadable. Can you do anything about that, Richard?" he asked.

"I can try, but it looks as though it's been covered in mud. Do you want to see the rest of the recording?"

"Yes, she hasn't got in yet so it may not be the car we want," said Charles.

A minute later he knew it was. They watched as Aisha opened the passenger door and got into the car, which was soon on the move.

"Is it possible to follow the car on your cameras, Richard?" Charles asked.

"It is, if all our cameras are working. Without the registration it won't be easy, though. I'll give you a call as soon as I've got anything worthwhile, OK."

"Thanks, I'd better get back to the office. Good luck," Charles said. As he walked back to his car he was thinking that staring at those screens all day would send him doolally. Ah, well, each to his own.

Mapley started his tracking of the Ford. He had a map in his head of the camera system in the area where he was looking, having studied previous recordings numerous times. He was able to switch between the cameras as the car drove along, hoping that the number plate would catch the light and somehow allow him to get the registration details. Not once was the image clear enough for any part of the number plate to be read, but that had been more of a hope than an expectation anyway.

He had a bit of a worry once when the car turned into a side street, before remembering that it was a dead end.

*So that's where you took her, you dirty bastard*, he thought.

After ten minutes he watched as the car came back onto the main road, noticing that the girl was no longer sat in the passenger seat. He was able to follow the car as far as the Groby Road before losing camera imagery. He switched, in turn, to all the cameras that covered each exit road, picking the car up again as it passed the Glenfield junction. The next camera was at the big interchange with the A46 but when the car hadn't appeared after a couple of minutes he accepted that it must have turned down the side road that led to Groby. There were no cameras covering that area at the moment so he reluctantly accepted that his search was over.

Reaching for the phone he called Charles and gave him what information he could, not forgetting to mention that the girl had not been in view the whole time.

While Mapley had been watching his screens, Charles had been helping the couple of constables who had been drafted onto the team. They were calling house rental agencies and compiling a list of all detached properties rented in the Leicester area in the last six months where the rental was still in operation. There were more than expected, caused by a firm relocating to one of the many industrial parks. Most of the workforce concerned accepted a relocation package and were renting while their houses were waiting to be sold in the old location.

He had been on the phone for the last hour or so, writing down names and addresses, when it rang in between calls.

"DS Charles, CID," he said.

"Hello Michael, Richard here."

"Hi, have you got an address for us? Or at least the street?" Charles asked.

"Afraid I can't get that precise, but maybe I have an area. The car turned off the Groby road just before the A46 lights, which could mean he was heading for somewhere in Groby itself. That was the first time it had left the main roads, by the way. Unfortunately, there aren't any cameras in that area. Sorry," said Mapley.

"If you'd managed to follow it to the front door, I would've been surprised, Richard. Very pleased, but surprised. We can check the rentals in the Groby area that haven't already been done, Smith must be somewhere and that's as good a place as any to start knocking on doors. Thanks, mate, I owe you one."

The two constables had overheard the conversation and were already back on their computer keyboards, finessing their search criteria to concentrate on all lettings in the Groby area.

Longman had seen the patrol officer who had helped to identify the Asian girl. As he had thought, there was nothing new to add from that quarter. The man felt really bad about not following up on the girl at the time, but Longman reassured him that there had been no reason for him to suspect anything other than a young girl being foolish. It had seemed to be a case of young people with very poor judgement of the risks involved. If the girl had met a normal punter she would have been at home now. Feeling ashamed of herself, probably, but alive. It was her bad fortune to get into that particular car. Once she had closed the car door there was nothing anyone could have done to save her.

Longman was walking back to his office when his mobile rang.

"DI Longman."

"Hello, Inspector. It's James Day here. Ricky's here at the depot, you said you wanted to speak to him when he got back."

"Yes, sir, thanks for getting back to me. Can Ricky come to police headquarters? It would be better to talk to him here."

After a moment, presumably while he told his employee that he *would* go and see the inspector, Day came back on and told Longman that Ricky would be at the station within the half hour.

"Thank you, sir. Much appreciated," said Longman, smiling. It was always a wonder to him just how many people did not like to enter a police station, almost as though there were a secret radar that would scan them for any past transgressions before locking them away forever.

He had time for a coffee before interviewing the reluctant Ricky, so he carried on to his office and poured himself a cup, wandering over to his sergeant's desk while he drank.

"Anything new yet, Sergeant?"

"Maybe, sir," answered Charles, filling Longman in on the results of the video search Mapley had done.

"Good work. The noose is starting to close, I feel. Do you want to come and see this Ricky, one of Smith's old work colleagues? He's coming in for a chat."

"Yes, sir. I think I could do with a break from this screen. How these two," he wafted his hand at the constables hunched over their keyboards, "keep going hour after hour is beyond me."

"You're getting old, Sergeant," one of them dared to utter.

"Cheeky bugger," said Charles, giving the man a friendly swat. "Back to your screen, slave."

Longman and Charles left their office and made their way to one of the interview rooms where they found Ricky waiting nervously.

"Is it true that you can't smoke in 'ere, then?" he asked as they entered the room and sat down opposite him, the scarred table between them.

"Not for a long time, Ricky. It is Ricky, I presume," said Longman.

"Yeah, Ricky Lester. What am I 'ere for then. The boss said you was wanting to know about Smithy. What's 'e done then?"

"What makes you think he's done anything, Ricky?" Charles asked.

"Well, 'e's not at work an' the boss said that you lot 'ave got 'is van, so 'e must be in trouble. Obvious, ain't it," Ricky said, then continued, "I always knew 'e would end up in bovver. 'As one of his birds reported 'im then?"

"Why would that happen, Ricky?" Longman asked.

"'E 'ad a mattress in the back o' that van, didn't 'e. I asked 'im about it once and 'e said it was for shagging 'itch'ikers, like. 'E knew we wasn't allowed to pick up passengers but 'e did anyway. Always boasting about what 'e got them to do. I'd told 'im that one day 'e would go too far and one of 'em would report 'im, but 'e just laughed. They all love it, 'e told me, especially up the arse. I didn't believe that, no bird I've ever gone all the way with has asked for it there."

Charles was suppressing a smile as he asked Ricky if he and Smith ever went for a drink together.

"Sometimes, but 'e couldn't 'old it. He used to talk all kinds of rubbish when 'e'd 'ad a couple. 'E even boasted about living in two 'ouses once. Who needs two 'ouses, especially if you was single, like we are?"

That bit of information made both Longman and Charles sit up.

"When did he tell you about having two houses, Ricky?" asked Charles, adding, "I don't suppose you know where these houses are, do you?"

"It was about a month ago now, and course I do, 'e took me round and showed me next day 'cause I didn't believe 'im. But don't ask me the numbers. Can't remember numbers for the life of me. One of 'em was over near Glenfield, think it was Meadow Lane or Road, somethin' like that anyway. Nice place, but too big for one person if you ask me. The other one was the other side of town, near Oadby. A big, detached 'ouse with a garage. It was in a dead end street, very quiet. Name reminded me of a fruit, one of those posh ones that you only get in Marks and Sparks. Avocado Grove, I think that was it. Couldn't live somewhere like that meself, the neighbours are probably all old codgers. I like somewhere with a bit o' life, see. Anyway, 'e told me never to tell anyone about 'is 'ouses. 'E said 'e was going to use one as a place to take the birds, an' the other was where 'e would live normal, like.'

Charles excused himself and left the room. He went back to the constables who were still busy searching the listings for properties that had been let in the Groby area.

"OK, you two. Forget Groby, the location has shifted. Have a look at detached houses in the Oadby area, with garage attached, and in a cul-de-sac. Could be called Avocado Grove, though I've never heard of it, if it is. It looks like our man has made his first big mistake, lads."

"Righto, Sarge, shouldn't take long. We'll soon have a list for you."

Longman was listening to Ricky Lester going on about his job when Charles re-joined them.

"'E never wanted to 'ire Smithy in the first place, but 'e didn't pay enough to get anyone else. Smithy didn't care about the money anyway, 'e said, 'e just wanted the van so 'e could travel round and see the country. Bollocks, I say, 'e just wanted a mobile shaggin' wagon. Anyway, you still 'aven't told me what 'e's done. What do you want to see 'im for then?"

"Just to help us with our enquiries, Ricky, that's all," said Longman. "Do you think you could show us where these two houses you mentioned are exactly?"

"Nah, we never stopped, 'e just pointed to them. One 'ouse looks like another to me, anyway. Is that it, then?"

"Yes, Ricky, I think it is. You can go home now," said Longman.

"Nah, I'll need a drink after all this. I'm off down the pub."

"Don't forget to take your car home first, we'd hate to catch you for drinking and driving," warned Charles.

Lester left the room and Longman and Charles followed him out, watching as he left the building.

"What do you reckon, sir, do you think he knows more than he's telling us?"

"I don't know, Sergeant. Possibly. He seemed to know more than I expected about our Mr Smith, that's for sure. I get the feeling that they did more than just have a drink together."

Ricky sat in his car and pressed the buttons on his phone.

"Yes," he heard.

"Smithy, it's Ricky. You'll never guess, I've been talking to the police about you. They want you for summat, they wouldn't tell me what. What you been up to then? One of them girls complained, 'ave they?"

"Shut up, Ricky, and listen. What did they ask you about me?" Josh asked.

"Nothin' much. Just said you could 'elp them with their enquiries, that's all. They didn't get any information out of me, I kept my mouth shut."

"I doubt that you could ever keep your mouth shut, Ricky. Never mind, they won't find me. Not unless I want them to. You didn't tell them about the houses, I hope."

There was a slight pause, before Ricky assured Josh that he hadn't mentioned the two houses to the police.

*I bet you didn't*, thought Josh. Never mind, nothing Ricky told them could stop him from completing his agenda.

"Don't call me anymore, Ricky. You will not see me again, goodbye." Josh hung up before Ricky could respond.

Right, Inspector, time to shake you up.

# Chapter 16

Helen Morrison was enjoying herself.

She'd been through Longman's freezer, finding it surprisingly full. There were steaks, chops, lots of fish and, filling up the space, bread rolls. Tom obviously liked to eat a varied menu. She'd decided to do a curry, using all of a packet of tiger prawns that were now defrosting. Thankfully there was a selection of cooking sauces in the cupboard. They really did take the pain out of making a good curry nowadays. There was also a container with just enough Basmati rice to give them both a decent portion.

Looking through his stock of wines she selected a merlot, smiling when she noticed it was from Chile. The French merlot was ok but Chilean was so much better, in her opinion. One more thing they had in common. Just in case, she also put a chardonnay in the fridge to cool.

Going into the living room, Helen made for the shelves full of CD's. Tom had quite a selection covering all sorts of tastes and after a short look she chose Madonna's Ray of Light. Setting the volume low she settled into the armchair and closed her eyes, letting the music wash into her.

Josh knew that the police would be busy in their futile search for him and decided that it was time to teach that interfering busybody of an inspector a lesson. He'd done his homework and found out that the inspector was unmarried and lived alone. That meant that he would have as much time as he needed inside the house. The inspector would be left in no doubt that it was not a good idea to upset Josh Smith.

Parking two streets away, Smith walked to Longman's house and at first strolled past on the other side of the street. Looking across, he noticed that the driveway was empty, and that there was a half glazed door at the side of the house. *Good,* hc thought, that would make it less obvious when he broke in. He felt in his pockets to check that he had the hammer and a roll of tape, finding that he still had the small plastic container with the chloroform soaked pad in one of his pockets too. Never mind, it could stay there now, he'd put it back in the glove box when he returned to his car. Josh had started to feel a bit apprehensive about breaking into a policeman's house. Longman could return at any time, he knew, and catch him inside. It was risk he had to take, that man had to be shown who was in control here. Josh had an *agenda*, and no police inspector was going to put a stop to that, oh no.

He reached the door and was about to start taping the glass when he heard music coming from inside.

He froze.

Surely Longman wasn't inside. There was no car on the drive and Josh would have put his shirt on the inspector chasing around trying to find the other house. He made a hasty retreat and when he was round the corner he stopped and collected his thoughts.

There was only one way to find out if anyone was inside so he got his mobile phone out and called.

*Typical*, thought Helen, *just get some decent music on and the bloody phone rings*. Then she smiled as she thought that it could be Tom letting her know he was coming home early.

"Hello," she said, picking up the handset.

Josh was shaken. There was a woman in Longman's house. He hadn't thought about the inspector having girlfriends, a serious omission on his part.

"Hello," he said, putting on a posh 'phone voice', "would it be possible to speak with Mr Longman, please? This is Philip Stonehouse, from the bank."

"I'm sorry, Mr Stonehouse, he isn't in at the moment. Can I get him to call you back later?"

"As long as it's before four, madam, that will be fine," he said.

"I doubt that, but if he does manage to get here in time I'll tell him."

"Thank you, madam, it's not terribly urgent," said Josh, and rang off.

*Well, well, Inspector, this puts a different perspective on things*, he thought. He had intended to wreck the house, leaving a message that he was not to be interrupted in his work. Kate Laxton *was* going to be punished, and *he* was the one who would decide how and when.

He thought about this development. The woman had sounded quite chirpy, as though she'd expected to be hearing Longman's voice. This was too good an opportunity to miss, and he thought quickly about how he could get into the house. Obviously, breaking in was no longer an option. He had to take whoever it was unawares, which meant ringing the bell and hoping that she would answer. He'd have to leave it for a half hour at least to let her get over the interruption of his call. Going back to his car, Josh sat behind the wheel and got the plastic box out of his jacket. Another job for you, I think, he told himself as he got the bottle of chloroform out of the glove box and recharged the pad.

By the time he wandered back to Longman's house he had a plan. A lot depended on the door chain being released by the woman. If she didn't let him in he'd have to leave Longman's punishment for another day.

He walked up to the side door and pressed the bell, hearing the ding dong from inside. After a moment the door opened, no chain, and she stood there. He saw a very attractive woman, probably in her thirties. She was dressed in the new fashion of jeggings, and a sloppy t-shirt.

"Hello, can I help you?" she asked.

"Sorry to bother you, but my car has broken down and, would you believe it, I forgot to charge my phone last night. If I give you the number, could you ring the breakdown people for me, please, madam?" Josh asked, starting to rummage in his pocket, ostensibly for the phone number.

"Of course, that won't be a problem. Could you wait here, please, while I get a pen and paper? If you told me the number I'm afraid I'd forget it by the time I got to the phone."

As she turned away from him he stepped forward and gave her a solid push in the small of her back, causing her to fall forward onto the kitchen floor. Before she could react he had dropped down onto her back, completely winding her. As she gasped for breath he pulled the pad out of his pocket, he'd already got it out of the box while supposedly looking for the breakdown service number, and pressed it over her mouth and nose. She couldn't stop herself from breathing in and the chloroform soon had her unconscious on the kitchen floor.

Josh stood up and looked for something to bind her with. There was a dishrag in the sink which he stuffed into her mouth, tying a tea towel round her head to keep it in place. He couldn't see anything that could be used to tie her up, so started going through the kitchen drawers. He found a roll of insulating tape which would have to do for the short term. Pulling her arms behind her back he made her as secure as possible, wrapping the tape round her wrists several times. He picked her up and sat her on one of the kitchen chairs, using the rest of the tape to bind her legs together. Her head flopped onto the table and he decided that she would be safe to leave for a few minutes, while he had a look round. He started upstairs, but found nothing of interest to him. He came back down and entered the living room, finding what he supposed was the woman's handbag on the coffee table. He grabbed it, and was about to start wrecking the room when he heard noises from the kitchen. *Surely she couldn't be waking up*, he thought, *she should have stayed out of it for a good while yet.* He went into the kitchen and found her starting to raise her head off the table.

"No, no, no, we can't have this," he said and used the pad to put her under again. He would have to get her back to his place, and quickly, so he decided to forego wrecking Longman's house. Going back to his car he drove round, backing it into Longmans drive. He opened the rear door before going into the kitchen for the woman. She was still out, her head resting on the table. Josh picked her up and carried her to the door. Checking outside and seeing nobody about, he carried her to the car and laid her on the back seat, covering her with the same blanket he'd used on the Asian girl. After closing the kitchen door, he got behind the wheel and drove to his house.

Helen stirred as he drove, instantly realising that she was in deep shit. She expected the worst, she'd heard all about perverts who got their jollies by tying their victims up and raping them, but at the end of whatever was going to happen to her she also thought that there was the chance of being released. She shuffled a bit, just to see how secure she really was, which got the drivers attention.

"Hello, you whore. What were you doing in Longman's house then? Are you his little bit of stuff? There was I, thinking that all his energies were channelled into catching me. How wrong I was. He probably couldn't concentrate on me at all, not with you waiting for him, ready to shag his brains out I bet. 'Can't say I blame him, I bet you have a nice body under those clothes, such as they are. Still, I'll soon be finding that out for myself. Best thing about all this is that while I'm seeing to you there's not a damn thing that your copper boyfriend can do about it. He'll know that I've got you, of course, you're going to tell him that yourself. In a day or two."

Josh had paused between each sentence, allowing time to let the words sink in. The final sentence, he noticed, made her eyes open wide.

Helen knew now that she was in the worst possible situation, as there was no doubt that this man was the one Tom wanted to apprehend. She tried moving her arms and legs, soon realising that they were securely tied.

Josh noticed her efforts, and smiled.

"Try all you like, my dear, it won't work. I can guarantee that. Don't even think that I'm going to let you go, either. You've had your last kiss and cuddle with that copper. He got one of my girls away from me so I consider this as a favour returned. It's his fault really that you're here with me now, so think on that over the next few days. Before you die."

They soon reached the house and Josh stopped at the end of his driveway and pressed the remote for the garage doors. Driving in, he closed them before opening the back door and pressing the pad over the woman's face again. Once she was limp he lifted her out and carried her upstairs to the bedroom, laying her on the bed. He tied her to the four corners, leaving the gag in place. He thought about cutting her clothes off and having her then and there, but decided to wait until she was awake.

There was plenty of time, no need to rush.

Josh suddenly realised that he was extremely hungry and decided to have a pizza. He had stocked the freezer with pizzas, burgers and frozen oven chips as he hated cooking and refused to pay the extortionate prices that restaurants charged, even though he could easily afford them. About the only time he would go out for a meal was when he fancied a Thai curry. He chose one, double pepperoni, and turned the oven on to heat up. Once it was cooking it would only take a half hour, he knew. *Might as well have a cold beer while he waited*, he thought. He sat in his armchair in the lounge – beer on the coffee table, pizza in the oven – thinking about his guest upstairs.

She should prove to be an interesting bonus, he reckoned. He'd gone to Longman's house to wreck it, to leave the inspector a clear message that he, Joshua Smith, was not someone to piss off. This would be much better. Longman would soon know that she was missing, but Josh wanted him to stew for a day or two before he got her to talk to him. Before he found out who had his little tart. That got him to thinking about how the investigation was progressing. By now they would be searching the Oadby area for the house where his ex-colleague and supposed mate, Ricky, 'thought' he lived. That had been quick thinking on his part when he'd gone to work to be asked by the little sod where his second house was. He hadn't remembered telling him anything about having two houses, but it must have slipped out. He hadn't drunk with Ricky again after that, no way was he chancing letting anything else slip. Anyway, they'd gone to see the houses, his real one and one over in the Oadby area that was a good enough place as any. There was no way he was going to show anyone, least of all Ricky, the real location of this house. His intention had been to use it to set up home with Kate Laxton. An unwilling partnership on her part, no doubt, but he had ways to make her accept the situation, he now knew. The drugs he'd used on the Asian girl had proved to be most effective and were readily available from various sites on the internet. He eagerly anticipated, in his mind, how Kate would react when he fed them to her. He made a mental note to order some more very soon, he had enough for the moment but would be using some to get that inspectors whore upstairs in the mood for sex. He could simply keep her tied up and rape her but, remembering how that little Asian had turned into a nymphomaniac once the drug had altered her perception of the situation, he wanted to have this one in the same manner first. Later on he would keep her clear headed, the fear and disgust turned him on just as much, as he enjoyed her in any way he wished. All these carnal thoughts had got him quite excited, and he forced himself into the kitchen to eat. He looked into the oven and saw, through the glass door, his pizza bubbling so he got it out and slid it onto a plate. He had a cutter and soon had the pizza ready to eat, the slices as neat and precise as he could make them. He'd brought his beer with him into the kitchen and had soon finished both it and the food.

*Right*, he thought, *now it's time to see to my guest*. He poured a glass of water and crushed one of the tablets up, adding it and giving the water a good stir. He carried the glass up the stairs and went into the guest bedroom where she was laid on the bed, wide awake and panic stricken, judging by the look in her eyes.

He'd gone through her bag while eating and according to the cards in her purse she was Mrs Helen Middleton. That was a turn up, the inspector shacked up with a married woman! *Whatever next*, he thought.

He looked at her and saw her shrink into herself, as though she could blank him out. That wasn't going to happen and he moved to the bedside, sitting down on the edge of the bed.

"Hello, Helen, I'm Joshua Smith. I suppose that your boyfriend has told you all about me. I kill people. Actually, to be precise, I kill women. First I enjoy having sex with them. Sometimes they enjoy it, and as I have rather a large cock, I 'always' do. Most often, though, they hate it. I wonder why? Why not enjoy having anyone you want to, whenever you want to? Ah, it's probably the way I go about it, isn't it. Maybe I should be gentler and treat them nicely. Do you think so, Helen?"

She couldn't answer as the gag was still in place, but he reckoned he knew what she would say anyway, and he didn't want to hear it.

"You must think me a monster, keeping you tied up. I promise you will be made more comfortable in a moment, but I suppose you're thirsty and hungry after your trip here. Chloroform doesn't taste very nice, does it, Helen? I've brought you a glass of water and later I'll get you something to eat. Now, listen to me carefully." He leant down and picked up a hammer from the floor. "See this," he waved it in front of her eyes, "if you make a sound I will smash your kneecaps into fragments. You would never be able to walk properly again, if at all. All you need to do is keep quiet and have a drink, understand?"

Helen was thirsty as hell and frantically nodded her head, wanting that water.

"Good girl, Helen," Josh said and untied the tea towel before removing the flannel from her mouth.

"You bastard," she spat, but quietly. She didn't want to make him use that hammer.

"Understandable under the circumstances, but I warn you, Helen, one more little outburst like that and you will be punished. Severely." Josh held the glass to her mouth and started to tip it. "Now drink."

She did, greedily. The glass was soon empty and she closed her eyes, savouring the quenching of her thirst.

Josh sat and watched, waiting for the drug to work. After a few minutes he saw her breathing quicken and she started moaning a little, twisting her legs and pushing her backside up off the bed.

"Why, Helen, whatever is the matter?" Josh asked.

"What have you given me, you bastard?" she hissed, but couldn't stop her body from wanting someone, anyone, to satisfy her. When he moved into her view and thrust his lower body towards her all she could think of was his cock and how good it would feel inside her, thrusting in and out.

"Get that thing out of your trousers and inside me now," she pleaded, now totally taken over by the drug.

"Certainly never let it be said that I ever refused a lady's request," said Josh, astounded once more at the effect this drug had on women.

He went to the dresser and got the large scissors he'd placed there earlier. It was a simple task to cut along the length of her clothes and she was soon covered only by the two loose halves of her top and trousers. He replaced the scissors on the dresser and came back to her. He gently pulled the top off her, letting it rub against her nipples as he did so. They came into view and were standing erect, two strawberry coloured tips stiff with excitement. The trousers were next and as they slid off her abdomen he saw her flinch and heard her give a gasp when the waistband brushed her pubic mound. As they fell away he was surprised to see that there were no panties.

"Well, well, now that is a sight to see," he said, noticing that the hair above her pubis was shaped like a heart.

*Probably for 'him'*, thought Josh, *but he won't be seeing 'that' again.*

He was quickly out of his pants and climbed onto the bed, straddling her. He could see how wet she was and he slid in without any problem, just a little gasp from her as she realised just how big he had become. *God, she was something else*, he thought after a few thrusts. He could feel her gripping him and she was soon coming, thrashing her head around and trying to open her legs wider to get him further inside. He decided that it would be best to keep her secure for the moment, and climbed off her, waving his still erect member in her face. She looked at his erection and licked her lips.

He was stood in the bathroom, drying himself off after his shower, when he heard her start to cry.

He walked into the bedroom, still naked, and saw her turn her head away, tears streaming down her face.

He'd gagged her once they'd finished, he didn't want her making any unnecessary noise once the drugs wore off. He'd also been thinking of different ways to feed her the drug, as he feared she would sooner be thirsty and hungry than take anything that may cause her to lose control again. He didn't think that his threat of breaking her kneecaps would work either, not now. She'd probably be happier if he killed her sooner rather than later anyway.

"Hello, Helen. Feeling a bit let down, are you? I'll bet you've never had as big a cock in you before. Felt good, didn't it. You'll be getting it again before long, then again, and again. You really are a fantastic lover, has the inspector ever told you that, Helen? You'll be able to speak to him soon, let him know that I'm taking good care of you. But not today, today I have a special treat for you, and me, as it happens." Josh went to the dresser and got the plastic container. Taking out the cloth, he put Helen under again. Once he was sure that she was unconscious he cut the ties, turned her over and secured her to the four corners of the bed once more.

Longman and Charles were parked at the end of Avocet Close. It was the nearest name they'd found to 'Avocado Grove' in the Oadby area. One of the houses there had been rented to a bachelor businessman, according to the rental agency. It was also the only detached house that had been rented in the area in the last six months. The name the agency had on their copy of the rental agreement wasn't Smith, but they had never expected it to be so that wasn't an issue. The problem they were faced with was that the car in the drive was a saloon, not the estate they were expecting to see.

"Maybe he keeps the estate in the garage, sir," said Charles.

"That's a possibility, Sergeant. I suppose we had better find out." Longman waved to the rest of the team, waiting by their minibus, as he got out of the car and they approached the house warily. There was no indication that there was anyone at home apart from the car in the drive, so they rang the doorbell and waited. After a minute there had been no response from inside so Charles gave the front door a really good thump with his fist.

"Always found that to be more effective than some of these weedy sounding chimes, sir," he explained to a bemused Longman, before standing to one side, allowing the ART to face the door.

Sure enough, they soon heard the door being unlocked and as it opened they prepared themselves in case Smith was armed.

"Just what the bloody hell do you think you're playing at?" demanded a deep voice.

Longman looked, and saw a very angry man standing in the doorway, staring down at the members of the armed response team. They, in turn, were staring at one of the biggest black men they had ever seen.

Longman stepped forward and the man turned towards him as he answered.

"Sorry about this, sir, but we were acting on what we thought was reliable information. We are looking for a serious offender and were led to believe that he had rented this house. It is quite obvious that you are not the man we had hoped to see open that door, sir. Please accept my apologies for any inconvenience caused."

"And you are?" asked the man.

"Detective Inspector Longman, sir, Leicester CID."

"Well, inspector, I hope you have success in catching your quarry. Now I would ask that you leave and please do it quietly. The reason I rented this place was to get some much needed peace, and up to now that was what I was enjoying."

"Once again, sir, I can only apologise," said Longman as they turned to leave.

Back in their car, they thought about what had just happened.

"That Ricky led us up the garden path, sir," said Charles.

"Or was led up the same path first, Sergeant. This may well have been engineered by Smith to divert us from our trawl of the rental agencies for a while. We'd better get back and carry on looking. He has to be somewhere and it's only a matter of time before we find out where. Best get on the phone and get your tame PC's to keep on searching. We had better call in on Mr Brandon on the way back, see what he's got for us. The autopsy on that young Asian girl might have provided some more evidence, although I think we have enough to put Smith away several times over already."

"OK sir, I hope that the ME has finished. I never have got used to seeing bodies get opened up. It doesn't seem right, if you know what I mean," Charles said.

"I do, Sergeant, and I can't say it's my favourite pastime either. However, sometimes, just sometimes, something gets found during these invasive examinations which helps us to catch the killer."

They were soon at the hospital and made their way to the morgue, finding the ME sat in his office writing.

"Hello, you two," he said as they walked in and grabbed a seat each. "I have some information for you that you won't particularly want to hear." Noticing that he had got their full attention, Henry Brandon continued. "I've completed my examination of the young Asian lass. As I suspected at the scene, she had been involved in having sex – quite brutal sex too. Her anus was torn which accounted for the blood in the pubic area, and her vagina showed signs of bruising, probably by having a foreign object forcibly and repeatedly inserted. The cause of her death was from gunshot wounds, she'd been shot twice in the back of the head. The weapon was 0.22 calibre, using the same type of round as was used on the previous victims. The toxicology report has provided some interesting information, however. She had traces of chloroform, which was expected, but there were also traces of a new drug. This drug has not been cleared by any clinical trials but has shown up recently during investigation into date rape cases, both here and in America. I have occasion to speak with other medical examiners now and again, and in the last six months this drug has been used in fifteen cases of suspected rape. Three of those cases involved male rape, by the way. This drug is far stronger than the normal ones, like Rohypnol to quote one example, and can be obtained from at least one internet site. It is expensive, but when it has the effect of not only removing all inhibitions but of heightening the recipient's sexual appetite, you can understand why it has become so popular."

"Let me get this straight, Henry. Are you saying that the victims actually want to have sex once this drug has been administered?" asked Longman.

"Exactly, Tom. Not only do they want sex, but from the interviews that I've read they demand it, in any way, with whoever is there. Man or woman."

"My God, this drug is the answer to a rapist's prayer. How come it hasn't been taken off the market?" asked Charles. "Surely it cannot be legally sold if it hasn't undergone tests."

"You are right, of course, sergeant. The sad fact is that if there is a market for sexual enhancement drugs then there will always be a supplier. If you're not aware that you've been given this drug, the first you will know about it will be when the drug wears off. By that time, of course, it will be too late."

"How long does the effect last?" enquired Longman.

"That really depends on the individual, Tom. Around four hours seems to have been the average. One male victim actually started to lose the effect halfway through being raped by a gang of four lorry drivers in America. They didn't stop, dumping him at the side of the road when they'd finished. There is also a case of a woman hiring a private detective to find whoever it was that used this drug on her, before leaving her in a hotel room to recover. Evidently, unlike other date rape drugs, this one lets you remember everything that has happened. This woman had never experienced sex like it before and wanted her attacker found so she could get a repeat performance."

"Well, Henry, thanks for the information. We know that Smith could be the girl's murderer, actually make that probably. Unfortunately, we're still no nearer to catching him. Now that he knows that this drug works I get the feeling that he will keep on using it, which means more women are at risk. Come on, sergeant, there's work to be done. Goodbye for now, Henry," said Longman, shaking the ME's hand as they stood up to leave.

Longman and Charles drove back to headquarters in relative silence. After briefly wondering to each other about the ethics of chemists who produced these drugs, they lapsed into their own thoughts about where to go from here. Smith was out there somewhere, taunting them. There must be a clue to his whereabouts somewhere in the information they had gathered so far. No one could just disappear.

They arrived back at headquarters to find it besieged by press vehicles, reporters standing in front of cameras recording messages for their news channels.

"I think we had better drive by, Sergeant, and find out what's going on before trying to get past that lot. I have a pretty good idea, though."

They drove past their place of work and Longman got on his phone and called the front desk.

"What's all the press for?" he asked the desk sergeant after identifying himself. He was told that it was all to do with the Asian girl.

"Thought as much," he told Charles, "the Asian girl's murder has stirred up a media hornet's nest. Let's go in the back way, I'll get on to the custody sergeant and ask for the gate to be opened."

They reached the high gate that led to the yard and stopped. It started to open immediately and they went through, the gates closing after them. Parking up, they went through the custody suite door and were making their way to their office when Longman's phone signalled an incoming call.

Grabbing it from his pocket, he looked at the caller ID. It was Kate.

"Longman here, ma'am."

"Inspector, can you come to my office immediately on your ·return, please?"

"Certainly, ma'am, we've just got back so I'm on my way now," he responded. Turning to Charles, he told him to keep searching through the letting agents. "We have to find his address, no matter how many houses we look at, or how many innocent renters are disturbed. He will be in one of them, he has to be."

At the end of the corridor Longman went left, heading for Kate's office, while Charles went straight on.

Emma was sat at her desk as Longman entered the ACC's reception area.

"Inspector Longman is here, ma'am, shall I send him right in?" she said into the desk intercom.

"Yes, please, Emma. Can you…"

"Coffee's, ma'am. Of course, once your other visitor has left…?" Emma interjected, then, giving Longman one of her smiles, she continued, "Go right in, inspector."

"Thank you, Emma," he said.

Longman entered Kate's office and noticed straight away that there was tension in the air.

"Inspector Longman, I would like to introduce Mr Kumar, the deputy mayor."

Longman shook hands with the man and sat in the other chair opposite Kate, who was perched on the edge of her chair, behind her desk.

"Mr Kumar is here to find out how we are progressing in the hunt for whoever killed Aisha Pahman, Inspector."

"This situation is intolerable, Inspector," said Kumar. "Why have you not arrested anyone yet?"

"I assure you, Mr Kumar, we are doing our utmost to find whoever killed Miss Pahman. My team are, at this moment, pursuing lines of inquiry that we are confident will eventually lead us to her murderer." Out of the corner of his eye he noticed Kate give him a surreptitious nod, so he continued, "we have reason to believe that the man who murdered Aisha is also responsible for several other deaths. The Assistant Chief Constable and I will be giving another television appeal later today where we will emphasise the danger posed by this man."

"You think that he will try again, Inspector? Just how many people has this man killed?" asked Kumar.

"Aisha was his fourth victim, sir. We were able to interrupt him before he could harm his previous victim, but, unfortunately, he wasn't apprehended."

"I was going to ask, and from what you have just said, I will ask you now. What did he do to poor Aisha before he killed her, inspector?"

"This is not for public discussion, Mr Kumar, I hope you will honour that. Miss Pahman was repeatedly raped before being shot in the head. This man, as I said, is extremely violent. We know who he is, but not where. I will promise you that we will find him and the full weight of the law will ensure that when we do he will spend the rest of his life behind bars," said Longman.

"And I promise you, Inspector, that if he is found by any of Aisha's relatives before you catch him, I fear he will not be available to the courts. I wish you success in your endeavours, and I would like to ask that I may be allowed to join you in your television appeal. I can ask the members of the Asian community to stay calm and to be aware of the threat posed by this monster. It may help, I don't really know, but it cannot hurt."

"That will be fine, Mr Kumar," said Kate, "the press conference will take place at four this afternoon. We'll see you then."

"Thank you," said Kumar, and got up to leave. Shaking hands with Longman, he looked him straight in the eyes. "I hope you find your killer soon, Inspector, before any more innocent lives are lost."

As soon as the door had closed, Kate motioned for Longman to take a seat.

"What do you think Smith is playing at, Tom. That note he left at the scene must be kept from the press. God, if they got wind of that poor girl being killed because we pissed him off…"

"I know, ma'am, it doesn't bear thinking about. We 'are' shortening the odds in our favour, however. All the detached houses that have been rented recently are being checked. Smith won't have travelled far from where he feels comfortable, which means that, sooner or later, he'll have to leave his hideaway. Every officer knows what he looks like, we've even had some photos retouched to show him with various hairstyles."

There was a tap at the door and Kate opened it for Emma, who came in with two mugs of coffee on a tray, which also had some biscuits on a plate.

"Hob Nobs, one of my favourites," said Longman, giving Emma a thank you smile.

Emma coloured slightly as she left, bringing a chuckle from Kate.

"You're honoured, Tom, she doesn't get her Hob Nobs out for just anyone."

# Chapter 17

Helen wished she was dead.

She had been tied to the bed for two days now, the only time she was not secured by her wrists and ankles was when 'he' allowed her to go to the toilet, and that was something she would rather forget. He kept the door open and stood there, looking at her, while she did what was required. She had been kept naked and he smiled as he watched her. He'd made sure of her silence, there was a gag tied round her head which prevented her from spitting out whatever he'd stuffed into her mouth. She could smell herself, and it wasn't nice. She would love to take a bath and wash his sweat, and worse, off her body. She nodded at the bath and he smiled.

"Why not, Helen. You smell worse than a pig so I can't see it doing any harm. I won't untie you though, you'll have to kneel in the bath while I wash you down. I have the hammer here, so don't even think of trying anything."

She finished her business on the toilet and hobbled over to the bath. He lifted her over the edge and she knelt on all fours, waiting for him to start the shower. The water started flowing and she gasped when it hit her, he had kept it on fully cold.

"Sorry about that, my dear, would you like some warm?"

He adjusted the temperature controller and the stream of water went from cold to nearly scalding.

She could feel every droplet as it hit, and pictured her back getting scalded, blisters forming. He turned the control again and the water became just warm. *Thank God*, she thought.

"Not for you, sweetheart, but if I'm to get you clean, 'I' don't want to get scalded," he told her, starting to scrub her with the loo brush.

He kept it up for another five minutes before getting tired of it, finally rinsing her off and lifting her out of the bath. She was sore, but now that her ordeal was over she felt better. He didn't offer her a towel, just led her back to the bedroom and tied her back to the four corners of the bed. She was relieved to be tied face up, even though she knew she was likely not to remain that way for very long.

He provided her with water, forcing her to drink. She knew it was drugged and tried desperately not to swallow but the threat of the hammer overcame her self-loathing at knowing what the drug would cause her to become. There was always the chance that, this time, it was just water. A couple of times it had been and, at those times, she was hopeful that he'd finally finished with her and would kill her. That was not in his plan, though, and the next time she drank the sensations had started again after a few minutes. She knew that she would soon be craving sex like she had never had it before. Her faculties were all functioning and her body responded to his touch as though 'he' was her chosen lover, not the brutal rapist that he really was. The worst part of it all wasn't knowing that as the drug wore off, normally after he'd finished, she would remember everything. It wasn't that she remembered pleading with him to take her, taking him in her mouth, asking him to take her in other ways too. She knew she was bleeding, she'd seen the blood when she'd been to the toilet.

No, the worst part of it all was that she knew she would be begging him to do it all again.

Josh was humming to himself as he climbed the stairs after having had a spot of lunch. He'd made his guest a jam sandwich, not really expecting her to want it but he knew how to make her eat. As he entered the bedroom he saw her stiffen, wondering, no doubt, if he would be drugging her again. He had wondered himself, and decided that he *would* have another bout of sex with her before she died. He'd crushed a tablet into the jam, and also dissolved one in the water. She would take one or the other, and if she took both, well, he would be interested to see the result of a double dose.

"Here you are, my love, a nice sandwich. You must be starving after all this physical exertion you've been doing. I know it's given me an appetite. Now, remember, no noise or I'll use this." He showed her the hammer.

Helen didn't care anymore, and as the gag came off and he removed the flannel from her mouth she tried to scream. All that came out was a dry croak, her throat was parched and it was all she could manage. Josh swung the hammer and it cracked onto her knee, not doing any real damage but causing enough pain to make Helen pass out.

While she was unconscious Josh removed the gag and poured the water into her mouth, working her jaw to make her swallow, before putting it back in place.

Helen came to after a couple of minutes, her knee throbbing with pain. She knew straight away that he had drugged her again as she felt herself reacting to the sight of him stood beside her, naked and ready.

"Hello, Helen, is there something that you need?" he asked, stroking himself.

"Yes," she hissed, "I want your cock, now. All of it. Inside me. I want you to make me come again and again, and then I want to swallow you."

"Hear that, Inspector? I bet you didn't know that your little lady could be so demanding. But then, you're probably not as well hung as I am. Helen just loves me fucking her brains out, don't you, sweetheart? Say hello to your pathetic policeman boyfriend, Helen," he said, and climbed on the bed, ready to give her what she was demanding. He'd rung Longman as she was coming to, knowing that she would want sex as soon as she saw him.

"Hello, whoever you are," she said, "why don't you come and join us, I would love to have two cocks at the same time. Ooooh!" Josh had just given a big thrust as he took the phone away.

"No contest really, Inspector. But, good as she is, she still isn't the one I really want. Tell that bitch of a boss of yours her turn is coming. I'm ready for her."

Josh rang off.

Longman stared at the phone in his hand, before placing it on his desk. He picked up his mug and threw it against the wall.

"You bastard," he shouted, "you absolute fucking bastard."

Charles, who had been busy looking at the latest list of rental addresses, looked up in surprise.

"Smith has got another victim, and he's just made her talk to me," Longman said, trying hard to keep himself from shouting it out.

"Surely that's good, sir. It means that she's still alive, at least," said Charles.

"Yes, Sergeant, though I have a feeling that she won't want to be when the drug he's fed her wears off. She was being raped and, because of the drug, she was enjoying it. I know this woman, Sergeant," said Longman, and proceeded to tell Charles about Helen.

"My God," was all Charles could say when Longman had finished. He reached for the phone his boss had put on the table and pressed 1471, hoping that he'd be rewarded but anticipating disappointment. A number appeared on the screen and he quickly reached for a pen and wrote it down.

"Looks like he's made another mistake, sir," he said. "We should be able to trace the name this number is registered to and from that we can only hope that he's been using the same alias to rent wherever he has got himself accommodated at the moment."

"Good thinking, sergeant. We need to hurry with this, God knows how long he will keep poor Helen alive."

Charles knew that there was an office, hidden in the depths of area headquarters, part of whose remit was the identification of persons to phone numbers. He was soon talking to their team leader, Sergeant Mark Chapman, who promised to call as soon as they had a name.

"I can't just sit here, Sergeant, knowing that bastard has Helen. There must be something we can do."

"We have the list, sir. It isn't complete yet and other officers are knocking on doors but there's still quite a few that need…"

"Then what are we doing sat here. There must be some on that list where the renter is a man on his own. Let's go, Sergeant, I would feel better doing something instead of just sitting here, waiting for that call back. I'm not too hopeful it will help. I think Smith allowed us to get that number, hoping that it would cause us to waste a little more time. We'll probably find that it's a pay as you go special from one of the supermarkets, nearly untraceable."

Longman headed for the door, Charles following with the list in his hand. Once they were in the car, Longman had a look at it and told Charles to head for an address in Anstey, not too far from Smith's own house in fact.

"He may have rented this place thinking that we wouldn't expect him to get somewhere so close to his old house, Sergeant. We can but hope," said Longman, as Charles started the car. The security gates of the rear compound opened and he drove out, nearly knocking over a reporter who was stood on the road just outside them. They were gone before the reporter could gather himself enough to raise his camera.

"Bloody reporters, our job would sometimes be a lot easier without their interference," mumbled Charles.

"Agreed for the most part, Sergeant, but they can be useful on occasion," said Longman.

They were soon at the address and as they pulled up an estate car was pulling out of the drive.

Charles parked so as to prevent the other car from leaving, and they got out and approached it warily, one at each side. Before they got up to it the driver opened his door and got out, angrily demanding why they had blocked him in.

He fitted the description up to a point, so Longman and Charles were immediately on their guard, watching the man carefully.

"Good morning, sir, we would like to have a few words, if you don't mind. I'm Detective Inspector Longman and this is Detective Sergeant Charles."

"I don't care who you are, lovey," the man said, then his face changed and he started to smile, "my goodness, this is all a wind up isn't it? I'll kill that bloody woman when I see her. God, you had me going for a moment there. I knew something was being planned but this is quite good. Where are you going to take me then? No, don't tell me, keep it a surprise. Are you going to put the cuffs on too? Make it look real?'

He stepped towards them with his hands in front of him in the surrender position.

Longman got his warrant card out and showed it to the man.

"I don't know who you think we are, sir, but we are not wind up artists," said Longman, realising this was not their man. His voice was thin and reedy and he was quite obviously effeminate, judging by the extremely tight jeans and the hint of make up on his face. "We're sorry to have bothered you, but can I ask why you thought you were being wound up?"

"It's my fortieth birthday, Inspector," he said, "I know, it doesn't seem possible, does it? My bitch of a secretary has been planning something, I just don't know what. Pity, it would have been nice to have been cuffed in the back of your car. Never mind, maybe another time." He flounced off back to his car and they went back to theirs and moved it out of his way. He gave them a cheery wave as he drove past.

"Bloody poofter," Charles commented. He'd never accepted that men could be attracted to their own sex, and didn't mind who knew it.

"That's as may be, Sergeant, but whether you agree with them or not they're here, and legal," Longman said. He himself found it difficult to understand the gay philosophy, as did most straight men, but had come to accept that it was no longer considered quite as taboo as it had been only ten years ago.

They drove to the next address and found the driveway empty, but there was a garage built on to the side of the house, so any vehicle could be inside. Charles rang the bell, getting no response. Longman tried the gate at the side of the garage and it opened, giving access to the garden. He walked round the back of the garage and found himself looking into a large conservatory. There he found the reason why no one had responded to the doorbell. There were at least a dozen people, all naked, on sofas, chairs, rugs and even an exercise bike. There was a fug of smoke in the air and he guessed that they were probably all high. No one took the least bit of notice of him until he rapped on the glass, then a tall blonde who was enjoying the ministrations of a black girl looked up and saw him. She just smiled and beckoned to him with her finger. Longman smiled back, but shook his head before retreating back through the gate just as Charles was coming to see whether his boss had found anything.

"Nothing to cause concern here, Sergeant. The door wasn't opened because they're having a bit of a party. Not the place we're looking for, that's for sure."

"Mark Chapman has been on the blower, sir. As we expected, the phone is a pay as you go, the call we got was the first it had made and there have been no more since."

"Damn, this was one time I would gladly have been wrong. Do we know which mast the call was routed through?"

"Any one of three, sir, all in the Groby area. Looks like the first area we were going to look at could end up being where he's rented."

"It's still a big area to check, Sergeant. Are any of the houses on your list in it?"

They had got back to the car and Charles leant in and retrieved the list from the door pocket.

"There are several on the list so far, sir. All of them look promising, but that's probably just wishful thinking on my part."

"It's a start, and as we're out and about, we may as well give them the once over," said Longman.

# Chapter 18

Josh was excited.

He'd had to go out to get some fresh milk and bread and was now back in the house, having a bit of tea. The local paper was on the kitchen table and he was reading about the young Asian girl he'd raped and killed. Aisha Pahman was her name, not that he cared. A beauty pageant runner up, no less. He wondered how many of the audience had looked at her with lust in their eyes while she had been parading in front of them. It was him, Josh, who had had her though, and the memory was still fresh enough to make him feel sorry that he'd killed her. Not that she would have been released, oh no, but if he'd kept her alive he could have had some more fun. The Asian community were demanding that the killer be caught, the police were saying that they were close to making an arrest, and the paper was of the opinion that the police had no idea of who they were looking for.

Oh, they have, he told himself, but they won't catch him.

He turned the page and another headline demanded his attention. There was going to be a dinner at the town hall as part of the celebrations for the inauguration of the new Mayor of Leicester. It was due to be held in two days' time and there was a list of the expected dignitaries that were due to attend. As Kate Laxton was the youngest ACC in the police force, and very pretty to boot, she was named, as well as some of the local bigwigs in the community.

That gave Josh an idea, but he would have to work fast. That bitch upstairs would keep, he'd intended to kill her and leave her body outside Longman's house during the night but he really couldn't afford any risks now. His mind started working, and he eventually came up with his plan to get Kate *bloody* Laxton. It was risky, but if it worked, he would finally be able to have Kate where he wanted her.

In his house, in his life, in his bed.

# Chapter 19

Longman and Charles were starting to get a little disillusioned by the time they reached the fourth house on the list. At two of the houses the door had been opened by pensioners. One of them was an author who had rented a house to get some peace and quiet which he reckoned would help him overcome the writer's block he'd been getting at home. The other one had just been widowed and couldn't face living in the family house any more. He was renting 'while the old place is up for sale'.

The third front door had been opened by a woman, and when they enquired as to the whereabouts of the man whose name they had as the renter she told them it was her.

"I feel safer," she explained, "using a man's name instead of my own. A single woman living alone just presents a target for some people." As she was talking she was dragging on a cigarette, all twenty stone of her.

As they were walking back to their car, Charles couldn't help remarking that any man would be brave indeed to try anything on with her. The fourth house looked deserted, no car in the drive and no lights showing from any of the windows. Charles rang the bell and they waited a half minute before ringing it once more. There was no sound at all so they accepted that it was probably unoccupied and went back to their car.

"Three out of four is good, sir. We can come back to the other one later. The team will find some more, no doubt, if they haven't done so already."

There weren't any more on their list, so they drove back to headquarters. Halfway back, it suddenly struck Longman that if a woman could use a man's name to rent somewhere, then the opposite may hold true also.

"That will change things a bit, sir, I must admit that when I briefed the search team I told them to look for houses rented to men. It never crossed my mind that he may have used a woman's name," Charles said when Longman told him. "I wonder how many houses that will add to our list?"

They walked into their office to find it deserted. Charles looked at his watch and realised that it was past six o'clock in the evening. He went over to the researcher's desk and picked up the list lying there. There were six sheets of A4 with lists of addresses. Some had been checked off, but there were still quite a few left to be investigated. All of them had male names as the renter.

"Guess they'll be busy again in the morning, sir," said Charles.

"Yes, Sergeant, I suppose they will," commented Longman distractedly. He was going down the list to see if there were any more addresses in the area where they'd been looking. There were another five.

"Got anything planned for tonight, Sergeant?"

"No, sir, nothing that won't keep," Charles said, picking up the list and following Longman back out of the office and down the corridor. They decided to get a quick bite to eat at a drive in McDonald's on the way to the first house, and were eating their not too healthy option when Longman's phone rang. He got it out of his jacket pocket and flipped it open, just as it stopped. He scrolled to the missed call page and found that the call had been from Smith, he recognised the number as the same one Smith had used on *that* call. He thought for a second before calling the number. He reasoned that if Helen was still alive there may still be a chance to keep her that way, and he had to know. If she was already dead there was no reason not to talk to her killer. The only thought that caused him to hesitate was that she may once again be under the influence of a drug and he didn't know if he could take listening to her talking like that again. Making his mind up, he pressed the call button. It was answered immediately, and he recognised Smith's voice straight away.

"Hello, Inspector. So nice of you to return my call. I suppose you'd like me to tell you that your girlfriend is still alive. Well,' Smith paused for a full ten seconds before continuing, causing Longman to wonder if the connection had been lost. "She *is* alive, but she isn't feeling too chipper. I think I may have given her too much of what she's been craving in the last day or two. I'm sure you know what I mean, but then again, maybe not. You don't have the same means of persuasion that I do, do you? Anyway, the reason for my call was to tell you that you have very little time left if you want to stop me from killing your tart. She has very nearly outworn her novelty value for me, and I don't keep things once I have no further use for them. Are you any nearer finding me, inspector? Do you hope to rescue dear Helen? I don't think you will. Tell you what, I'll give you three more days, starting now. If you haven't caught me by then, your beautiful Helen will cease to exist. By the way, she's listening to this call. So, live or die, it's up to you now, inspector, bye."

Longman started to speak, hoping to start a conversation with Smith. He reasoned that something might get said that would help him with finding the man, but Smith didn't wait and Longman was left hanging, feeling totally frustrated.

"Smith again?" asked Charles, seeing the look on Longman's face.

"Yes, Sergeant. Things have just taken a turn, and not in our favour." Longman filled Charles in on this latest development before getting up from the table, his meal forgotten. Charles picked up the rest of his burger and followed, finishing it off by the time they had reached their car.

"There's not a lot we can do tonight, sir," he said as they buckled up, "shall I drop you off at home? I can pick you up in the morning, the team will be back in at eight and we can continue the search."

"Does Chapman's team work a shift, Sergeant? It may help us to know if Smith has moved since he called last."

"If it doesn't, I'm certain that Mark would come in and check for us. Everyone knows that this case has started to take priority, too many innocent girls have died for it not to have done."

Charles had somehow known that his boss would not want to call it a night, so he got on his phone and was soon talking to Mark Chapman, who said he would meet them at his office in half an hour.

"Probably wolfing his dinner down and explaining to his wife that sometimes the job required him to respond to urgent requests, sir," said Charles, starting their car and moving out onto the road.

"Yes, Sergeant, let's hope that he can help us. The clock is ticking."

"Well, sir," Chapman said after an hour spent on his computer, "I can tell you that the latest call was made from the same location as the previous one. It also looks like we may be able to narrow the search area down a little bit, but that's only because there was a mast down for servicing when he first rang and now it's back on line. The first area we had was this one," he got an image up on his screen that showed the three masts that had 'seen' the first phone call Smith had made earlier. He scrolled through and got another image on the screen. Now there were four masts that had seen this latest call, and that made determining the location of the caller slightly easier. The intersection of the reception coverage circles had reduced the common area down by about a third.

"It's still quite a large area, and it's nearly all urban sprawl. A few thousand houses, I'd guess, sir," Chapman said.

"We don't need to check them all, Sergeant, only the rented ones," Longman told him. "I really appreciate you coming in to do this, it may well mean the difference between life and death."

"Wow, that's a first for me. Good luck, sir. If you need any more help, just call."

With that, Chapman requested a print out of the screen shot before turning his computer off. Charles thanked him also and they left Chapman to lock up. Once they were back in their office they got themselves a coffee before sitting at the conference table with the printout before them. Charles had the list of rental addresses in front of him, using a highlighter to mark off the addresses that had already been checked.

"None of those five we were going to check fall within this new area, sir. There may well 'be' some more but that we won't know until the team carry on with their phone calls tomorrow."

"I know, Sergeant, but I can't even contemplate sleeping while that monster has Helen. God knows what further hell she's being put through as we sit here."

Charles knew what his boss meant, but neither of them would put into words just what they thought Smith could be doing to Helen.

"Being too tired to think straight won't help, sir. We both need to get some rest, even if it's just a couple of hours. I'll get on to the desk, see if there's any accommodation available."

They both knew that it was against the rules to sleep in the cells, but now and again the desk sergeant would bend them a bit if an investigation had reached a critical point. Longman knew that he wouldn't sleep at home, thoughts of Helen would prevent that, so he nodded and listened as Charles cajoled them a 'room' each for the night.

Longman couldn't settle. He kept thinking of Helen, hoping that what he had heard were not to be the last words he would remember her speaking to him. If he ever got his hands on Smith the man would regret the day he was born. Truth be told, if anyone other than Charles got to know about his relationship with Helen, he would probably get taken off the case. He knew Charles wouldn't say anything, he probably wanted to get his hands on Smith just as much as Longman anyway.

Eventually he must have drifted off because he was rudely awakened by the slamming of a cell door in the early hours. He got up, stretching the ricks out of his shoulders, and went in search of the washroom. After a quick wash he headed for the office, where he found Charles already sifting through sheets of A4 printouts.

"Morning, sir, sleep well?"

"Yes, surprisingly. Can't understand why our guests moan about the conditions? Those narrow shelves with thin mattresses are perfect, we should be in the town accommodation guide."

Charles had discovered early on in their working relationship that his boss had a funny sense of humour, so, accepted the answer with good grace, acknowledging that his question should not have been asked.

"So, Sergeant, what do we have? Judging by the lists you're going through there are some new addresses to check. I doubt very much that Smith has had an attack of conscience and given himself up so let's get onto it, shall we?"

"Actually, sir, I was going through all the lists that we already have, looking for any addresses that could possibly be in our search area but were discounted because of the mast coverage area. There's always the possibility that, on a good day, those masts can 'see' a little further. The team who'll be building the list up with our revised parameters won't be in for another hour, sir, but as soon as they arrive I'll get them back onto it."

"Right," Longman automatically looked at his watch. "Of course. So, have you found any more?"

"Yes, there are another two that are just off the edge of the area that Chapman provided, but they do fit our criteria regarding the type of house. One has been rented for the last two years, the other was rented only three months ago. Both to supposedly single men. A Mr Harold Westlake and a Mr Sean Golightly."

"Strange name, Golightly. In the absence of anything else let's go and see him first. Is there a telephone number?"

"Yes, sir, I tried ringing it but it wasn't picked up. I left our number on the answer machine, asking Mr Golightly to contact us."

"Fair enough. The other one?"

"Mr Westlake was definitely in. He gave me a right earful for waking him up. He works shifts, he says, and had only been asleep for an hour. I asked him if he would be in later on this morning and he told me, in no uncertain terms, what I could do with myself. I think it would be in order to call on him first, sir, rather than Golightly," said a smiling Charles.

"Most definitely; can't have members of the public insulting a police officer, can we?"

Josh decided to stay inside all day. There was no reason to go outside as everything he would need to carry out his plan was available on the internet. As soon as he'd received order confirmations, and delivery times, he turned it off and went over the details of his idea again and again. He couldn't find any flaws, but still felt apprehensive. Such a lot depended on it going right.

*Everything* depended on it going right.

He started to fantasise about what life would be like once he had Kate, *his* Kate, under *his* sole control. He would tell her what he wanted her to do, and when, knowing that the drugs would prevent any disobedience. Indeed, she would be pleased to do whatever he wished. The times when she wasn't under the influence of the drugs he would watch her, tied to the bed or chair. She would loathe him at those times, he knew, but he would still be her master.

Thinking about Kate, he decided to pay his guest a visit. Should he take her some food and water before or after having sex? He decided on after when he went into the bedroom. Helen was laid on her stomach, asleep, a cushion underneath her causing her bottom to be raised up, and available.

Josh was quickly out of his clothes and as he climbed onto the bed, Helen woke up. She had hardly opened her eyes before she felt him, then as he entered her she wanted to cry out in pain. She couldn't though, he had kept her gagged and all she could do was scream inside her head. It wasn't long before he'd finished and he climbed off her. She was convulsed with sobs by this time, the tears streaming down her cheeks onto the pillow. His face loomed in front of her and he told her to be still while he cut the ties and turned her over, securing her again quickly. She didn't have the strength to fight him, and knew that if she even tried he would hurt her again with the hammer. Her knee was giving her so much pain she actually looked forward to the drugs. She accepted that they would cause her to want this creature in every sexual position she, or he, could think of, but while she was under their influence the pain seemed to stay in the background.

Once she was face up, Josh removed the gag and fed her the sandwich, washing it down with a glass of doctored water. He waited and, sure enough, within a few minutes she was breathing faster and looking at him with lust in her eyes. He didn't really feel like it again so soon, and told her that this time she would have to want. He stood up, seeing her eyes drop to look at what she was craving.

"You'll just have to use your imagination, my sweet. I'll be back later."

As she lifted herself up, offering herself to him, he laughed and left the room.

# Chapter 20

"I really don't know why I have to attend this bloody dinner. Just because I'm the youngest Assistant Chief Constable in the force." Kate had never really enjoyed these dinners. Her husband had heard all this before and knew that she would go whether she wanted to or not. If the Chief asked her to attend she couldn't refuse, it was all part of the job. Be available to chat, without discussing policy too much. There would be the usual bores who would try to tell her how to do her job, there always were. This time, though, Richard couldn't accompany her as he'd been called to Paris to discuss the plans for a new detention centre. As it was to be a shared cost venture between Britain and France he'd been invited to attend because he was the architect. The French wanted to modify the design to save on building costs but Britain wanted it to be built as per the original design.

He would much rather have gone to this dinner with his wife.

"You'll be fine, darling, and if you go dressed like that you'll knock 'em dead." He ducked as Kate threw her flannel at him. She was stood at her sink in their en-suite, in her bra and panties and, whenever he looked at her, he was always amazed that she had agreed to be his wife. She was beautiful, but had never become conceited with her looks. She didn't use the gym and had not a lot of use for makeup. God, he loved her.

He knew that there was a murder investigation in progress, and that his wife was closely monitoring its progress, but what he didn't know was the exact nature of her involvement. If he had he would never have agreed to her attending this function without him by her side.

Kate finished her toilet and came into the bedroom. Richard was sat on their bed and patted the quilt, giving her a lascivious look as he did.

"Forget that, husband of mine. I have to get ready for this dinner, so you'll have to wait until after you return from your little holiday in 'Gay Paree'. Speaking of which, shouldn't you be going? You'll miss your flight if you don't get a move on."

"Yeah, you're right. Peter is coming by to pick me up. He should be here any minute. The firm decided that he needs the experience so I'll have to listen to him going on about their new baby boy, no doubt."

Kate knew that Richard was getting desperate to start a family, he was two years older than her and didn't want to leave it for much longer. They had agreed that she would give this new post two years and then she would take leave and try with him for a baby of their own. His colleague and friend, Peter, had just become a father for the first time and boy, didn't everyone know about it.

As if on cue, there was a hoot from outside and Richard looked out of the bedroom window to see Peter's car parked at the end of their drive.

"Best be off, darling, see you in a couple of days." He gave her a big kiss and a pat on her behind. "Enjoy your dinner and keep off the red, you know it makes you randy. Ow!" He rubbed his arm where Kate had playfully thumped him.

"And you keep away from the Mademoiselles, just looking at them makes *you* randy."

He went downstairs and Kate went to the window. She watched him get into Peter's car and he looked up at her and waved as the car pulled away.

Kate turned away from the window and sat on the bed. She always felt so alone whenever he left on a trip like this. It would pass, she knew, and told herself not to be so maudlin'.

Too early to get dressed yet, so she shrugged herself into a dressing gown and sat on the bed. Fluffing the pillows up, she turned the television on and leant back against them. Flicking through the channels, she found a programme about the frozen wastes of Antarctica. *Perfect*, she thought, and settled down to watch. A little after six she decided that she had better get herself ready and headed for the spare bedroom nearest to the bathroom, which they had turned into a dressing room.

Her dress uniform was laid out on the bed. The silver rank badges shone and her shoes gleamed.

As she looked at it she was once again reminded of just how far she had come since she started training all those years ago. Her mood quickly changed as the memories of those days had triggered another, and this one was not as pleasant. Smith was still out there somewhere, and he had told her, through his messages, that he was close to finishing his agenda. Kate was at the top of that particular list and wondered how long it would be before Smith made his move on her. She knew that she was being watched whenever she was away from the office, even though she hadn't been told of any protection.

Tonight, though, she had been allocated an official car. She was due to be picked up in just under an hour, at seven. Plenty of time to give Inspector Longman a call, see how the manhunt was progressing.

Before she could call him though, her phone rang.

"Hello, Kate Laxton here," she said.

"Hello, Kate Laxton, Joshua Smith 'here'. I'm just letting you know that you'll soon be able to chat to me face to face. I'm going to have you here as my guest before long. At the moment I have a friend of your Inspector Longman here, has he told you? She is a bit broken, though, as she never knows when to stop asking for sex. Why don't you talk to Kate, Helen?"

The next thing Kate heard made her blood run cold.

"Hello, Kate. Why don't you come over and join us, Josh keeps saying he'd love a threesome and his cock is plenty big enough for both of us," she heard Helen say, and was just about to say something, anything, to try and get through to the woman when she heard Smith's voice again.

"I'm sure you would love to join us, Kate, and you will. But I think *I'll* collect *you*, I'm sure you realise that I can't give you my address. See you soon, my lovely."

Kate sat there for several minutes going over what she'd heard. Why hadn't Tom told her that Smith had a new victim, and, more to the point, why had he kept the fact that he was now involved on a personal level from her? She called his number.

"DI Longman."

"Hello, Tom, Kate. How's it going?"

"Hello, ma'am," he said, which told her he wasn't alone. "It's a slow job. We've called on all the houses in the area and nearly half of them were empty. Whenever we can we leave messages on the answerphone machines or put notes through the door asking the tenants to contact us as soon as possible. Of course, if Smith is in any of these he is hardly likely to answer the door or return the call. It does narrow the field a bit though, as each house that does respond can be checked off the list, as long as it isn't Smith that is. The good news is that while we are doing this we are visible, so if he is within our search area he may have spotted us and, if so, should remain inside."

"Why haven't you told me that he has another woman captive? Before you answer I'd better tell you what's just occurred." Kate proceeded to tell Longman about Smith's call, hearing his sharp intake of breath when she reiterated what Helen had said.

"How well do you know this woman?" she asked.

Longman knew that he was in trouble. He should have reported the fact that he knew Helen Morrison, and couldn't blame Kate for wanting an explanation. He told Kate about Helen, how she had come to him for help and ended up staying.

"Only until she gets herself sorted," he hastened to add.

"How involved are you with her, Tom?' Kate asked, wanting him to tell her that he wasn't forming any kind of relationship with this woman.

"I like her very much, ma'am, and before you ask what you really want to know, the answer is yes, we have started a relationship." There, it was out, and Longman felt a relief that he'd told someone other than his partner about Helen.

"You do realise that I should remove you from the investigation, Inspector."

"Yes, ma'am," he'd picked up on the use of his rank instead of his name, accepting that Kate was annoyed, "I do. But I would prefer to be kept on the case. Smith has given me three days, during which time Helen stays alive. After that who knows. He may keep her alive, he may not, but putting someone else on the case now would waste valuable time, ma'am. There will be no possibility of me being alone with

Smith, I can promise you that. We're getting very close now, I can feel it."

"Very well, Tom, but I want to be informed of *all* developments as they happen in future. No more surprises, please."

"Of course, ma'am. Our list of possible addresses is reducing all the time, but there are still a lot to check. We *will* find him, and hopefully we will find Helen Morrison alive."

"You know that I am out at this civic reception tonight, so I won't be available until the morning. I suppose that you and Charles are carrying on this evening?" she asked.

"Yes, ma'am, we'll be going back to some of the addresses that had a negative response earlier. Before you ask, both myself and Charles are wearing body armour under our jackets. I doubt that Smith would even answer the door, if we happened upon his address, though. But every person that does means one less house on the list and improves our chances of getting Helen out of this alive."

"Well, good luck, Tom," Kate said, ending the call.

Charles had heard his boss's side of the conversation and guessed, from what Longman had said, that the ACC had somehow found out about Smith having another victim.

"The bastard rang the ACC at home, Sergeant. 'And' he put Helen on the line while she was under the drug's influence. He said that he was close to 'collecting' the ACC. That was *his* word, Sergeant. Just how on earth is he hoping to get to the ACC? We have a car outside her house on a watching brief. Every visitor is checked, all deliverymen are checked and even the postman can't deliver mail until our men have given it the once over. Whenever she isn't at home she's here. I really don't see how he will be able to get within a mile of her, let alone get close enough to physically overpower her. To answer your unasked question, Sergeant, I *am* being left on the case. It's getting too time critical to change horses mid-stream so the ACC has agreed to let me carry on, on the understanding that I don't have a go at Smith when we do get him. As if I would, eh, Sergeant? Let's hope the bastard resists arrest, that would make it all bets off."

# Chapter 21

Josh was nearly ready. He checked himself in the mirror and decided that he would pass a cursory inspection. He was humming to himself as he went into the guest bedroom.

"How do I look, Helen? Smart enough, do you think? You'll soon have a playmate, although it will be a woman. I doubt that you'll mind, though. I have ways of making you want different experiences, don't I?"

Helen was laid with her head on the pillow, still tied to the four corners of the bed. She was suffering, not only with memories of her wanton behaviour every time he drugged her, but physically too. He had been so rough with her that she was continually bleeding from her anus, and he never gave it a chance to stop before he was buggering her once more. She knew she was getting weaker. She hoped that when his next victim arrived he would leave her alone, but it was a forlorn hope, she knew. He would have his way with both of them together before killing her. She'd been told by him often enough that the only thing she could be sure of was her death at his hands. *That could be soon*, she thought, looking at him. She was under no illusions about what he could do, she knew he'd only kept her alive for his pleasure. She also knew that she had demanded sex from him, the drugs didn't stop her from remembering that; but deep down, she wasn't the one he really wanted. This Kate Laxton, whoever she was, would be his next target. All Helen knew was that, if he succeeded, her life was over.

"See you soon, sweetheart, be good," Josh said as he walked out of the room. He went downstairs and put his new black shoes on, before going through the kitchen and into the garage. He checked his pockets for his latest toy for the tenth time and, finding everything in its place, started his car. He opened the garage door with the remote and backed out, pressing the button to close the doors when he was clear. He drove steadily towards the little village where Kate lived, finding the place he'd chosen on the map quite easily. He reversed his car down the track that led to a farmhouse and left it on the side of the road, far enough down so that it couldn't be seen by passing traffic.

Locking it, he headed back towards the main road, stopping when he reached a suitable tree to wait behind. The road was little used, but he knew it was the most direct route from the city to the village, *her* village.

He'd been waiting for only ten minutes when he saw a large black saloon appear at the bottom of the slight incline. He kept himself out of sight until it was a couple of hundred yards away, relieved to see that it was the only car in sight, before running out onto the road, waving his arms above his head. As expected the car slowed to a stop and the driver wound his window down, ready to ask what the trouble was.

He never got the chance.

As the open window came alongside, Josh pulled his 'toy' from his pocket and the driver got two darts in his neck, delivering fifty thousand volts. He slumped back into his seat and Josh quickly opened the door and released the driver's seat belt, pushing the inert form over to the passenger side. He got behind the wheel and drove the car up the track, parking near to his own car. Transferring the unconscious driver to his own boot space, Josh used cable ties to secure his wrists and ankles before covering him with a blanket.

Josh retrieved his jacket and put it on, also donning the chauffeur's cap he'd bought on the internet along with the Taser. He backed the car down the track, swung out onto the road and headed for Kate Laxton's house. He was sweating, knowing that in the next few minutes he would have Kate in the car, with *him*. He reached the entrance to her driveway and was stopped by a policeman who wanted to know his business. He lowered his window.

"Here to pick up her ladyship for the civic reception at the town hall, mate," Josh told him, reaching towards the glove box.

"Fair enough, no need to get the paperwork out, we were told you were coming. We expected you five minutes ago, though."

"Bloody tractor held me up till it turned into a field. Shouldn't be on the bloody road in my opinion," Josh explained.

"OK, off you go. She's probably spitting feathers waiting."

Josh closed his window and drove the short distance to the house, turning the car round so it was facing back towards the road. Before he'd stopped, he saw Kate locking the front door. She walked quickly to the car and got in the back before he could get out to open the door for her.

"You're a bit late, driver, better get a move on," she said, settling into the seat and putting on her seat belt.

"Yes, ma'am," Josh said, knowing that his appearance was changed enough for her not to recognise him. Amazing the difference a wig made. He set off down the drive and as he turned into the road the policeman who had stopped him on the way in gave the car a smart salute.

Josh smiled, knowing that it would be the last salute she would ever receive. He accelerated and before long he was approaching the track where his car was parked. He turned in and stopped. "What's the problem, driver? Why have we stopped?" Kate asked him.

"Because I need to see your face when you realise who I am, bitch," said Josh as he brought the Taser up and pointed it over the back of his seat. As Kate's face showed her realisation of who she was with he fired the gun and the two little darts hit her in the chest. She immediately felt the voltage course through her and she slumped back against her seat, unconscious within seconds. Josh was quickly out of the car and, opening the rear door, he carried her to his own car. He laid her in the back, alongside the driver who was still unconscious.

"Don't worry, mate, it's her I wanted, not you," Josh said before pulling him out and dumping him at the side of the track. He used his shoe to nudge the driver into a ditch and heard him make a splash as he reached the bottom. Not knowing, or caring, if the driver was face up or down in the water, Josh returned to his car and saw to his new passenger. She still looked to be unconscious but as he neared the car she started to move. He got his little plastic box from the door pocket and soon had the soaked pad over her nose and mouth, sending her under again. He tied her as he had tied the driver and covered her with the blanket. Getting behind the wheel he set off for home, thanking his lucky stars that it had all gone according to plan. He would love to see the faces of that bloody inspector and his team when they found out that he'd outwitted the lot of them.

He, Joshua Jeremiah Smith, was better than them.

He was soon at his new home and parked inside the garage, waiting for the door to close. When it had slid into place he gave a huge sigh and switched off the engine. Looking over into the area behind his seat he saw that the blanket had slipped and her eyes were looking straight at his.

They were beautiful eyes, even though they were flashing angrily. She couldn't speak, the gag he'd tied round her head prevented that, but she didn't need to speak to show her anger.

He smiled.

"Hello, Kate. Remember me now, don't you? You're going to pay for humiliating me. The women and girls I've had, killed, and left for you, have all been leading up to this. It's your fault that they're all dead. All I ever wanted was to be top of the heap once, that's all, just once. But you, the perfect bloody copper, just 'had' to be better than everyone else, all the time, didn't you. Well, this time *you* are second best, and there's nothing you, or that interfering inspector of yours, can do about it. I've won, and *you*, my dear Kate, are my prize."

*He's bloody mad*, thought Kate. *Stark staring mad.* She knew she was in serious trouble now, and wondered if he'd already killed Helen Morrison. From what he'd just said it seemed that way, but no doubt she would find out very soon if that was the case.

He got out of the car and, opening the boot hatch, he reached in and pulled Kate out by hooking his hands under her arms. Picking her up in a fireman's lift, he carried her through the kitchen and up the stairs, dumping her on his bed. She was laid on her back and he'd never wanted anything as much as he wanted her.

"Not yet, my darling, not yet. I know that you'll soon be begging me to fuck you, but I'm afraid that you'll have to wait a little while longer. I have unfinished business to attend to first. Perhaps you'd like to watch? I'll have to put you under again first, I'm afraid."

Josh soon had Kate unconscious once more and carried her into the other bedroom, tying her to the chair at the foot of the bed where Helen lay face down, bruised and bleeding. Once he'd secured Kate, he went over to the bed, cut Helen's ties and turned her over before tying her again. Helen was too weak to do anything to stop him and lay there, looking down her body at the woman he'd tied to the chair. *This must be Kate*, she thought. Poor, poor woman. If she was the one he'd been leading up to then heaven help her. At least now she knew that her own ordeal at the hands of this monster would soon be over. She had no way of knowing how much time was left, if any, of the three days he'd told Tom he would keep her alive, but she guessed that his promises weren't worth much anyway.

"Don't worry, dear Helen. I told you that I would bring you someone to play with and I have. Don't you think she is beautiful? Would you like to have her instead of me? Or maybe you want to have us both together? You may not feel like it now, but you will." Tell you what, "I'll make her prettier for you."

With that, Josh got the scissors and started cutting the uniform off Kate. She was soon sat in only her underwear that her husband had admired so much only a few hours ago. Josh could hardly contain himself at the sight. She was everything he had hoped for and he rubbed his hands over her breasts, visible through the thin, lacy material of her bra.

He had an agenda, though, and Kate would have to wait for a little while longer before becoming his lover.

# Chapter 22

There was an air of quiet panic at police headquarters.

Longman was beside himself with worry. The car that had been dispatched to collect Kate had not turned up at the reception and the driver was not answering any calls on his radio or phone.

At the moment the police officer who was on gate duty at Kate's address was being contacted.

"Hello, this is DS Charles. Has the car shown up yet to pick the ACC up?" He jotted something down and handed it to Longman as he asked, "what time did it leave, and in what direction?" Longman saw that he'd written down a registration number and make.

*Oh, shit*, thought Longman, he's got her. It suddenly struck him that Smith had actually given them a clue earlier when he said that he would be 'collecting Kate' and felt incredibly stupid for not realising before.

He got onto traffic straight away with the car details and hoped that the car could be intercepted before anything happened to Kate. He was told that all the pool cars were fitted with locators and that he would be informed of its location within minutes. True to their word, they got back to him quickly, telling him that the car was stationary, and the location.

"I'll meet you there," he said, giving Charles the nod. They were soon in their car, blue light on the roof and two tones blaring, speeding towards a farm on the outskirts of the village where Kate had her house.

They saw the blue flashing lights down a track as they turned onto a long straight bit of road that led over a small hill to the village. Turning onto it they saw a body being dragged out of a ditch and feared the worst. Longman stopped the car and was out of the car and striding towards the scene before Charles had got his seatbelt undone. He soon joined Longman and discovered that the body that had been pulled out of the ditch wasn't Kate Laxton. One of the traffic police turned to Longman and told him who it was.

"Ray Gamble, sir. He's been one of the pool drivers for several years, ever since he finished with us. Whoever did this wants stringing up, in my opinion."

The driver had seemingly been overpowered somehow, tied up, then pushed into the ditch. It was unfortunate that the ditch contained water as it looked like he must have drowned, unable to help himself.

The traffic officer, Sergeant Tyler according to his badge, continued. "The ME's on his way, sir. We've looked in the car and it's empty. There are wheel tracks over there so it looks as though the ACC was transferred to another vehicle."

"Let's get the area secured, Sergeant. I'll get a team out here to do the business. There may be something the kidnapper left behind." Privately he doubted it, but one could always hope.

"Right, sir. I've sent my partner up to the farm to see if they noticed anything. I'll park up at the junction with the road, if you could tell him to join me when he gets back I'd appreciate it." He gave Longman a perfunctory salute and got back into his patrol car, moving it back down the track.

"Let's get to work, Sergeant. There may be something here to help us. I have a couple of coveralls in the boot, we don't want the incident team to get all shirty with us when they arrive, do we?"

Sergeant Charles hated the one piece coveralls. They made him sweat, and he hated that. But this was different, the ACC was missing presumed abducted by Smith and he got into the coverall quickly and followed Longman to the pool car. At first Longman just opened the doors and looked in, finding it completely empty. The boot was next and when he looked in he saw some thin wires in the corner. He motioned for Charles to have a look.

"What do they look like to you, Sergeant?"

"I know exactly what they are, sir. Taser wires. Now we know how the driver was overpowered, no one can withstand being Tasered. He probably used it on the ACC too. She's done the self-defence course, same as we have, and there is no way Smith could have abducted her without a fight otherwise. And I've a feeling that he would have come off worse if he'd tried."

They reached in and picked up the wires. At one end were the spikes that had gone into the driver's neck, still with bits of flesh attached. The other end had the magazine that the wires had been coiled up inside before being fired. There was a name on the magazine, together with what could be a serial number. Charles got his notepad out and copied every bit of information stamped on it.

"We may be able to trace the gun that goes with the magazine, sir. It all depends on how efficient the supplier is at keeping records." He got on his phone and scrolled through the directory. Finding the number he required, he called it and a familiar voice answered.

"Hello Patrick, Michael Charles here. I've got a little job for you, and it has the highest priority."

"Ah, Michael, me boy, since when did you ever have a job that wasn't the highest priority? I thought that we were quits now, anyway, after last time."

Patrick O'Hare was one of Charles's contacts, a nefarious type who could find out most things about the supply and disbursement of weapons that were not on the police register. He had found himself almost redundant when the situation in Northern Ireland had eased but still had a lot of contacts in the criminal underworld. Charles had saved his life almost by accident three years ago when he arrested a man who had started a fight with O'Hare. The man was about to pull a flick knife from his pocket when Charles joined the fray, knocking him to the ground and keeping him there until more help arrived.

Since then, O'Hare had been of help on a couple of occasions when certain enquiries would have taken a lot longer if the proper channels had been used.

Charles knew that O'Hare could refuse at any time but hoped that his help could be obtained just once more. He explained the situation and waited. O'Hare didn't hesitate.

"Of course, Michael. Give me the details and I'll get back to you." Charles reeled off the information and closed the call.

"If Smith had the Taser delivered Patrick should be able to find out the address. If he bought it over the counter he would have been asked to prove his identity and that may yield something to help us. It's a case of waiting for him to call back, sir, I'm afraid."

"In the meantime, Sergeant, we shall carry on with the address search. I feel that we're starting to close in on Smith, let's hope that we find him in time to save the ACC."

*And Helen*, he thought.

They saw the traffic officer approaching from the direction of the farmhouse and waited.

He came up to them and Longman introduced them both.

"I have a registration number, make and model of a car that was left here for about ten minutes earlier on this evening, sir. The farmer noticed it when he returned from one of his fields, he could only just get his tractor by." He noticed Longman's face starting to show impatience and quickly reeled off the car's description.

"Thanks, son," said Longman, "your sergeant is parked down at the junction. Would you like us to stay until the forensic team arrive?"

"No, sir, I'll be fine here."

Longman and Charles got into their car and, with a lot of to-ing and fro-ing on the narrow track, managed to turn it so it was facing back towards the main road. As they approached the police car they saw it move aside to allow the forensic minibus to pass.

Longman pulled over and lowered his window, motioning for their vehicle to stop. As their window was lowered he filled them in on what they had discovered so far, telling them that the information gleaned from the Taser cartridge was being investigated already.

They carried on towards the scene, but before he could get going again, Longman noticed the ME's car pulling onto the track. It stopped and Henry Brandon rolled down his window.

"Hello again, Tom. What have we got this time? Another young woman left by our psychopathic friend?"

"Not this time, Henry. It's a male driver, but his passenger was our ACC so anything you get that could help us…?"

"Of course, Tom. You don't need to ask. Was he shot?"

"Not quite how you would expect, Henry. It looks as though he was Tasered before being tied up and rolled into a ditch. Unfortunately the ditch contained some water so he may have drowned."

"That's where I come in, I suppose. Ah, well, onwards and upwards. I'll let you know as soon as I have anything at all."

"Thanks, Henry. Bye." With that Longman raised his window and pulled onto the road, heading for Police headquarters.

Charles was on the radio, requesting a check on the car they believed was Smiths. He was told an address and as he closed the connection he couldn't help grinning.

"Another mistake, you bastard," he said, immediately getting Longmans attention. "We have an address, sir. It's in the Groby area, which fits in with the search area."

"Call the ART, Sergeant. Ask them to meet us near there. This will need careful planning as there's no way of knowing how Smith will react."

They were feeling much more confident as they approached the outskirts of Groby. The address they had been given was in a cul-de-sac and they parked two streets away and waited for the armed response team. They didn't have to wait very long and Longman was soon in discussions with the officer in charge. He had to accept the fact that they were better equipped than himself and Charles and, knowing that Smith had a firearm, they were both told to stay clear of the house until the ART had secured the suspect. Longman wasn't happy at all, Charles noted, but they had to abide by the wishes of the team leader.

He had sent one of his men to do a quick recce of the house and when he returned they discussed how best to proceed. It had got towards dusk and a lot of houses had lights on inside, so when the man returned with the news that the only light in the target house came from one of the bedrooms they decided to go for a normal entry. This would involve breaking through the front door and using flash bang devices that were designed to disorientate any occupants, making the job of subduing them easier and also safer for the officers.

The team approached the house carefully, using the cover provided by the thick privet hedge that surrounded the property.

Getting to the front door, half the team carried on and waited by the French windows at the rear of the house.

At the same instant, both teams smashed through the doors and ran into the house, shouting, "Armed police, stay where you are and put your hands in the air," as they ran upstairs. They entered the room which had the light on and found a man, half dressed in his dinner suit, and a woman who was sat at the dressing table wearing a long evening gown and with make up half applied, staring open mouthed at them as they crammed into the room.

"What on earth is this?" the man asked, clearly scared nearly to death.

"Are you Philip Sinclair?" he was asked.

"Yes, what is all this about?"

"We have the suspect secure, sir," the team leader said into his radio mike, "You can come in now. We are upstairs, first door on the left, with two occupants. One male and one female, both alive."

*Thank God for that*, thought Longman and Charles as they made their way through the debris of the front door and climbed the stairs. Longman was wondering where Helen could be as with only two persons the odds were that it would be Smith and Kate.

It was neither.

As they entered the room the first person they noticed was a woman sat at the dressing table, in shock by the look of her. She was at least fifty years old and was very overweight, as was the man who the team had got to sit on the bed with his hands on his head.

Longman felt the weight of disappointment settle across his shoulders like a physical thing.

"You can check the rest of the house, but it looks like Smith has fooled us once again," he told the ART team leader. "This is not the man we are looking for." He turned to the man on the bed, "You can lower your hands, sir, I think you need an explanation and an apology. There are a couple of questions that I would like to ask you first though."

"Before you ask, what are you going to do about my house? It sounded like you've broken the front door at least, and those explosions have probably done some damage too." He looked at his wife and carried on, "She's scared stiff as well, wonder she didn't have a bloody heart attack."

*Nice to get your priorities in the right order*, thought Longman.

"There are procedures in place, sir, for any damage that has been caused to be repaired to your satisfaction. But I do need to ask you if you own this car." Longman read the make and registration of the car seen parked on the farmers track.

"That was my car, but I sold it a couple of months ago. Bloody hell, the chap who bought it assured me he would put the change of owner slip in the post for me. He seemed to be an honest looking bloke so I thought it couldn't do any harm. I take it that you lot think I still have it?"

"Yes, I'm afraid so, sir. Can you describe the man who bought the car at all?"

"Average sort of height, white of course. Dark hair that hung down to his collar, bit hippyish if you ask me. Nothing wrong with a good short back and sides, in my opinion. Paid cash, I recall. No quibbling either."

"Did he give you his name, sir?" Asked Charles.

"Yes, he did. A strange name too. Joshua Jeremiah Smith. I take it, looking at your faces, that you were hoping I would be him. What on earth has he done that necessitates armed police officers breaking down doors?"

"Nothing for you to worry about, sir. I will arrange for someone to come and repair the damage, and once again I offer my apologies for disturbing your evening."

"That's all right, didn't want to go to the bloody dinner anyway, if truth be told. Just a load of boring old farts talking about their golf handicaps while the women chatter about nothing in particular." He didn't notice the disappointment on his wife's face, or if he did he didn't care.

Longman and Charles made their exit, followed by the ART team. They waited outside until someone arrived to temporarily secure the doors. Fortunately there was another door on the side that led directly into the garage, so the occupants could at least come and go while they were waiting for new doors to be fitted.

As they unlocked their car, feeling thoroughly disillusioned, the radio crackled into life.

Charles grabbed the mike and identified himself.

"Can you both come back to headquarters immediately, the Chief Constable's here and wants to see you now," they heard.

"On our way," Charles said, "be about ten minutes."

He switched on both the siren and the little blue lights normally hidden from view. They were inside headquarters and making their way towards the Chief's office within the ten minutes he'd estimated.

They'd each been wondering why the Chief would summon them to his office out of hours. Normally, no matter what the facts of the case were, the Chief didn't interfere directly with the investigation. He must know something that he needed to tell them personally, that was all they could come up with. They reached his office and knocked.

"Come in, both of you, come in," he said, opening the door wide. "I have something to tell you that couldn't be said over the radio or even the telephone. Sit down, please."

Longman and Charles both sat, and the Chief did the same, settling himself in his chair behind his desk.

"We must think positive, detectives. Smith has our ACC, Kate, and we must hope that his intentions are not to harm her immediately. Certain senior officers know about what I am going to tell you but you are not to repeat it to anyone outside this room, are we clear on that?"

"Yes, sir," they both said, wondering what was coming.

"To quickly take you back, you will remember the failed kidnap attempt on Princess Anne, back in '74."

They both nodded and the Chief carried on, "It was decided that senior figures in public service, not just the Royals, would get an extra measure of protection after that debacle. It was too close for comfort. What I am about to tell you is very sensitive and must never be discovered by the media, heaven only knows what headlines they would come up with. Indeed, some of the people involved don't even know about it. Kate is one of them, which in my mind was a mistake but I was overruled. You may think that what I am about to tell you is straight out of a Bond movie, but I assure you it is not. Inside Kate Laxton is a chip that is akin, albeit much smaller, to the locating chips fitted to expensive cars. This chip can be activated by transmission of a coded signal from any of our traffic cars that have the necessary

199

equipment installed. The operators know what it does but have no knowledge of the name allocated to each code. It's a simple matter to locate the point of origin of the responding signal, the one sent from the chip inside Kate. At the moment we have four cars that have this kit installed and they have sent the activation signal. We should soon find out where she is being held, so I have instructed the ART to be ready once again to assist you. I'm sorry that I couldn't let you know prior to your operation about this. I had to get permission from above, and he was getting ready to attend a dinner with the PM."

Longman and Charles were nonplussed by this revelation from their chief. Now they 'would' get their hands on Smith, hopefully finding Helen still alive and Kate unharmed. He'd only had her a few hours so Longman tried convincing himself that Smith would be saving her until he'd finished with Helen. *Please let us find them both alive*, he thought.

"I've sent a message to Kate's husband and he's on his way back from the airport," the chief constable continued. "His flight had been delayed so he will be coming straight here. He understands the bones of the situation and will be with me in my car. We'll not get in your way, but I think you will agree that he deserves to be there when you bring Kate out."

"Actually, sir, I don't agree," said Longman, "there is a strong possibility that Smith could have drugged her and, if that is the case, I would not advise that her husband should be aware of the full effects this drug causes." Longman explained to the chief what had happened to Helen Morrison when under the drug's influence.

"Ah, I see, Inspector. In that case I'll keep him here at headquarters. You will apprise me of the situation as the operation progresses and once they are out of his clutches both women are to be taken to Leicester Royal afterwards for checks."

No mention of the possibility that one, or both, of them may not be alive, noted Longman thankfully.

# Chapter 23

Helen wanted to hide herself away from the gaze of the woman sat in the chair. She knew she was looking at Kate Laxton, she also knew that Smith had some plan for them both which would not be good news for either of them. Her own life was over, she had accepted that she would be killed by Smith and welcomed the release it would bring. If she was honest with herself she would like to live, but could see no way that anyone would find them in time. No, whatever Smith wanted, he got. It was at these times of lucidity that she remembered Tom, dear sweet Tom. He would be beside himself worrying about her, she knew. If only she had had the chain on the door she would still be there, waiting for him when he came home each day.

If only.

Her reflection was rudely interrupted by Smith coming into the bedroom, with two glasses of water. He offered one to Kate, by placing the rim of the glass to her lips. She was thirsty as hell, a reaction to the chloroform, and drank it all down. Helen watched her face as Smith brought the other glass to her and poured it into her mouth. She drank it all down, knowing what would happen but not caring any more. Sure enough, after a few minutes she felt the familiar stirring and her breathing quickened. She could see Kate was feeling some effects also, as she was straining at her bonds and looking at Helen's naked body with undisguised lust in her eyes. She herself was looking at Kate's breasts, the nipples starting to stiffen and show through the thin lace fabric of her bra. She knew that what she was feeling as she looked at Kate was wrong but she couldn't help herself.

"Why don't you ask Josh to untie you, then you could join me here and we could fuck each other like only women know how," she heard herself say, still looking at Kate's breasts. She wanted to rip the bra away and take them in her mouth, until the other woman was begging for her to do more.

Josh looked on and was once more amazed at the effect that these little pills caused. He decided that he would give Kate a chance to see what she would be begging him for later. Getting undressed, he got onto the bed and started on Helen, who was ready to do whatever he wanted as long as she was eventually satisfied. Kate watched, unable to join them but vicariously feeling his every thrust. Josh was enjoying this and decided that he would let them both come down from their drug induced state before starting on the next stage of Kate's humiliation. He put his dressing gown on and left them, going downstairs to make himself some supper. All this activity had made him quite peckish.

Helen became calm before Kate and watched in shame as the woman kept looking at her sex and licking her lips. Eventually she saw realisation dawn as the drug's effects wore off. Kate closed her eyes, unable to look at the broken body of the woman she had been lusting after just a few minutes earlier.

"What the hell has just happened?" Kate asked.

"You'll get used to it, Kate. It is Kate, isn't it?"

"Yes, and you must be Helen."

"I was. I'm not really sure who I am any more. He's kept me either tied up or drugged since I've been here. I thought at first that I was going to be raped and killed, like the ones Tom told me about, but for some reason he's kept me alive. He's phoned Tom, that's your Inspector Longman by the way, several times while I've been under the control of whatever drugs he's been giving me. As you now know, these drugs have quite an effect. I don't like to think what Tom must be thinking of me."

"Don't worry about Tom, Helen, he knows that Smith has these drugs and you should feel no shame about any of this. We must be positive, I'm sure that we'll be found soon and Smith will be locked away," Kate interjected.

"Yes, well, I hope you're right for your sake, Kate. All I will offer you in the way of advice is, don't annoy him. It won't be nice but he has the upper hand here and if you fight him he'll use force. Just look at my knee. That was done two days ago."

Kate had noticed that Helen's knee was swollen to nearly twice its normal size.

"He used a hammer," Helen continued, "I think my kneecap may be broken as it hurts like hell. Thing is, the drug acts as an anaesthetic as when I'm under its influence I can't feel any pain. It's a bugger, knowing that I need the drug's painkilling effect, but at the same time knowing that when he does I'll turn into a whore. I saw your face when he was here and you know what I'm talking about. You couldn't help yourself from wanting to be on the bed with us, joining in. No, don't turn away," she said as Kate tried to hide her disgust at herself from Helen. "It's not your fault, and I know it isn't the real you when you look at me that way. This drug alters. everything, God knows what, if any, lasting effects it may cause." She thought to herself that she would probably not be alive to find out now that he had Kate, but wasn't going to tell her that.

They both went silent as Josh came back into the room.

"Keep chatting, girls, you really do need to get to know each other better. Tell you what, Kate, why don't you join Helen on the bed. Just give me a minute and I'll free you from the chair. Ooops, silly me, I need to do this first," and Smith pressed his chloroformed pad over Kate's mouth and nose until she became unconscious. Going over to the bed, he made Helen drink a glass of water, liberally dosed with the drug, before cutting Kate's ties and carrying her over to the bed. He laid her, face down, on top of a protesting Helen before securing her to the beds four corners. He went back to the chair where he settled down to watch the fun. Helen's protests soon turned to moans as the drug took effect and she felt Kate's body against her own.

After a few minutes Kate began to stir and was soon awake. She realised straightaway her position. She was laid with her face resting on Helen's shoulder and the rest of her body was mirroring Helen's, both of them secured by their hands and feet to the bed. As she looked at Helen she realised that the other woman's breathing had become ragged and her body was moving underneath her.

"Come on, Kate, can't you feel my nipples getting hard," Helen said, thrusting against Kate.

Kate was appalled. Smith had obviously given the drug to Helen only, leaving her to endure the other woman's drug fuelled body as it jerked at her own. Smith was watching from the chair, unseen by Kate although she knew he was there.

"You filthy bastard," she spat, then yelped as he put the lit end of a cigarette to the sole of her left foot.

"Don't call me names, my darling Kate. If you do that again I *will* use the hammer. You've seen what it's done to Helen's knee. Now be a good girl and let Helen enjoy her last bit of pleasure."

He got up from the chair and released one of Helen's hands.

"Now we'll see how well you can resist," he said, looking into Kate's hate-filled eyes, before sitting back in the chair.

Two of the four traffic cars agreed that the signal was coming from the house on the corner of the cul-de-sac further down the street. They had initiated the search a half hour earlier and the other two cars had not received any signal back from the chip that had been inserted into Kate Laxton during her biopsy. They had themselves taken some time before getting a return and were nearly ready to start questioning whether the chip was working when they began to receive a signal. They'd followed the signal, and it had led them to the quiet suburb of Groby, to the house they were now observing. They'd called the information in and the ART was on its way, having been held in readiness at the nearest police station. Longman and Charles were also en-route and were expected very soon.

All of the officers involved knew the importance of catching the suspect. He'd been responsible, allegedly, for the deaths of three women and was holding at least two more captive.

As they approached the location, Charles turned their blue lights and siren off. They didn't want to alarm Smith. It had been agreed that the ART would try to determine the position of the occupants in the house before going in. If they could get Smith while he was away from his captives there was a better chance of them not getting hurt. Longman didn't think he would kill Kate out of spite but he couldn't think the same about Helen.

The ART got their equipment assembled and started to listen to the noises coming from inside the house. This kit enabled them to pinpoint exactly where each of the occupants were so they could plan their entry route. It was soon apparent that the only sounds were coming from the bedroom at the front of the house, directly over the bay window. This had a flat roof that had been balustraded to give the bedroom a balcony. There was a pair of French windows giving access, opening inwards. The team leader decided that this would be their best way in and they started preparing themselves.

As soon as the bedroom was entered the rest of the team would go in through the front door, accompanied by Longman and Charles. Longman wanted to make the arrest, but Charles was ready to intervene in case Smith resisted. He didn't think his boss would stop at simply restraining Smith if that happened. Hell, he wasn't too confident that he'd be able to stop himself from giving the man a beating, after what he'd been told about Smith's treatment of Helen Morrison.

The ART was ready and had their ladder against the wall. The chosen two, one of whom was the team leader, made their way up the ladder and flattened themselves against the wall either side of the windows. On an agreed signal they broke the glass in the doors and threw a flash and bang grenade inside. As soon as it had gone off they charged through the now glassless doors into the bedroom. Smith was cowering in a chair facing the bed, dressed only in a short dressing gown, stunned into inaction. There was no firearm in sight, just a hammer on the nightstand, so the team leader shouted for Smith to lie down on the floor and put his hands behind his head. By this time the rest of the team had charged through the front door and when they heard the shout of "Suspect secure" from upstairs they moved to one side and allowed Longman and Charles to precede them up the stairs.

Longman entered the bedroom and stopped dead in his tracks with what confronted him. He saw Kate first, tied face down on the bed and sobbing uncontrollably, her shoulders heaving. She was virtually naked, dressed only in some very thin lace panties. Her bra had been ripped off by the look of it and, as he moved to one side of the bed, Longman saw Helen underneath Kate, her hand inside Kate's panties. Helen was moaning and still rubbing her hand against Kate, oblivious to the intrusion. Longman realised that she must be under the drug's influence again, at the same time knowing, hoping, that Kate wasn't from the way she was sobbing. The two members of the ART had got Smith on the floor and were in the process of applying handcuffs, none too gently Charles noticed.

"You perverted bastard!" Longman shouted, landing a kick in Smith's exposed groin before Charles, reluctantly, pulled him away.

"That won't help, sir. Let's get Kate and Helen sorted out first, he's not going anywhere."

Longman found a pair of scissors in the nightstand drawer and cut the ties binding the two women. As Charles took his jacket off and wrapped it round Kate, Longman ripped the sheet off the bed to cover Helen. She was still responding to the drug's stimulating effect and tried to grab him between his legs, telling him to get his clothes off so she could make him hard. He had to get his own handcuffs out to secure her hands behind her, effectively neutralising her. She started thrashing about and he held her shoulders until she finally started to come out of her drug-fuelled state. As she did, she realised who was holding her and fell against him, crying her heart out. He couldn't speak and if she hadn't been holding onto him so tight he would have killed the snivelling bastard who was laid face down on the floor.

He nodded to Charles, giving him the go ahead.

"Joshua Jeremiah Smith, I am arresting you for the abduction and rape of Helen Morrison, the abduction," he looked at Kate who shook her head, "of Assistant Chief Constable Kate Laxton, the rape and murder of Anna Horton, the rape and murder of Lucy Middleton, the rape and murder of Aisha Pahman, and the murder of Raymond Gamble. You do not have to say anything, but it may harm your defence if you do not mention when questioned something that you later rely on in court. Anything you do say may be given in evidence. Do you understand?"

He got a muffled "Fuck you" from the man on the carpet. Charles waited until the medics, assisted by Longman, had taken the two women out before hoisting Smith to his feet and helping him into a pair of trousers. As they reached the landing,

Smith stumbled and Charles momentarily lost his grip on the man. Before he could regain it Smith ran to the head of the stairs and threw himself down them head first. He tumbled down the stairs and landed in a heap at the bottom, moaning. Charles walked slowly down and noticed straight away that one of Smiths legs was at a funny angle. He lifted the man up and then released his hold, allowing the man's broken leg to take his weight. Smith screamed and fell down.

"Oh, dear me, you must have broken your leg. What a fucking shame," Charles said, leaning on it as he bent over the man, who was now in total agony. He'd just got back up when Longman came back from the ambulance.

"Best get the medics to take him away, Sergeant. I've called for another ambulance, if you would accompany him to the hospital I'll arrange for a guard. Why couldn't he have broken his bloody neck, like he wanted, it would have saved us all a lot of trouble."

# Chapter 24

"A man has been arrested in connection with a series of murders he is alleged to have carried out recently in the Leicestershire area. Joshua Jeremiah Smith was apprehended at a rented house in the suburb of Groby last night. Inside the house police found two of his victims, still alive. Their names have been withheld, but we believe they are both female, one a respected public figure. Smith, who was injured whilst resisting arrest, is due to appear before Leicester magistrates later today. We will have more details in our later bulletin. In other news, a proposed strike by bus drivers in Nottingham…"

Longman turned the television off and leant back in the chair.

"Thanks, Tom," said Kate. She was sat behind her desk, having been given a clean bill of health by the hospital. It would take a while for her to forget her ordeal at the hands of Smith, she knew, but she owed her life to the two men sat in her office. "And thanks to you too, sergeant. Mike, isn't it?"

"Michael, ma'am," said Charles automatically, before realising who had asked the question.

"Of course, Michael," Kate said, with a chuckle.

"How is Helen this morning, Tom?" she asked, knowing that he'd been by her bedside all night, reassuring her every time she awoke.

"It will take a while, ma…Kate," he said, noticing her eyebrows start to lift, "she's been treated for her injuries, but the mental scars will take a lot longer to heal. She really had expected Smith to kill her once he had got you in his clutches. In one way she would have welcomed it, she said, which makes me hope they lock the bastard up and throw the key away."

"How did you manage to narrow your search down to that address? I thought there were far too many houses left to check for you to have whittled it down to that one so quickly."

Longman realised that she really didn't know about the miniature locating beacon inside her, so he threw caution to the wind and told her. If she hadn't been meant to know, so be it. After what she'd been put through he reckoned she deserved to have the information.

"Well, I guess that must have been done during the biopsy they said I had to have when I first heard about the promotion. Sneaky sods. Actually, I suppose it's a good job I didn't know or I might have acted differently with Smith."

"We're going through the house for any more evidence linking Smith to the other murders, although we already have enough to put him inside for quite a few years. We discovered a rifle in the other bedroom, hopefully ballistics will match it to the rounds that were recovered from Aisha Pahman. Would you believe we already have submissions from his solicitor asking for the charge against Smith relating to the police driver to be changed to manslaughter? That won't happen, ma…Kate. The ME's report states quite categorically that the driver was dead before he was rolled into the ditch. His heart had given out when the Taser charge hit him. Smith hasn't got a prayer."

Two weeks later, Longman walked a shaky Helen from his car to the front door of his house. She was leaning heavily on him, trying not to put any weight on her injured leg. Her kneecap hadn't been broken, but Smith *had* caused a crack that would take a while to heal properly. Her wounds had started healing, although the psychological effects of her ordeal at Smith's hands would take a long time to diminish. He had been at her bedside as much as possible, holding her every time the tears started.

"You can stay as long as you like, Helen. I won't pressure you in any way, just relax and try to get over everything in your own time. Any time you need to talk, about anything, I'll be here."

Helen stopped and looked at him long and hard then, smiling, she said, "Tom Longman, I'm not a bloody invalid! It might be a while before we can make love but please, please don't shut me away. I've come to realise during the last couple of weeks that I love you, you big lunk. I want to become part of your life. I want to become part of you, Tom, without reservation. It's just going to be a while before I eventually *do* join you in that shower."

They both knew that she meant when the injuries had properly healed. Smith had been quite brutal.

"Helen, I think the feeling is mutual. Ever since we first met I haven't been able to keep you out of my mind. If that is love then I love you," said Longman quietly, surprising himself. He had never before in his life uttered those words to anyone, not even his parents. Helen looked at him, her eyes starting to fill with tears, before wrapping her arms round his neck and resting her head against his chest, crying happily.